Escape From Phoenicia

The Sequel to
Adventures of Regen the Bremen

By M. L. Hollinger

TotalRecall Publications, Inc.
1103 Middlecreek
Friendswood, Texas 77546
281-992-3131   281-482-5390 Fax
www.totalrecallpress.com

ISBN: 978-1-64883-0907
UPC: 6-43977-40907-2

Library of Congress Control Number: 2021935896

FIRST EDITION
1   2   3   4   5   6   7   8   9   10

This book is dedicated to all the readers of my first book who encouraged me to write a sequel

Preface

This book is the result of a lifetime enchantment with space travel. When my grandmother gave me Wiley Ley's book, *By Rocket to the Moon*, in 1947 she had no idea it would launch me on a career in aerospace engineering. I was fortunate enough to be part of several major projects in the military space program and played a minor role in the Space Shuttle Program. Now that I am fully retired, I've devoted my time to writing novels and short stories. If this were 3021 instead of 2021, and I were forty years younger, I'd be Regen.

Introduction

In the first book, *Adventures of Regen the Bremen*, we left our hero on the planet Phoenicia happily united in love with the Lady Herion. Things are going very well for them until Herion is diagnosed with a terminal disease called Bryllion's Syndrome. It is a genetic mutation peculiar to women of Phoenicia and has no cure known on that planet in spite of their advanced medical science.

Regen is convinced she could be cured elsewhere in the galaxy, but he has no spaceship. On top of that problem, escape is forbiden and any attempt is punishable by death. His old enemies from the ruling council are still bent on his demise, and they hatch a plot to give him just enough capability to try an escape but not enough to actually accomplish his goal.

An unexpected ally comes to the rescue, and they make good their escape. However, they still must find a cure. Will they be successful? Will Herion live? Read on.

Chapter 1

The moan of the tunnel train's brakes rouses Regen from his nap. He studies the annunciator panel at the front of the car.

"Gunla Island, two more stops to home, boy." He reaches into the steel cage tied down where the row of seats ahead of him should be and pats the leathery head of the vile creature inside.

He leans back in his seat just as a tall blonde enters his car followed by a burly man in a dark blue toga trimmed in gold and wearing a police badge on a chain around his neck. Behind him an efficient-looking brunette carrying a computer/communicator gets scant notice. She's not at all pretty, and her dark brown toga falls nearly to her ankles.

In contrast, the blonde's toga is a bright white trimmed in purple, indicating some sort of government official. It ends just below her hips showing off her long, shapely legs. The woman clearly knows her best feature and flaunts it. The face is acceptable, but not remarkable. He decides to resume his nap.

★ ★ ★ ★ ★

The Lady Polla steps into the first-class car and stops immediately. The first row of seats on her right are missing, and in their place sits a steel cage containing the strangest animal she's ever seen. It looks like the bastard offspring of a small velociraptor and a huge rat. The head and front paws are reptilian, while the rear half is covered in dull gray fur and sprouts a naked pink tail.

Behind the cage in the next row a tall, muscular man is about to doze off. The seats next to him are vacant, though the car is nearly full. It's clear most passengers want no part of the creature in the cage.

The animal piques her curiosity, but not as much as the sight of a male occupying a first-class seat. She studies him for a moment.

His skin glows with the bronze tint of a man used to the outdoors, contrasting with the powder blue toga trimmed in white. Salt and pepper hair and a weather-worn face give the appearance of an older man, but black hair, a dark black beard and the absence of any tell-tale wrinkles or age spots belie that impression. She can't see his eyes, but he radiates an aura of intrigue. She decides she must get to know him better.

"Excuse me, I've never seen an animal like that before. What is it?" she asks.

Regen opens his eyes and sits up in his seat before answering. "He's a skeen, and you've never seen one before because he's the only one on this planet."

"May I touch him?" She starts to reach into the cage.

Regen takes her wrist in a gentle grip, stopping it short of the cage. "I wouldn't advise it. He bites."

The bodyguard reacts to Regen's action, but the lady waves him off. "It's all right Mikka, you and Joanna have a seat over there. I want to find out more about this animal."

"Yes, Lady," the guard replies and leads the brunette assistant to seats on the other side of the aisle.

"May I sit here?" she asks.

"Sure, love to have the company." He watches as she sits, making no attempt to control the rise of the mini-toga.

She offers her hand. "My name is Polla."

Regen takes her hand in a gentle grasp and raises it to his lips. "I'm Regen. A pleasure, ma'am."

Polla smiles at the anachronistic gesture and continues, "You don't usually see a man sitting by himself in the first-class section of a tunnel train, let alone one with a pet that's not in the baggage car. How do you rate such treatment?"

"All it takes is money. It's amazing what 100 D_p (Drachma) will buy you on this train. Besides, Hitler doesn't like it in the baggage car."

"Hitler, what an odd name." She studies the animal while mulling the name over in her mind.

"I got it from a book I once read about some planet at the edge of the galaxy. Seems this guy, Hitler, was some kind of dictator a dozen centuries back. The name seemed to fit a skeen."

"Is he a pet?"

"Yep, I raised him from an egg, and he used to keep me company on long flights. Now he helps me make a living here by eating up Runiga."

A glow of recognition lights Polla's face. "You're the out-worlder who came here two years ago to be with the Lady Herion."

"That's right. Two more stops and I'll be home with her again. I've been gone quite a while, so I got her a present." He reaches into a bag under his seat and produces a small box. He opens it to reveal a pair of fire opal earrings.

"Think she'll like these?" he asks as he passes it to Polla.

She sits back in her seat and studies the earrings. "What woman wouldn't? These are lovely." She passes the box back to Regen.

"The finest opal I've ever seen's mined here on Phoenicia, and it's cheap. The earrings only set me back D_p 10,000."

Polla laughs. "Maybe cheap to you. I understand you're one of the richest people on this planet, male or female."

"Money don't mean that much to me. I came here to be with Herion, and I'd have given it all up for her."

"You don't mind a planet ruled by women?"

"Nah, I never cared much who ran things anywhere I traveled. I figure you're some kind o' government high muckiuty-muck by your toga and the groupies."

Polla feels she should be irritated by this man's insolent attitude, but she is amused by his audacity. Besides, he's so good-looking, she doesn't want to let pride come between herself and what might be a pleasant sexual encounter.

"You guessed correctly. I'm the Governor of Euclid Province. Tell me, why did the Council let you live?"

"It wasn't easy. Herion helped a lot, but I did what I had to do to get the Council to let me stay here. I don't pay much attention to them now. I'm happy just doing what I'm doing and being with Herion."

"It must have been hard for you to give up your spaceship."

"It was, but I don't need it now. I'll spend the rest of my life here on Phoenicia with her."

Polla cocks her head to one side and smiles at the big Bremen. "You have a funny attitude. Phoenician men usually don't stay with one woman very long. We don't have anything like marriage here, but you might as well be married to Herion."

"Well, that's the good part about this planet. I love the ladies, and Herion doesn't seem to mind if I have other women as long as I come back to her. I don't know if she has any other men while

I'm gone on business, but it wouldn't bother me if she did. We don't need to be married to love each other."

"I'm amazed the Council didn't execute you after they found out about your views on male/female relationships. You could infect our planet with this virus-like idea of living with one woman."

"Well, I guess she still swings some weight with the Council, and that keeps Gilda and her buddies from going after me."

"I remember stories about your trial. It's a good thing Gilda's not Council Chair any more. She had a reputation for executing any out-worlders who stumbled across our planet, no matter who they were."

"I'm just lucky I had the right woman on my side," Regen says.

"Herion runs the game preserve on Kamara Island, doesn't she?"

"Yes, and I'm glad she has that job. I couldn't live underground like most of you people do." Regen shudders at the thought of spending all his time in one of the subterranean cities, even if they do have artificial skies and fake weather.

"We try to present a primitive appearance to any aliens who might find this planet, like you did."

"You do a damn fine job of that. I never had a clue you folks were so far advanced. Say, Kamara's part of your territory, isn't it?" "Yes, and I'm well acquainted with the Lady Herion's work at the game preserve. I've heard about you too, and I'm glad I finally got to meet you." A chime sounds and she points to the annunciator panel. "I get off at the next stop. Why don't you get off with me, and let me show you around? I don't have any appointments until later this afternoon. We could tour the city, have lunch and still have some time left before I have to be anywhere."

Regen considers the offer. *She isn't bad looking, and I wouldn't mind spending some time with her, but I just can't today. I'd better explain.*

"I'd sure like to do that, but I just can't today. I really need to get back home for a while. Maybe some other time?"

"You're always welcome in Spara, and everybody knows how to find the Governor."

A mechanical female voice announces, "The next stop is Spara, capital of Euclid province."

Polla rises and blows a kiss to Regen. "I hope the Lady Herion is well, but don't forget my invitation." Her entourage also rises and follows her to the exit.

"How could I?" Regen mumbles as he studies the long shapely legs revealed by an ultra-short toga. *I love this planet.* He watches Polla from the train window and sees two women in official government togas embrace her. She kisses one of them quite passionately, and he wonders if she swings both ways. In the last two years, he's found it was a common practice on Phoenicia.

The train accelerates smoothly out of the Spara station and Regen sits back for the short haul to Kamara.

★ ★ ★ ★ ★

Herion is not there to meet him at the tunnel train station, Apalon meets him instead. *That's odd, but she must be busy with something.* He uses the remote control to lift Hitler's cage off the platform and sets it to follow him. These days the skeen seems to enjoy the ride, though it took him a long time to get used to the idea of floating on air. He walks to Apalon, Herion's administrative assistant. The usually smiling face now shows a great deal of concern.

"I'm so glad you're back, Regen. The Lady Herion needs you."

"What's wrong?" Regen suddenly feels dread he'd not experienced since coming to Phoenicia.

"I'll let her tell you all about it." He gathers Regen's luggage, and they take the elevator to the island's surface. Apalon has a skimmer car waiting. The ride to the game preserve seems to take forever, though it's only a few minutes. On the way he presses Apalon for more information.

"You gotta tell me what's wrong with Herion," Regen demands.

"She's sick. That's all she wants me to tell you until you see her."

"Sick? She hasn't been sick a day since I came here. You Phoenicians are the healthiest people I've ever seen. What's the problem?"

"I think she'd like to tell you herself. I'll take you to her."

The game preserve soon comes into view. It consists of several buildings made with native materials to resemble aboriginal villages Regen remembers from other planets in his travels. The gamekeepers live in huts raised from the ground two meters on stilts and roofed with thatch made from the fronds of a common jungle tree. The animal cages sit inside a compound walled off from the rest of the facility by a steel fence made to resemble bamboo.

Apalon stops the skimmer at the small clinic serving the game preserve. The island's doctor meets them at the door.

"Regen, I'm glad you're here. Herion's been anxious to talk to you in person." The somewhat thick figure of Dr. Michaela is even too big to be hidden by her combination lab coat and toga, but she has a lovely face and a kind manner.

"Doc, you're worse than Apalon. Is she dying?"

"She wants to tell you about it herself. This way." She leads Regen to a room where Herion lays in bed hooked up to several machines.

"Thank Astarte you're here, Regen. Come kiss me," she says.

Regen moves to her and kisses her gently on the forehead because of the oxygen tube in her nose. She pulls the tube away. "Not that kind of kiss you big stud."

Regen smiles and kisses her fully on the lips.

"What's wrong with you?" he asks.

"The day you left I had a dizzy spell and almost fell off the North cliff. Regia and I were checking out the birds that use those cliffs as nesting sites this time of year. I'm lucky she caught me before I went over the edge. I had Doc Michaela check me out when we got back, and she ran some tests. She says I've got Bryllion's Syndrome."

"I never heard of that. What is it?" Regen says.

"It's a genetic disorder that sometimes manifests itself in people my age. We live a long time, and the scientists tell me that's the cause. Our genes sometimes can't cope with the longevity. It causes us to lose our balance at first, but it gets worse."

"How much worse?"

"It will eventually kill me." Herion turns away from him and drops her head on her chest.

The big Bremen feels a pain in his gut he's never experienced before. The life or death of people around him hadn't mattered much until he met this woman. Hitler is the only other thing capable of evoking this response. He takes her in his arms, oblivious to the beeps and electronic protests from the gear attached to her. He turns her to him and sees the tears streaming down her cheeks.

"Don't cry, there must be something they can do for you."

She sobs even harder and buries her face in his chest. "I've seen this in other women. There's nothing they can do but give me some pills that delay the inevitable. I'm going to die, Regen."

He pushes her to arm's length and lifts her chin. "Look here, I won't let that happen to you."

She shakes loose and collapses on the bed. "You big oaf, this isn't something you and that skeen of yours can muscle your way through. The tests are all positive. I've got it, and there's no cure. I've been through all of the possibilities while you were gone. There's no hope for a mistaken diagnosis."

"Hey look, Michaela's a great gal, but she isn't the only doctor on this planet. We need to get you a second opinion."

Herion composes herself a bit and manages to sit up. "Don't be foolish, darling. The tests are the same here or in the finest research hospital on the planet. The only thing Michaela can't tell me is what variety I've got, but that doesn't matter. All of them are fatal, eventually."

"Well, we're going to get you to another medic to make sure there hasn't been some kind of screw-up." He passes her a box of tissues, and she begins to dry her tears.

"It won't do any good."

"It won't hurt any either."

"Regen, be sensible. I thought I'd resigned myself to my fate until you showed up all optimistic and ready to take on the universe. Don't give me false hope. I don't want to drop into the pit again."

"All I know is in the rest of the universe modern medicine can cure anything. There's gotta be somebody somewhere who knows how to lick this thing."

"Our medicine is very advanced, and they've been doing research on this for years with no success." Tears begin to form in her eyes again, and Regen fights back the urge to break down and sob. He has to be strong for her now.

"Look, I know if I could get you off this planet there's bound to be someplace that can cure this, this, what is it?" Regen asks.

"Bryllion's Syndrome, and I doubt it very much. Our genetics aren't like other races' genomes. I doubt anyone else has ever heard of it."

Regen squeezes her hand and sits back in a chair. "Damn, I can't even get on the Interplanetary Web to check it out. This place is cut off from civilization real good, thanks to your Council."

"We don't need the rest of the universe, Regen. We've done very well for centuries without them. You have to resign yourself to this for my sake. I'm only worried about what will happen to you after I'm gone."

"What can they do? I'm a full-fledged citizen now. I can speak the language and I pay off your priests on a regular basis. I even helped some of the new Council members get elected. Lots of people on this planet owe me favors."

"Don't forget, Gilda's still around, and she's no fan of yours."

"She isn't in charge anymore."

"I know, but she still has many powerful friends. If I'm gone, she can come after you without fear of losing the support of people who owe me favors. She'll find some way to do away with you."

"If my spaceship wasn't at the bottom of the ocean, I'd get us both out of here damned quick. I could get us to Terma. I've got a lot of friends there."

Herion squeezes his hand and sighs. "What would you do for money? Even if you could leave Phoenicia, you'd never be able to take your wealth with you."

"I've been broke four times before and always made it back on top. There's a gal there on Terma that's got all the money I couldn't bring here. She'd stake me 'til I could get back in business again. If she can't, I got a real, honest-to-God princess who'll set me up first class on Bardour. Fact is, she's probably queen there now. I'm not worried about money, all I'm worried about is you."

An orderly appears bearing a tray of food. "Are you hungry, Lady?" she asks.

"Yes, I am. Will you bring Regen a tray also, please?"

"Yes, ma'am." She sets the tray on a table next to the bed and leaves.

Herion looks at the food and grimaces. "Same bland stuff they've been feeding me all week."

Regen peruses the tray and snorts his disgust at the selections. "If they bring me that stuff, they'll just have to feed it to the disposal. The only part that looks edible is that yellow stuff."

"Furga root," Herion says. "Supposed to help you build up some kind of beneficial enzyme. It's not bad." She pulls the table across her bed, tears the covering from the plastic fork and begins to eat.

Regen decides to pick up the conversation. "I got

propositioned on the way home by a gal named Polla—said she's the governor of Euclid Provence."

Herion dabs at her mouth with her napkin. "She's a little heavy in the hip, but not bad looking. You should have accepted the offer. You might need her on your side someday."

"Has she got a ship?"

Herion stops eating and looks at Regen with a bright expression. "As a matter of fact, she does."

"She does?"

"It's on the old side, but it is a spaceship."

"How old?"

Herion stabs another morsel with her fork and chews a moment before answering. "Exactly 5,690 years old."

"That's the current year, 5690," Regen says. Then it suddenly dawns on him. "It's 5690 ΞA, but I never bothered to ask what the ΞA meant."

"It means 'year of the Ark' in Phoenician, and ΠA means 'prior to the Ark'. We number our years from the time we boarded the Ark and set out to find a new home."

Regen snorts in disgust. "Fat lot of good that does me. Being that old, it's probably all rust by now."

"The Ark on display is only a mock-up. You couldn't use it, but there are several shuttlecraft with it that are real. They're just as old, but they may be restorable," Herion says.

The orderly brings in Regen's tray and sets it on the small table near the wall. "Would you like something to drink, sir?" she asks.

"Got any Gordian Bourbon?" he asks.

"No, sir. No alcoholic beverages in the clinic."

"Water's fine," Regen concedes.

He pulls the table to him and picks at the offering a bit. "Tell me about these shuttlecraft."

"The Ark is the ship our ancestors came here on. They used the shuttlecraft as lifeboats and for ferrying people between the Ark and the planet. They're all in a museum in Spara."

"A museum piece, eh? How does that help?" He pulls the cover off the desert bowl. "Hey, this is bread pudding." He digs into that with gusto.

"If you take Polla up on her offer, she'll probably show them to you. They might be something there you could use." Herion pushes her tray away. "If you don't have any appointments on your schedule, why don't you call her tomorrow and make a date?"

"I want to see you back on your feet first." He scoops the last of the pudding out of the bowl and takes a long sip at the water flask.

"The medication's got it under control now. They're releasing me in the morning, and I can get back to work. Take a few days and see what she can do for you. You can tell me later if she's any good in bed. She's twenty years younger than me, you know."

Regen pushes his tray away and climbs into bed next to Herion. He puts an arm around her and kisses her gently. "Aren't you scared she might woo me away from you?"

"If I were, darling, I would never have suggested you meet with her. You've always come home to me. Now, go get some sleep. You have to be well rested to do your best for her. She may be the answer to your problem."

Regen kisses her again and leaves for their hut, as ordered.

Chapter 2

The next morning Hitler awakens his master by pouncing on his bed and dropping a dead runiga on his chest.

"Aw shit, Hitler. You know I don't like that." He sweeps his pet off the bed along with the runiga. Hitler gobbles up the prize since his master shows no inclination toward having it for his breakfast.

Regen sits up on the edge of his makeshift bed. He can't get used to the futons the Phoenicians use. They're fine for making love to Herion, but he can never find a comfortable position with his bones so close to the hard floor. The clock reads 0930, and he swears under his breath. "Damnit, I wanted to be up to help Herion get back home." He glances at her sleeping area and notices it hasn't been disturbed.

Hitler rubs against his bare legs. "I know, boy. You want some breakfast. I guess that rat didn't do the job."

Hitler coos imploringly and runs for his bowls.

Regen fills one bowl with the dry kibbles Hitler craves every now and then and adds cool water to the other bowl. He leaves the skeen to his breakfast while he showers, shaves and dresses for the day in his tan toga. He grabs the box containing the earrings and walks to the clinic.

Herion is dressed and sitting on the bed while Dr. Michaela scans her with a diagnostic unit. He knocks on the door sill. "You ready to go?" he asks.

Dr. Michela stops scanning and smiles at him. "She's stabilized now, Regen. You can take her home."

Herion embraces her doctor. "Thank you for all you've done for me," she says.

"I'm sorry I couldn't give you better news, but you're responding well to the medication. You'll be fine for quite a while on this dose, and we'll check you over periodically from now on. Be sure to come in if you feel any relapse."

"I will doctor. Thank you again."

Michaela kisses her and turns to Regen. "Take good care of this lady, or you'll answer to me, understand?" Her voice is pleasant, but Regen knows she's deadly serious.

"I'll do just that, Doc," he says.

Regen sits down on the bed next to Herion. "I bought you a present on the way home, but I didn't think yesterday was the right time to give it to you." He holds up the small box, and Herion recognizes the name inscribed in gold script across the lid.

"Xergans, you really do care about me. Either that or you did something really naughty while you were gone."

She opens the box and sucks in her breath. "Oh, Regen, they're lovely." She removes the plain loops in her ears and replaces them with the fire opals before moving to a mirror. She studies the effect for a long time.

"They sure look good on you now that you seem to be doing better," Regen says.

"You really know how to please a woman in so many ways." She moves from the mirror and throws her arms around him.

"I'm a lucky guy to have such a fine woman to please," he says before he kisses her.

Herion breaks off the kiss and moves to the bed. "Let's get out of here." She places her loops in the box in place of the opals and drops it into a small duffle bag. After zipping it shut, she hands it to Regen.

"Where are we going?" he asks.

"I really need to get back to work. Apalon's been bringing some work to me, but I need to get out in the field again."

"Now don't overdo," he says.

"Don't worry. All I have to do is take it easy and not put myself in jeopardy of falling. I have a year or two of decent health before the bad times kick in." She turns from him, but he pulls her back.

"Look, that's enough talk about dying. We'll make the most of what time we got left, and I'll keep trying to find some way off this planet. Far as I'm concerned, nothing's changed. As long as you can do things, we'll do 'em. Now get over feeling sad." He kisses her again with a zeal conveying all of his will power through their lips.

Herion holds the kiss a long time before breaking off. "I'm sorry, my love. I promise not to dwell on it anymore. I'll do as much as I can for as long as I can."

"That's the spirit," he says.

She smiles at him and pulls away from his embrace. "I need to get back to my duties, and you need to call Polla. Just let me know you're going before you leave."

"Don't worry, I'll let you know."

Herion leaves for her office hut, and Regen makes a date with Polla for that afternoon.

★ ★ ★ ★ ★

Polla's limo driver is waiting on the platform when Regen's train arrives. He's holding a placard with "Regen" scrawled on it in wide ink marker. Regen finds him easily, and enjoys the luxury of the ride to the capital building.

Polla is in a meeting, and he has to wait in her outer office, but the long legs of her clerks provide all the entertainment he needs as they fidget under their open-faced desks. The staff being all female, he calculates they're not worried about an over-sexed Bremen getting a good look at their assets.

The meeting breaks up and several women he recognizes come out. The first one is Lunna. She's still a member of the Grand Council, having been re-elected for her final term only that year. Regen has been a major contributor to her campaigns.

"Regen! How good to see you," she says.

"Good to see you too, Lady." He rises and offers his hand, but she pushes past it to embrace him and plant a passionate kiss on his lips.

She pushes him back to arm's length. "You still look great. What brings you to Spara?"

"I got some business with Governor Polla." He doesn't think it wise to inform her of the real purpose of his visit.

Lunna leans close to his ear and whispers, "I'll be in town all week for these meetings. I'm staying at the Poseidon Hotel, room 356."

He whispers his reply, "I'd love to, but I have to get back to Herion soon as I can. She isn't well lately. I'm headed back to her as soon as I finish with Polla."

"Sorry to hear that. What's wrong with her?" Lunna's face shows genuine concern for her friend.

"It's Bryllion's Syndrome."

The name changes Lunna's expression from concern to anguish. Her hand flies to her mouth, and tears begin to well up in her eyes. "I can't believe it. She's always been so healthy. Are you sure?"

"The local doc says that's what it is."

"She needs to get to Jupiter hospital in the capital for a second opinion. She can stay with me while she's there."

"I'll tell her. I've been wanting her to do just that."

"Give her my love, and tell her I agree with you." She kisses him again and leaves the room crying.

The other women greet him formally, and Polla is the last one out.

"Good morning, Regen. Are you ready for our day together?" She offers her hand, and he raised it to his lips.

"How can a busy lady like you take a whole day off for a guy like me?" he says.

"When you're the Governor, you can do what you like." She turns to her assistant. "I'll be out all day, Verina, but you can get me on my communicator if it's an emergency."

"Yes, Lady," Verina replies.

"Come on, Regen, I've got a lot of things you'll really enjoy seeing." She takes his arm and pulls him from the office.

The limo is waiting for them. After entering Polla says, "What would you like to see first?" She moves close to him, lifting her toga high on her leg.

Regen feels himself being aroused but remembers his mission. "The first thing I'd like to see is the Ark." He discreetly pulls her toga down to cover her leg. "The best parts of this visit can wait until later."

She smiles at him and pats his thigh before instructing the driver. "To the Founder's Museum, Nicko, and call ahead to have the curator meet us."

"Yes, Lady." The driver nods into the rear-view mirror before Polla closes the partition between them and the driver.

"Why are you interested in the Ark?" she says.

"Besides my interest in spacecraft in general, I'm curious to see what kind of technology you people had so long ago. It's hard for me to understand why you decided to stay isolated from the rest of the universe when you were so advanced that far back."

"We used to trade with the rest of the galaxy up to about 2500, but when a few planets decided they wanted to enslave us, we shut ourselves off from the rest of humanity. We defended ourselves against several attempted invasions, and over time, people just forgot about us."

"The universe hasn't changed any since then. I still know a few places that'd come here and try to take over if they knew about you."

"We still have very sophisticated means of defending ourselves, but all of that technology's top secret. We've come a long way since the Ark."

She shifts in the seat and lets her toga reveal a bit of her chest. "Tell me about your planet."

"Brem isn't much. Not as green as here and a real violent place. Most arguments are settled with fists, laser pistols or worse. I got out of there soon as I found out I could do better elsewhere."

"Is Brem typical of the rest of the universe?" she asks.

"No, most planets have firmly established law and order. At least, in most of their countries. There isn't a planet that hasn't got someplace where your fists or your gun's are the only law there is. This is the closest I've found to a perfect place as there is."

"We have crime, but no place is beyond the law here. A

criminal could never hope to find a safe haven on Phoenicia," she says.

"Herion tells me there's some pretty wild spots on this planet—places where nobody wants to go."

"Those places also have some pretty dangerous wildlife. Any criminal trying to hide out there'd turn himself in to save his skin. That is, if the big lizards didn't eat him first."

The limo pulls up to a large building and stops by the front door.

"Here we are," Polla says.

The driver opens the passenger door and helps Polla out. Regen follows her.

"Wait for us," Polla orders.

"Yes, Lady," he says.

She leads Regen into the building where they are immediately dwarfed by the largest spaceship he's ever seen. The thing stands a good 100 meters high and is over 100 meters wide. It stretches for over 1,000 meters into the building, as well as he can estimate it. The exterior is a dull gray color and shows hundreds of cable runs, ducting, solar panels and hatches, but no windows. A large sensor array covers what he guesses is the front end of the craft. He gives a soft whistle of appreciation.

"That's one huge ship," he says.

A woman in a light blue toga approaches them. "It's an honor to have you visit, Lady," she said as she bows slightly to Polla. "Welcome to the museum. I'm Marga, the curator."

"It's my pleasure, Marga. This is Regen. He's visiting from Kamara, and he's interested in the Ark," Polla says.

"A pleasure Mr. Regen. If you and the Governor will follow me, I'll give you a personal tour. I'm taking you through the sections of the ship open to the public, but if there's anything else you want to see, just let me know."

Regen nods his agreement, and they walk to the ship. Several groups of students are also touring the vessel under the supervision of their teachers, and quite a few other visitors are in line to wait for a guide, but Regen's group sweeps past all of them through a gate marked "Museum Personnel Only."

Regen can appreciate the size of the ship even more as he gets closer. There's nothing like this in the universe today, and the power required to propel the monstrosity has to be beyond even the craziest engineer's wildest imagination. Marga leads them into an elevator which takes them to an entrance ramp half-way up the side of the beast. They walk across the ramp to a docking point and an ordinary-looking air lock. It's open on both ends, which Regen assumes is a concession to the museum staff, since in normal operation it would be impossible to have both ends open at the same time. They enter an administrative area.

"This is the reception station," Marga explains. "Of course, the Ark was built in orbit, and shuttlecraft ferried the passengers and crew to and from the surface, docking at this airlock. All passengers and crew checked in here to get aboard. The passenger list contained over 50,000 names, and the ship required a crew of 2,500 men and women. The crew was nearly all female, but the passengers were equally male and female. Our home island population numbered over 700,000, so selection for this trip was quite an honor. Only the best and brightest were allowed aboard."

"What happened to those left behind?" Regen asks.

"They perished with the other humans on our home planet when our sun grew too large."

"Didn't anybody else there know about spacecraft?" Regen asks.

"We were the most advanced civilization there at the time. Several other nations tried to gain access to our Ark, but our armed forces held them off until we launched."

"That must have been a bloody mess," Regen says.

"Those left behind sent us videos, and they are very sad. We don't show them now, they're too grim and graphic. I'm sure you can imagine the chaos of those final days when our planet was being torn apart by volcanic activity and the atmosphere was becoming a thick soup of toxic chemicals. We don't know if anyone survived that epoch. We only have the super-nova to remind us of our homeland now. This time of year, you can see it on a clear night if you look to the Southwest about 40 degrees above the horizon."

"I have no idea about where my home planet might be from here. Do you folks have any charts of the inner galaxy?" Regen asks.

"We know something of the inner galaxy, but not the exact location of your home planet. It's all quite irrelevant, of course, since you're now a citizen of Phoenicia." Marga says. "This way to the flight deck, please."

She leads them through a maze of companionways to a control center featuring many items with a familiar look to Regen.

"That there looks like an MS 236 star tracker," he says.

"Well, that's not the designation we have for it, but it is a star tracker," Marga says.

"And this's a communication panel," Regen says as he moves to a wall filled with keyboards and displays.

"Right again, Regen," Marga says. "You know a lot about spacecraft."

"I used to fly them, but I never knew how to build one. The innards of all this stuff's a mystery to me."

"I assume you know Regen flew here from the inner galaxy two years ago to be with the Lady Herion," Polla says.

"I did know, and I think it's quite romantic," Marga says, and her eyes take on a tender look.

"Yeah, and it was worth it, too," Regen says.

The ladies laugh at his coarse summation of the relationship, and Marga leads them down another series of companionways to rows of cabins.

"These are the cabins for the passengers. I'll show you a typical family unit." She opens a door to a spacious living area. The furnishings are very utilitarian, but look comfortable. She shows them two bedrooms with bunk beds lining each wall, a bath area and a small storage closet.

"They couldn't bring much along from the looks of that closet," Regen says.

"No, they were very limited in the area of baggage, as you can imagine," Marga says. This cabin could accommodate a small family—perhaps one woman with only four or five children. There were a few large cabins, but not many. The bulk of the ship's mid-section was devoted to cabins. There are a total of 8,000 family cabins and eight dormitories for the single passengers. The passenger section consists of 16 levels with 500 cabins to a level. This way to the common areas of the ship."

The passenger section ends in a large open area spanning half the width of the ship. It is a park with green plants, flowers and fountains.

"This area was maintained as green space by a very complex life support system. Today, we use simpler means to retain the effect. There were other green spaces on alternate decks. Follow me through that opening to see the recreation area."

They pass through the gardens to a space devoted to various play areas. Many of the courts are unfamiliar to Regen.

"I haven't seen any of this before. Did you quit playing these games?" he asks.

"We've modified them over the centuries, and some have been dropped altogether," Marga says.

She leads them on through dining halls, cargo holds and theaters to another airlock that appears to be the exit.

"Is this it?" Regen asks.

"This is only a mock-up or the Ark's flight deck and living areas," Marga says. "The actual Ark couldn't be landed on Phoenicia, of course. Once it was unloaded completely, any useable items were stripped from it, and the ship was destroyed," Marga said.

"I understand you do have some of the ship's real shuttlecraft, though." Regen says.

"We do. The ship used them as lifeboats. We'll go down and have a look at them," Marga says.

Regen smiles. They're what he'd come to see in the first place.

Three smaller craft rest at the foot of the exit elevator. They seem to be identical in every respect. Marga opens one for Regen's inspection.

"This is more like it. I can tell it's real by the smell." He takes a deep breath and exhales strongly. "Yeah, I remember this all right."

This shuttle is configured for passengers with seats on either side of a central aisle. Each row consisted of six seats, three on each side, and there are six rows. A small cargo area at the rear of the cabin holds what are probably fake containers. Regen heads for the control deck.

There is only room for one other person on the control deck, and Polla allows Marga to accompany Regen. The Bremen takes a seat in the commander's chair and surveys the controls.

"Pretty advanced for its age. What kind of propulsion did it have?"

"It was a heavy water fusion system. A bit antiquated by today's standards, but it got the job done back then," Marga explains.

"You're right about it being an antique. Let's have a look at it."

"You'd have to go to the bottom of the Great Ocean to do that. The propulsion system was removed long ago because of its high degree of radioactivity."

"I'd still like to see the engine room, if that's possible."

"I'll take you there, but we can't stay too long. There's still a lot of residual radiation in that area."

Marga leads him to the rear of the ship and opens a hatch leading to the engine area. It is marked with symbols indicating a severe radiation hazard, and Regen holds back a bit.

"Don't worry," Marga says. "The radiation levels are much lower after 5,000 years. If you don't stay down there too long, it's no more than a couple of X-rays."

Regen drops into the engine bay and looks around. He'd heard of heavy water fusion units but was not familiar with their details. He calculates they must have been huge from the size of the room. It will easily accommodate a modern Warp drive system. He climbs back up to the main deck.

Marga closes the hatch immediately. "Is there anything else you'd like to see?"

"Do you mind if I look around a bit on my own?"

"Not at all. If you need access to any closed areas, just let me know."

Regen continues to inspect the shuttlecraft closely. He checks the wiring and the plumbing. He tests several panels for corrosion and notes many places where the seals are non-existent due to deterioration from contact with the atmosphere's oxygen. Even though there is no natural sunlight in the underground city, many rubber components are reduced to little more than black and gray powder. Restoring the ship to flyable condition will take a lot of money and a substantial amount of time. He turns to Marga.

"Are all three in the same shape?"

"Yes, I'm afraid they are. We just don't have the budget to restore these craft as we'd like to."

"They're in pretty good shape for being that old. I don't see any significant corrosion anyplace."

"They were made of a special alloy that's still a closely guarded secret today. It also helps that we keep the museum at a constant temperature and reduced humidity. As you noticed, many of the rubber and plastic parts have deteriorated considerably, but the basic structure of the craft is still sound."

"It's a shame you can't get the money to restore 'em. I'll bet at least one of these could be restored to flying condition."

Polla speaks. "There's an historical society that wants to do just that, but they haven't had any luck convincing the Grand Council to give them the money."

Regen rubs his chin and stares at the shuttlecraft. "Maybe I can help out. Tell me how to get in contact with those ladies."

"Actually, a man's in charge of that society. I've got his number back in my office if you're finished here," Marga says.

Regen turns to Polla with a surprised expression. "I didn't think you'd let a man run anything on this planet."

"We don't, unless it's something we don't really care that much about. The nut cases in that restoration society fall into that category. Nobody wants to spend that kind of money just to create a joy ride for the tourists," Polla says.

"Joy ride?" Regen says.

"Yes, the society would use a restored shuttlecraft to take museum visitors on a short ride to outer space. They see it as a fund raiser to help support the museum," Marga says.

"Sounds like a good idea to me," Regen says. "I suppose you could use the extra cash," he asks Marga.

"We always need money, Mr. Regen. Admissions don't come close to covering our expenses, and our appropriation from the Grand Council is quite small. The gap of several hundred thousand Drachma remaining must be solicited from our donors and several philanthropic trusts," Marga says.

Polla looks at her watch. "I'm afraid we're out of time today. She can give you the contact data for the society, and we'll be just in time for lunch at the Athenian."

"Sounds good to me. Let's go," Regen says as the trio heads for the museum office.

Chapter 3

Over lunch Polla quizzes Regen about the shuttlecraft.

"Why all the interest in antique spacecraft?" she asks.

"I'm a pilot, and I always liked spaceships. It seems a shame to just let those shuttlecraft go to hell." He cuts another bite from the largest steak available on the fancy restaurant's menu.

"It'll cost a fortune to fix up one of those things. It's too much to ask of the donors, and the Council will never approve the funds." Polla sips at the excellent red wine she ordered

"Like Marga said, they don't seem to care much. I've got some money to spare, and it can't cost that much to make 'em flyable."

"Are you sure there isn't some other reason you want one of those shuttlecraft restored?" she asks as her eyes probe him over her wine glass.

"Maybe if I could get one into flying condition, they'd let me fly it every now and then." The wistful expression conveys more of his intentions than he really wants to show, but the thought of being behind the controls of a spaceship overwhelms all chance of concealment.

"You said Herion wasn't feeling well. If something should happen to her, what would hold you on this planet?"

"Don't get me wrong. I'd hate to lose that woman, but there are lots of fine women around here, including present company." He raises his glass in a toast to her.

Polla almost blushes, but her political acumen stops it short. She sets down her glass and reaches across the table to take one of Regen's hands.

"The day's almost shot for business.   Let's go to my apartment, and perhaps I can verify your judgment of me."

"Soon as I finish this steak, love."

Regen dives into his meal and finishes quickly. While he eats, Polla called her office and cancels the rest of her day.

★ ★ ★ ★ ★

Herion meets Regen at the tunnel train station. He enfolds her in his arms and kisses her as if he'd been gone a month instead of two days.

"It's good to see you up and around," he says.

"I'm feeling well. Besides, I have to stay healthy to keep up with Hitler while you're gone." She pulls away from him and takes his arm, leading him from the platform to a waiting skimmer.

"Hasn't he been behaving himself?" he asks.

"He goes crazy when you're gone. We have to keep him in his cage much of the time or he'll kill every animal on the island."

A porter loads Regen's bag in the skimmer, and Herion takes the driver's seat.

"Don't you feed him?' Regen asks.

"He eats everything we give him, but then he goes out and kills anything he can find. He really misses you, I guess."

"Well, I'm home now. Any jobs come in for us?" Regen leans back in his seat and lets the salt air blow the atmosphere of the underground city out of his head.

"No, nothing on your schedule," she says.

"Good, I need to go visit some historical society people about restoring one of the Ark's shuttlecraft."

Herion stops the skimmer and turns to face him. "Those

things are 5,000 years old. You don't really think you can get one of them in flying condition, do you?"

"I don't know. Won't know until after I talk to that historical society guy."

"Even if you did succeed, I doubt one of them could get you to the planet you were telling me about. That's where you came from when we first met, wasn't it?"

"Yep, an' I got some idea about how far away it is and no idea in what direction, but maybe I can find out."

"All that information's very closely held by the Grand Council. Their people programmed your ship when we sent you away the first time."

Regen smiles at her and pats her thigh. "Yeah, but you brought me back?"

"I did, but the Council doesn't know that."

"But they know I got back here some way, and they probably also know you had a lot to do with it."

"They think they didn't succeed in fully clearing your ship's navigation memory, and you used it to find your way back. They didn't know about the statuette. I made that using data I pirated from one of the technician's computers while she was busy with Apalon. For some reason I held on to the data. It's on a chip that's well hidden in our hut."

"Why didn't you tell me?"

"I never thought you'd need it again, but I had to hide any evidence I'd helped you come back," Herion says.

"Well, that changes things. We'd at least have a chance of finding Terma if we do get a shuttlecraft in flying condition." Regen sits silent wrapped in thought about their chances of making good an escape.

★ ★ ★ ★ ★

Hitler scratches at his cage door violently the moment he spots his master, and Apalon opens it in response. The skeen runs to Regen and jumps into his arms.

"Oooooofff, you're getting too big for this," Regen says. It's a good thing the skeen's master is a Bremen. A man of lesser build would have been bowled over by the impact. It nuzzles its snout against the big man's toga and coos a greeting.

"I'm glad to see you too. Now get down." He dumps the skeen on the ground, but it stays close to his heels as they walk to Herion's office.

"You'll have to excuse me. I have some things I must attend to this morning, darling," she says.

"That's okay. Hitler and I need to speak with that historical guy."

Regen finds an unused console and consults the contact information Marga gave him. Soon he's speaking with the head of the Ark Restoration Society, a certain Doctor Padopolous.

"Mr. Regen, it's a pleasure to talk with you. Marga tells me you have an interest in restoring one of the shuttlecraft."

"Sure do, but I'm surprised they let you run this show? I'm used to women running everything on this planet."

"I'm retired from the Phoenician Space Force with the rank of Fleet Commander. I was the only man to reach that rank, the rest of the senior officers are women. The Council doesn't trust a man with a lot of rank, so they took me off flying status and put me in charge of the PSF research program. I missed flying, so I took early retirement after a few years of piloting a desk. I volunteered for this job because I figured if we could restore one of the shuttlecraft to flyable condition, I could still get some stick time in every now and then."

"Well, it's good to talk man-to-man and pilot-to-pilot for a change," Regen says.

"Tell me, why are you interested in the shuttlecraft?" Padopolous asks.

"I love to fly, too. This planet doesn't have airplanes, and the PSF are the only people with spaceships. Like you, I figured if we got one of the shuttlecraft back in shape, I could at least get some time in every now and then. Besides, I like your idea of selling rides to make some money for a good cause."

Dr. Padopolous strokes his beard a moment before responding. "I see, those craft hold 36 people. I think we could charge 50-100 Drachma each, which should cover expenses and still leave some profit for the museum."

"You could be the primary pilot. I'd do the flying on a volunteer basis when I'm around, and maybe we could get some other retired pilots to help out in that regard."

"Yes, but it'll take a lot of money to restore something that old to working order, and the Council doesn't seem to want to give us any. I've tried for several years, and it's a long, sad story."

Regen sits back in his chair and puts his feet up on the credenza. "I've got all afternoon, Doc. Tell me about the shuttlecraft and how much it'll take to get one flying again."

"Well, the big money will be in getting a new drive system. The structure isn't in bad shape, but all the seals are gone and the wiring's shot. We can re-wire pretty easily, but we'll have to make new molds for the seals, and that's expensive. The other systems haven't been checked out thoroughly yet. It's hard to say what shape they're in."

"What other systems are we talking about?" Regen asks.

"There's no artificial gravity system. Back then, the crew and passengers were strapped in and all the cargo was tied down. There is a rudimentary food service system. The shuttlecraft were the Ark's lifeboats, and the food synthesizer could provide minimum rations for 38 for two weeks. The life support system was also good for two weeks. The fusion drive was not capable of warp speeds, so any planet they found had to be within two week's journey at sub-light speed. Basically, they were only good for moving people and cargo from a planet's surface to the Ark and vice-versa."

Regen cursed inwardly. *Those things aren't going to do the job unless I can modify them considerably. We could live with no gravity, but we aren't going anywhere in two weeks at sub-light speed.* "Tell me, Doc, how much are we talking about to do the job?"

"I submitted a budget of D_p5.5 million a few years back, and the Council turned it down. I bring it up again every year, but the answer's always 'no'. I'd say you're looking at over D_p7 million for that project today. I don't think the Council would even consider that number."

"I've got some money to throw in on the deal, but not that much. Let me think about it for a while. I'll call you when I've decided what to do. Thanks for the info, Doc."

"No problem. Call any time."

Regen terminates the call and slams a fist down on the credenza hard enough to attract the attention of several workers in the operations center and cause a couple of monkeys in a nearby cage to begin howling. He looks at the icy stares with a sheepish grin. "Sorry," is all he can muster.

That night he briefs Herion over dinner.

"Looks like my idea of using one of the shuttlecraft is no good."

"Why's that?" she asks as she dives into a plate of mixed greens.

"First thing, the drive system's gone. That really makes it an expensive proposition. It'd take more money than I've got to fix it up. Besides that, the life support system's only good for two weeks. We'd have to get where we're going in less time than that even if I could rig some drive that's good for Warp 200 or better. I'll have to come up with another plan."

"Suppose you could get hold of, what did you call it?"

"A Warp drive."

"Yes, suppose you had one. Could you get to this planet you mentioned in less than two weeks?"

"No way. You guys rigged my navigation system so I couldn't find my way back, but my clock still worked. It took 35 days to get back to Terma, and the same to come back here." He pushes his plate away and reaches for the bourbon. He pours a healthy shot and knocks it back. "The whole idea's silly. Even if I had all the funds I needed, I don't know what course vector I'd need to get us there."

"Did you forget I have the chip I used to make the statuette?" Herion said.

"Okay, we could use a shuttlecraft if I could find a Warp drive, and if the life support system'll work for the time we need, but those are big 'ifs'."

"I can't help you with those things, but I'm sure you'll find some way to work it all out."

They finish dinner and take a long walk on the beach before retiring.

Chapter 4

In the capital city of Astartia others are considering Regen's latest actions. Ex-Council Chair Gilda studies the transcripts of his conversation with Dr. Padopolous while the new Council Chair, Selenia, sips a glass of white wine and enjoys the antics of Gilda's pet monkey. Gilda's apartment is underground, as all other buildings in the capital are, but a cool breeze blows through the delicate draperies at each window.

"How curious. This Bremen suddenly has an interest in making the Ark museum profitable. I don't believe it for one minute. He's up to something," Gilda says as she shut down the video unit.

"Lady, your suspicions may be well founded. I understand the Lady Herion has Bryllion's Syndrome and the doctors give her less than three years to live. With her dead, Regen has no reason to remain on Phoenicia, but he'd need a spaceship to do that."

Gilda sniffs in disbelief and holds out her glass for a nearby servant to fill. As the servant pours, she speaks. "His interest in Papadopolus' old project may mean he wants to use on of the old Ark's shuttlecraft."

Selenia laughs. "Those things are over 5,000 years old. It would take more money than even Regen has to make one of them spaceworthy. He'll have to come to the Council for a grant, and I'm sure they're not in the mood to spend that kind of money on the museum. It takes enough of the budget as it is."

"Don't sell him short. He's a very resourceful man with several supporters on the Council. A few well-placed bribes might swing a vote in his favor even if they suspect he's planning an escape," Gilda says.

"I doubt a restored shuttlecraft would be able to outrun the PSF. If they caught him attempting an escape, they would put him exactly where you want him, strapped to the garrote post."

Gilda smiles grimly envisioning Regen's eyes bulging as the executioner tightens the strap around his neck. She'd take the final turn of the screw herself. She takes a sip of wine and places her glass on the communication console. "Then we should see he has a chance to escape."

Selenia laughs and waves her hand in a dismissive gesture. "An admirable thought, Lady, but I don't see the Council giving him a modern drive unit. He'd need a Warp drive to reach the inner galaxy, and there's no need for that kind of unit to merely haul visitors to low orbit and back."

"Then we'll have to make sure he can get hold of a Warp drive by some means," Gilda says as her smile changes from one of morbid enjoyment in Regen's execution to one of sly cunning. "We just need to make sure he can't outrun the PSF."

Selenia nearly chokes on her wine at that announcement. "What are you saying, Lady? Do you want him to escape?"

"I'm saying we must be sure he has just enough capability to make an attempt, but not enough to escape our justice. We must see that the Council provides the right kind of drive unit."

"Yes, but the only sensible request would be a gravity interaction unit? What they want the shuttlecraft for would not require a warp drive," Selenia says.

Gilda turns thoughtful. "Hmm, you have a point." She thinks for a moment before continuing. "A new gravity interaction unit would also be expensive. What about a unit from a confiscated ship?"

"The PSF have some units they've used for research purposes. We could propose use of such a unit as a means of reducing the cost of the project, but those units would be capable of warp speeds," Selenia says.

"I'm sure the Council will demand the PSF disable the Warp drive aspect of such a unit, but we must be sure the components needed to restore its function are accessible to Regen by some stealthy means. He will have to obtain them illegally and, thus, compound his offense. We will have him in double jeopardy when he's captured trying to escape."

"Elektra has oversight of the PSF in this session. I'll have her look into the matter," Selenia says.

Gilda swirls the wine in her glass and stares out the window. "Yes, but don't let Elektra know of this plan. She has a tendency to talk too freely. Keep her in the dark."

"She is an ally against Regen. I hate to deceive her."

"You and Elektra were with me two years ago, but that was a public hearing. She could talk to anyone about that. The fewer people in on this plot, the better. Someone might fall under the spell of that brigand and tip our hand. I never could understand why the women of this planet go crazy over him."

"You have to admit that he is an excellent specimen of that sex. It's his eyes that attract most women, so I'm told," Selenia says. "Women who've lain with him tell me I should try him out, but I don't really care to lie with men."

"I've had many men, and I have no desire to bed Regen," Gilda says.

"I understand your feelings, but he's kept his nose clean since his trial. He may cause women's hearts to go soft, but an escape attempt would force even the most starry-eyed bitch to condemn him," Selenia says.

"Yes, and Mallana and Gisellia are no longer on the Council. That takes two votes away from him in any case," Gilda adds as she raises her glass in a toast. "To the demise of Regen the Bremen," she says.

Selenia responds in kind and adds, "Hear, hear."

★ ★ ★ ★ ★

Regen leans back in his chair and swivels the monitor screen to Padopolous. "Looks good to me, but why did you only ask for a gravity interaction drive?"

"It's all we need for our work. Besides, I figured that's the only thing the Council would approve."

"You're right, I guess. Go ahead and send it in." *The first thing is to get the ship. Maybe I can find some way to get hold of a Warp drive later.*

Padopolous hits the "send" key on the communication console and pours two glasses of wine. He pushes one to Regen and says, "Here's to success."

"I'll drink to that." Regen raises his glass and touches the offered goblet. "If this thing goes through, we'll toast that with champagne."

★ ★ ★ ★ ★

General Regna, the commander of the PSF, is never comfortable talking to members of the Grand Council. She learned through painful experience that what they said seldom reflected the true purpose of their visit. They live in a world of subterfuge and double dealing a military officer rarely has to contend with, and she is not good at the game. Selenia and Elektra are the most devious of the bunch. Anything said to them is sure to backfire into serious trouble or result in drastic budget cuts. She sharpens her mind in preparation for the encounter just as they enter her office.

"Lady Selenia and Lady Elektra, how good to see you again." Regna lies, but she knows it is the expected greeting.

"General, you're looking as lovely as ever." Selenia embraces the Commander.

"Thank you, Lady Selenia." She turns to Elektra, "Lady Elektra, you don't seem to age." She knows Elektra is vain about her looks.

"You flatter me, General, but thank you anyway."

"Please sit down and tell me what brings you here." The ladies take chairs as Elektra surveys the rather plush office.

"Is that a Chagran original?" She points to a rather large painting on one wall.

"Oh no, only a very poor copy, Lady. My salary is generous, but not that generous." Regna uses every bit of her guile to suppress any nervous tic that might give away the fact it really is an original.

"Not as poor as you may think, General," Elektra says. "But we didn't come here to discuss your taste in art."

Her protestations of disinterest do not convince Regna. She knows her next visitor will be an art appraiser, and males mental plans to banish the item from her office until the fuss dies down. "What can we do for the Council today?" Regna asks.

Selenia speaks. "We have a proposal for a project to help make the Ark Museum self-funding. The Historical Society proposes to restore one of the Ark's old shuttlecraft to flying condition and offer rides to low orbit for the visitors to the Ark Museum. Their major problem involves the propulsion system.

As you may be aware, the shuttlecraft used a fusion unit for power. Since it would be impractical to reproduce such a unit, not to mention creating a major radiation hazard, they've asked for a gravity interaction drive."

Regna breaks in. "The PSF would be pleased to support the Council with our procurement expertise in this area. Micron, Inc. makes an excellent unit as does Nebulex. We could combine your requirement with our next purchase and insure the lowest possible price."

"Thank you, but we had something less expensive in mind," Elektra says. "We understand you have several units from confiscated ships that may be serviceable."

"We do. In fact, the unit removed from the Bremen's ship would do the job, and it should be in excellent condition. Our scientists were very interested in that system, and they found several useful technological advances we've since applied to our own drives. I believe they're finished with it now. If they haven't destroyed it, you could certainly have that one."

"Destroyed it?" Selenia asks.

"Yes, we destroy all confiscated units as soon as we've finished with them."

"Could you check that out for us now, General?" Elektra asks.

"Certainly," she replies. Regna punches a code into her communicator and a woman in a laboratory coat appears on the screen.

"Yes, General," she replies.

"Doctor Wilma, is the Bremen's drive unit still available?"

"Yes, sir. It isn't scheduled for destruction until next year. We always keep units for a year after we've finished testing in case some follow-on work is needed."

"Good. The Council may have a use for it. I'll let you know as soon as a decision is made. Please make sure it's kept in working condition until then."

"Yes, General. Is that all?"

"Yes, I'm meeting with representatives of the Council now. I expect they will have a decision very soon. Goodbye."

The screen goes dark, and the General speaks, "You heard?"

"Yes. I think the Council would approve use of that unit, but I understand that drive also has Warp capability," Selenia says.

"Oh yes, all confiscated drives are Warp capable," Regna says.

"Would there be any way to separate the Warp drive from the gravity unit?" Elektra asks.

"I'm afraid not. The two systems are highly integrated, but there may be a way to disable Warp capability," Regna says.

"How would you do that?" Selenia asks.

"I'm not sure of the specifics, but all drives must be switched from gravity interaction to Warp drive in normal usage. I'm sure our scientists could find some way to prevent use of Warp capability. I'll have them check for that right away if you like," Regna says.

"Please do, General, and report their findings to me personally as soon as they're available," Selenia says.

"Yes, Lady, immediately. Is there anything else I can do for the Council today?" Regna asks.

"You could sell that Chagran, and turn the money in to the Council." Elektra rises and Selenia follows her example.

Regna rises and bows slightly as she mumbles through clenched teeth, "Have a good day, Ladies."

Chapter 5

Several days later, Regen and Herion are enjoying a quiet evening together when the communicator sounds its lilting melody. It's her favorite, and Regen never changed it.

"I'll get it," Regen says as he rises from the couch they rest on together. He moves to the console and finds the call is from Dr. Padopolous.

"What's new Doc? Hear anything from the Council?"

"That's what I called about. They've approved our grant request, and they're going to furnish us with a drive system from the PSF. We can start work next week."

"What kind of drive did we get?" Regen asks.

"I don't know. It's out of a confiscated ship, but the PSF says it's serviceable for gravity interaction mode. You can see it in two weeks when they deliver it to the museum. In the meantime, I've got all the contracts ready to go for the restoration job. Drop over any time you like."

"I will. I got a job next week, and I'll come by on the way home. See you then, Doc." Regen signs off and returns to Herion.

"That sounds like good news," she says.

"I don't know about that. The drive from any confiscated ship would have to have Warp capability besides gravitational interaction, and I can't see the Council shipping us anything like that. They've probably disabled the Warp Drive function some way."

Herion lifts herself on one elbow and pulls his face to hers. "I have every confidence you'll find a way to get it working again.

Now, forget about that and make love to me. You're going to be gone at least two weeks on your new job, and I need something to tide me over until you get back."

Her kiss convinces him to put drive systems out of his mind.

★ ★ ★ ★ ★

Selenia accompanies the team delivering the drive unit to the Ark Museum. Padopolous' mouth drops open a moment when she exits the cargo unit first, but he recovers quickly.

"Lady Selenia, I wasn't expecting you. What a pleasant surprise," he says.

"Tell these men where to unload the drive system, then we need to talk, privately," she says.

Padopolous turns to an assistant. "Have them put it in the warehouse. We won't need it for a while." He turns back to Selenia. "This way, Lady."

He leads her into his private office and closes the door behind her. "Please have a seat, Lady," he says.

Selenia makes herself comfortable in the only chair available besides the one behind Padopolous' desk, and he asks, "Would you like some refreshment?"

"No, thank you. I need to get back to the capital, but I had to deliver this message personally."

He sits down, swiveling his chair to face her. "Go ahead, Lady." He picks up a recorder and turns it on, but Selenia quickly reaches over the desk and turns it off.

"Our conversation here is strictly between you and me. No one else is to know anything about what I tell you. Is that clear?" Her tone is unmistakable and implies   dire consequences for any breach of trust.

"You have my word, Lady," he replies.

"Good. The unit I just delivered to you is capable of both gravity interaction and Warp drive modes. We have disabled the Warp mode, but it can easily be reactivated with this." She places her briefcase on his desk and opens it. She removes an electronic circuit rack and places it on the desk before him.

Padopolous picks up the unit and studies it for a moment. "I see, but why do you give this to me?"

"This is the most sensitive part of what I'm telling you. Someone may want to make the shuttlecraft Warp capable. You must keep this rack in a secure place and only allow access to someone specifically authorized by the Council. Should any unauthorized person gain access to this item, you will notify me immediately. Do you understand?" She leans closer to him to emphasize her point.

His face becomes a picture of puzzlement, but he decides there is no point pursuing the reasoning behind her instructions. "I understand. I have a very secure safe here in my office." He points to a sturdy-looking cabinet in one corner. "Only I have the combination. I'll place it there now, if you like."

"Not necessary. I trust you to do the right thing." She rises and offers her hand. He takes it and kisses her ring of office. "Goodbye, Dr. Padopolous. Good luck with your restoration program."

"Thank you, Lady. I'll keep the Council advised of our progress."

"See that you do. I'm looking forward to an excursion when it's completed." She walks out of his office as he looks after her with his mind in a confused state.

Why leave this with me? I'd think they'd want to keep it in their own custody. Who would want to use a Warp drive? The craft's no good as part of the PSF, and its life support system gives it only limited range. It can't fight, and anyone wishing to escape Phoenicia couldn't reach the closest civilized planet. It doesn't make any sense, but if that's what the Council wants, I'll carry out their orders.

He opens the safe and places the rack inside. *Welcome to your new home.*

★ ★ ★ ★ ★

Two weeks later, Regen stops off at Spara on his way home to check on the progress of the shuttlecraft restoration. Marga is not too keen on allowing even a caged Hitler into the facility, but Regen assures her his pet is used to crowds.

Padopolous set up the restoration area in full public view. Only glass walls separate the patrons from the workers. Regen walks into the area and quickly finds Padopolous.

"Hey, Doc, did we get that drive unit yet?" he calls.

Padopolous looks up from his drawings. "Regen, welcome back. Yes, we did. I was waiting on you to uncrate it. This way, please." He indicates the path with one arm.

"Do you mind if I let Hitler out to run a bit? He's been caged up for quite a while."

"No problem, he can't get out of the work area." Padopolous smiles as Regen opens the cage door and the skeen darts out to the glass wall, running into the barrier before realizing the situation. The men and women working on the restoration hold their breaths as the animal reels back in a state of stupor. They know of Regen's love for the evil creature, and they fear he might become violent if it suffers any serious damage. They are all relieved when the big Bremen begins to laugh loudly.

"Come here, Hitler," Regen calls, and the skeen staggers to his feet and joins his master. Regen looks his pet over carefully and pronounces him no worse for the blow. "He's okay. He's just has to learn about this place."

A moment of tender affection from his master seems to revive Hitler, and the skeen begins to prowl the confines of the work area to test the limits of his freedom. After a tour of the glass perimeter he moves into the storage area Padopolous indicated earlier.

"Let's have a look at this engine," Regen says.

"Looks like Hitler's going to find it first," Padopolous says as he leads the Bremen to several good-sized crates stacked in one corner of the large room. Hitler is busy sniffing at the crates with great interest.

"Looks like he's found something he likes in those boxes," Regen says. "You might have brought in some kind of rat with the engine."

"I doubt that," Padopolous says. "They told me this stuff came straight from the PSF testing labs, and they're pretty clean places."

Both men are surprised to see Hitler stop at one corner of the largest crate, lift a hind leg and urinate on the wood.

"Why did he do that?" Padopolous says.

"He's markin' his territory. I haven't seen him do that for a while. He must think he's going to live here," Regen says. "Let's open this big one first." He points to the one Hitler just anointed.

Padopolous calls for two workers who pry open the crate to reveal a large mechanism Regen recognizes as a warp drive master controller.

"That looks a lot like the unit I had on my ZHS 1160," Regen says. He moves closer to inspect it in more detail.

"This nameplate's in Morcan. My ship was made in Morca,

but I thought it and everything on it was at the bottom of the ocean."

Padopolous joins him at the unit. "It could be yours. The PSF's allowed to dismantle all seized ships before they're sunk. If there's any advanced system on it, they reverse engineer it for use on our defense craft."

Regen pats the shiny steel cover and smiles. "This is a damned good unit. Hey, that's why Hitler pissed on it. It smelled familiar to him, but they'd obviously cleaned his scent off it, and he needed to re-mark it."

"Makes sense, but we don't need a Warp unit. Will it do gravity interaction too?"

"Sure, it's all built in together. You just flip a switch on the control console to go from one system to the other. Let's open up the other crates."

Regen inspects each crate's contents and turns to Padopolous. "It's all here except for one piece."

"What's that?" Padopolous asks.

"There's one electronics rack missing. You need all of this to get the gravity interaction, but you can't do Warp speeds without that rack."

"Well, we don't need Warp speed anyway. The PSF probably kept that unit for some reason." Padopolous feels his mouth going dry and sweat beginning to form under his lab coat. He has the missing rack in his office safe, but there is no way he can let Regen know it. The Council would have him garroted for betraying their secret. *Do you suppose Regen's the one Selenia was talking about when she said somebody may want to use the rack?*

Chapter 6

Herion meets Regen at the tunnel train station and they take the elevator to the surface. Regen releases Hitler, and the skeen quickly vanishes into the jungle.

"How did the job go?" she asks.

"Routine, no problem there, but I got a surprise when I visited the Ark Museum."

"Oh, what was that?"

"The drive unit they sent was the one from my old ship."

Herion stops and turns to Regen with a surprised expression. "They didn't sink it with your ship?"

"Evidently not. Padopolous said the PSF probably checked it out to see if it had anything they could use. He says they do that with all the confiscated ships."

Herion resumes walking toward the skimmer. "Yes, they always check them over for any advanced technology, but I didn't think your ship was that advanced."

"It wasn't, as far as the propulsion system went, but they may have wanted the stealth stuff."

"Stealth?"

"Yeah, I had a pretty good system aboard, but it wasn't working too well because it got shot up while I was doing that job for the Princess on Bardour."

"It's Warp capable, then," Herion says.

"Nope, they pulled out the electronics rack that engages the Warp drive. It can only do gravitational interaction without that piece of the puzzle. I'm sure that's the Council's doing."

"It's only logical as far as they're concerned. You don't need it for orbital work, do you?' Herion says.

"No, but I'll bet they've got that rack someplace where I'll never be able to get to it."

"Hmmm, she might have just ordered the PSF not to send it with the rest of the gear. Maybe Padopolous still has some friends in the Space Force research section. He could check that out for you. If the Council's got it you're out of luck," Herion says.

"I'll think of some story for the Doc that'll get him to check out the PSF. If we can eliminate them, maybe you can pull some strings to check out the Council," Regen says.

"I still have some clout there, but Selenia and Elektra are very tight with Gilda, and if they're behind this, nobody's going to buck that trio of harpies."

"I hear you. We'll just have to take it one step at a time."

They board the skimmer and start for the game preserve. On the way, Herion stops in a small clearing and points to a cascade of flowers descending from the branch of a tree. "Look, the Moura tree is blooming. Let's go have a look." She pulls Regen out of the skimmer, and they move to the flowers.

"They're pretty, all right, but what's for supper?"

She playfully punches his shoulder. "You incurable romantic. Don't you remember? This is the clearing where your ship landed the first time."

"Well, I guess it was a good thing that rat back on Bardour sabotaged my navigation system. Otherwise, I'd have never met you. I'd probably be wasting away in some whorehouse just drinking and gambling."

Herion turns away and begins to cry. "At least you'd be free to do that instead of being a virtual prisoner here with me."

Regen turns her around and sweeps her into his arms. "Look, there's one thing I'm sure of, the best thing that ever happened to me was falling in love with you. I'd rather be here than anywhere in the universe." He kisses her tenderly and presses her tightly to his chest.

Herion returns his embrace and looks up into his deep blue eyes. Those eyes that first betrayed his feelings for her and caused her to risk all to bring him back. Those eyes which drew women to him in lust now shine with a tenderness reserved for only her and his wretched pet skeen. She even feels honored to be included in that exclusive circle. "I love you so much, and I don't care if you're lying through your teeth. I'm just glad you chose to love me."

"No other woman even came close to you, darling."

He kisses her again, but their intimate moment is interrupted by one of the gamekeepers.

"Lady Herion, there's …Oh, I'm sorry."

Herion pushes Regen away and wipes her red eyes with a part of her toga. "It's all right Yarina. What's the problem?"

"The Magus monkey's out and we need the tranquilizer gun to get him back in his cage, but the main problem is Regen's skeen has him cornered in the storage barn. I'm glad I found you two together."

"Take us there," Herion says, and she and Regen fall in behind Yarina as she leads the way to the problem.

They reach the storage barn to find a small crowd watching the spectacle. The monkey is busy swinging from rafter to rafter with Hitler racing back and forth beneath him.

Regen begins to laugh.

"What's so funny?" Herion asks.

"That monkey knows Hitler can't climb, and Hitler knows that monkey can't stay up there forever. We've got a real stand-off here, but I'll bet Hitler can wait him out."

"Well, we're not going to wait around for that," Herion says. She turns to Yarina. "Here's the key. Go get the tranquilizer gun."

"Yes Lady." Yarina races out and soon returns with a long case.

Herion opens the case and selects one of the darts. She opens the vial of tranquilizer and measures some into the dart. Yarina speaks. "Isn't that too much for..."

Herion silences her with a finger to her lips. "It's not for the monkey," she says in a low voice. She loads the gun and quickly aims the dart at Hitler before Regen notices the target is his skeen.

"What the hell?" Regen watches with mouth wide open as Hitler staggers about for a moment before collapsing on the floor. "I thought you were going to shoot the monkey."

"Think a moment, darling. If I shot the monkey, one of two things would happen. One, he'd fall to the floor, and Hitler would be upon him before you could stop it. I'd lose a prize specimen and you'd be facing Council disciplinary action for not keeping your pet under control. Two, the monkey would fall asleep up in the rafters, and someone would have to climb up and get him. That's totally unnecessary, as you will soon see. Call him down, Yarina."

The woman claps her hands and calls to the monkey. Seeing Hitler is no longer a danger, the monkey clambers down from the rafters and jumps into Yarina's arms.

"You see? Now I'll revive Hitler." Herion selects a syringe

from the case and loads it with antidote to the tranquilizer. She turns to Yarina. "You'd better get him back in his cage before the skeen wakes up."

"Yes, Lady." Yarina takes the monkey back to its cage while Herion revives Hitler.

The skeen staggers to its feet and scans the rafters with a mournful expression.

"Come 'ere, boy," Regen calls, and the skeen runs to his feet. The big Bremen kneels and rubs the thing's head. "It's okay. I'll get you a couple of rats for dinner."

★ ★ ★ ★ ★

That evening Regen calls Padopolous. "Hey Doc, I been thinking about that missing rack. Are those PSF boys sure it'll work for gravity interaction without it?"

"They're pretty sharp, but I'll talk to them tomorrow to make sure and let you know what I find out."

"Okay, call me as soon as you hear from them."

Regen signs off and turns to Herion. "The Doc's going to talk to the PSF boys in the morning. What do we do if the PSF's still got the unit?"

"You'll have to think of some excuse to get your hands on it. You're the technical type, I'm just a naturalist and animal biologist." She moves closer to Regen and begins to massage his neck and shoulders. "Maybe if you relaxed a bit."

"You know I won't get much relaxing with you doing that," Regen says.

★ ★ ★ ★ ★

Padopolous signs off from Regen and stares at his safe. *Regen must be the one Lady Selenia was talking about? He seems very interested in making the shuttle capable of Warp speeds, but why? As*

I remember, he argued very strongly with the Council to stay here with Herion, and they seem to be as happy as ever. If he suddenly wants to get away from Phoenicia, the shuttle's his only hope, but it's only a slim hope. I'll keep all of this quiet until I'm sure about his motives, and those of the Council.

★ ★ ★ ★ ★

The next afternoon Regen answers Padopolous' call. "What'd you find out, Doc?"

"I told them about your concern, and they assured me the gravity interaction section would work just fine without that rack. They were awfully evasive about where it was. I'll bet they're still using it for research and don't want the Council to know they've still got it." He has an easy time lying about the rack to throw Regen off the scent and deflect curiosity back toward the PSF.

"Just make sure it's not in one of those crates. I wouldn't want your guys to throw it out with some packing material, okay?"

"Sure, I'll supervise it myself. I'll let you know if we find it," Padopolous says.

"Okay, I got a job that'll keep me away for a couple of weeks, but I'll stop on my way home and have a look myself if you don't find it."

"No problem. See you later."

Regen signs off, and Herion steps from behind the communications camera. "If the PSF's got it, it's probably torn apart by now so they can see what makes it tick. If the Council confiscated it, you can bet Hitler it's in a vault in the capital somewhere under Gilda's control," she says.

"You're probably right. Either way, I'll never get hold of it." Regen slumps into a chair and pours himself a large glass of

Gordian bourbon. "You want any bourbon?"

"No thanks." She moves to his chair and lifts him to his feet. "I still have some friends on the Council. I'll make some inquiries while you're gone. Meantime, put down that glass and come to the bed. You're going to be gone a long time, you know, and drinking dulls your sensual skills."

"Speaking of that, I will need something to tide me over until I get back." He sets his glass on a table and follows her to the bedroom area.

Chapter 7

Restoration of the shuttlecraft is going well. The structure is in better shape than expected, and rewiring is going smoothly. Padopolous finds he has plenty of time to ponder the electronics rack in his safe.

One thing's obvious—the Council wants someone to be able to use the ship for Warp speed work on a moment's notice, but who? The closest planet's Diron, but it's primitive with no modern comforts. I can't imagine any of the Council members wanting to go there. Gerba's a more desirable destination, but it's over 25 light years away. The shuttle's life support system'd be marginal for that journey, considering any Council member would want to bring an entourage of staffers and sycophants along. Beyond that, several modern planets might be reached by three or four people. I'd better keep a close eye on planetary politics until I can sort it all out.

★ ★ ★ ★ ★

Herion is at the tunnel train station to meet Regen, but instead of pulling her into his arms he holds back pointing to the sling supporting her left arm. "What happened to you?" he asks.

"Oh, it's nothing. I just broke my arm when I fell the other day." Herion shrugs it off as if were a mere scratch, but she knows Regen won't accept that explanation.

"Just broke your arm? How did you fall? I thought you were supposed to be careful about that stuff." A porter brings up Hitler in his cage, and Regen tips him before turning back to Herion.

"I was being careful, but our Codder snake was up in a tree, and she'll only respond to my voice. I had to get on a ladder to coax her down, and as I was reaching for her I got vertigo and fell. They tell me it's all part of my problem."

"You never should have climbed that ladder, damnit." Regen stomps off toward the game preserve, and Herion looks after him perplexed.

"Regen," she calls after him, but he doesn't turn around. She sets her jaw and catches up with him. She runs ahead of him and turns to face him, stopping his progress with her good arm. "Look, I can't just sit around and wait to die. I have to keep going in my job, and that means taking some chances every now and then. Now stop acting like a spoiled child."

He pushes her hand away from his chest but holds it for a moment before pulling her to him and kissing her tenderly. "I'm sorry. It's just I don't want anything to happen before I get a chance to take you someplace where they can help you."

She lays her head on his chest and sighs. "I know, I know. Let's get to our hut, and I'll fill you in on what I found out while you were gone."

★ ★ ★ ★ ★

At the game preserve Regen lets Hitler run, and he and Herion climb into their home. He finds some wine for Herion and poured himself a large shot of Gordian Bourbon. "Okay, what's up?"

"The gossip around the capitol is that Gilda's up to something, but nobody knows what it is. She still wields enough power to intimidate the usual gossips. I did learn that Selenia was the one who worked with the PSF to get the drive system, and my source in her office said she didn't have any of the pieces for it when she got back to the capital. That doesn't mean Selenia didn't hand the unit over to Gilda before she went to her office."

"Padopolous thinks the PSF still has it. I checked out all the crates and boxes at the museum and couldn't find it. Maybe he's right." Regen takes a swig of bourbon.

"Wait a minute. Gilda knows I'm sick, and she's probably figured you may want to get away from Phoenicia when I'm gone. Don't you see? It all makes sense now. That unit's someplace where you'll be sure to find it when the time comes. She's betting you'll not be able to outrun the PSF. They'll catch you, and she'll laugh while they execute you for trying to get away."

"She's probably right about that. That shuttlecraft's heavier than my ship. I doubt it can do Warp 200 even with my old propulsion system. I imagine those PSF interceptors can do better than 200. I'll never make it unless we can surprise them some way."

"That means she's got someone who'll tip her off when you make your move. I wonder who that could be." Herion sips her wine as she ponders the problem in silence.

"Then it wouldn't be in the capitol. It'd have to be somewhere in the museum where I could get my hands on it easily. That means somebody in the museum or somebody close to us is working for Gilda. They'll let her know the minute we try to leave. Luckily, we got some time to find out. That shuttle won't be ready to go for another six months or so. They're making good progress, but you can only go so fast. I'll sniff around to find that rack. I figure once I find it, I'll have a pretty good idea who the rat is."

At that point Hitler runs into the room and jumps on Regen's lap. Herion begins to laugh.

"What's funny?" Regen asks.

"Hitler should come in handy finding a rat."

The Bremen strokes the skeen's chin and muses, "That rack's got to be close to the shuttle. You just may have put your finger on the solution."

Chapter 8

It was runiga season, and Regen and Hitler are busy on islands far away from the Ark Museum. Padopolous keeps him up to speed through daily messages, but Regen still feels the need to see progress in person. One evening the message raises the priority of an in-person visit considerably. It reads:

The food synthesizer unit has to go. It's too corroded to repair, and we can't afford to replace it. Luckily, we won't need it for giving the patrons joy rides. Hope the runiga hunts are going well. Let me know when you can stop by to see how well the rest of the project's going.

"Damn." Regen knows they won't need the unit for the stated mission of the shuttlecraft, but it's vital to his scheme. He and Herion face several weeks in deep space, and he doubts they can stand the extra weight of real food.

Hitler jumps to the bed beside his master looking for attention, and Regen strokes his head. "We got a problem, fella. I knew we had to carry a bunch of rats for you, but we can't eat rats. I have to find some way to keep us humans alive until we get to Terma. You got any ideas?

The skeen coos his response and shifts his head to expose another area for Regen's attentions. The next day, Regen rearranges his schedule so he can visit the Ark Museum between jobs.

★ ★ ★ ★ ★

"It's good to see you, Regen." Padopolous greets his partner with genuine enthusiasm. "Things are really going well. Have a chair, and let me fill you in on how far we've come since your last visit."

Regen releases Hitler from his cage to run inside the working enclosure and sits down opposite his partner in the project. "I got your message about the food synthesizer. That's too bad. The people taking the ride'll want some kind of snack, and I figured a taste of space food'd make the experience realistic." He says.

"So did I, but we can't repair it, and we can't afford a new one. We'll just have to take some snacks along on each trip."

Regen knows he can't afford to arouse any suspicions by revealing his disappointment. He has to put on a good show for Padopolous' benefit. "I guess it's silly to put a lot of money into something we really don't need. Any other problems?"

"No, the rest of the structure's good. Only a few bulkhead replacements here and there. We've replaced all the old wiring and anything that looked too rotten to use. We should have new seals in three weeks. The water recirculating system's good. That was a real surprise. It only needed some new seals, and they were a standard size. We're just getting into the life support system. It's old technology, and we'll probably want to replace it with a modern unit for safety purposes."

"Have we got money in the budget for that?" Regen asks.

"I think we've got enough. I planned on that originally, but if we'd need any more of your funds for anything, that should be the place to put them."

"I agree. Looks like it's all going well. I think I'll look around for a while before I head for Kamara to see how Herion's doing."

"No problem, I'll be on the floor if you have any more questions." Padopolous moves to the rear of the craft to supervise some work there, and Regen heads for the crates holding the drive unit. Hitler is nowhere to be seen, and he hopes the skeen hasn't found a way to enter the museum. The animal would certainly cause a panic among the visitors.

Once again, he checks the crates for the missing control circuit rack with no success. He remembers Padopolous keeps a bottle of Gordian bourbon in his office and heads for that area to console his frustration. Entering the room, he sees Hitler sniffing curiously at the scientist's safe.

It's a drab gray floor safe standing about a meter tall and appearing as formidable as any battle tank. The keypad on the door holds the usual ten digits plus some Phoenician symbols to complicate the safe cracker's job. A large chrome handle completes the picture. He's seen Padopolous put papers inside the thing, but he didn't paid any attention to the combination.

"There's nothing in there, boy. The old guy only keeps his scientific papers in that safe. Get over here."

Hitler looks up at his master and coos imploringly while he paws at the steel door.

"You'd think there was some kind of rat in there, or something, the way you're acting. Get away from there." He kicks at his pet, but Hitler only moves out of his reach, returning to the safe as soon as Regen turns his back.

"I give up. Go ahead and sniff all you want." Regen sits down at Padopolous' desk and opens the lower left-hand drawer to obtain the whiskey. He pours a healthy shot into one of the spare coffee mugs and leans back in the swivel chair with his feet on the desk.

I wonder what he's got in that safe. Whatever it is, Hitler sure wants it. I'll just go out and ask him about it. He starts to rise but sits back down at once. *Hey, he acted the same way when the crates with my drive system arrived. I wonder if the missing rack's in there.*

He begins to look around the office. *People don't like to memorize safe combinations. I'll bet he's got something around here that reminds him what it is.*

He checks the computer for any hint of a secret area with safe combinations and finds nothing requiring a password. The desk is fairly neat for a scientist, and there are no hidden drawers. No scribbled numbers appear under the desktop or on normally inaccessible locations. The safe itself is devoid of markings, but Regen checks the numerical equivalent of the brand name as a possibility. There are no pictures or plaques on the walls that might serve as a mnemonic for the combination, only a large periodic table marked in the Phoenician language. He walks over to it and studies the display. Three elements show faint smudges of fingerprints: iron, lead and phosphorous.

Funny he should think a lot about those things. An idea suddenly occurs to him. He writes down the atomic numbers; 26, 82, 15. He tries several combinations of the numbers with no success before resuming his seat and pouring another mug of bourbon.

There must be some symbols in the combination. Let's see, iron starts with φ, but there's no φ. Lead starts with Π and that's one of them. Phosphorous is also φ, so Π must be the symbol.

He takes a swig of bourbon and mixes Π into the sequence until the sound of a metallic "click" tells him he's found the correct order. He opens the safe, revealing the missing component.

That little weasel's had this all along. He's the one in cahoots with Gilda. As soon as I got hold of this, he'd clue her in, and I'd be dog meat. He's just waiting until that shuttle's finished to give me some hint about this thing so I can steal it and make a try at getting off this planet.

Regen closes the safe, much to Hitler's discomfort. "Well, boy you're just going to have to keep away from this safe until we're ready to make our play. Now that I know Padopolous is the guy. We can't tip him off."

The skeen gives its master a puzzled look then paws at the safe again.

"It's the cage for you when we're around here, that's for sure." Regen coaxes his pet back into its cage with one of its favorite treats and secures the door carefully just as Padopolous walks in.

"I see you found my stash of your favorite bourbon," he says.

"Yep, but I had to cage up Hitler. I think he's found a way out of the work area, and we can't have him running loose in the museum."

Padopolous laughs at the thought of the skeen scaring the daylights out of the school field trips. "I don't know, it might be fun seeing what happens." He pours himself a shot of bourbon and sits down.

"Well, it looks like things are going good here. I want to drop by and see Herion before I go on to the next job. Give me a call if you run into any problems." He sets Hitler's cage to follow him and shakes Padopolous' hand before leaving.

"Say hello to her Ladyship for me, and have a nice trip. I'll keep you up to speed," Padopolous says.

Chapter 9

Herion's face brightens at the sound of the voice behind her. "Hey, how about taking a break." Regen walks up to her desk and throws his arms around her.

She turns and kisses him on the cheek. "What a pleasant surprise. I thought you were on your way to Gaida today. Why didn't you call me?"

"It was a last-minute decision. Padopolous told me about a problem on the restoration, so I rigged my schedule to check it out. It also gave me a chance to stop and see how you were doing. I got three hours before the next train. Let's take a walk."

She rises and turns to an assistant. "Finish that report on this year's falugga run for me will you please, Wanda?"

"Yes, Lady. I'll take care of it." Wanda smiles broadly as she moves to Herion's desk. She nods to Regen on the way.

The pair go to their hut and Herion pours him a glass of bourbon. She starts to undress, but Regen stops her.

"We can do that later. I need to tell you about that missing electronics rack."

"Oh, did you find it?" she says as she re-wraps her toga.

"Padopolous's got it."

"Padopolous? He's always acted like he's as much in the dark as we were."

"I know, I figure he's Gilda's agent in all this. We can't trust him with anything now."

Herion pours herself a tumbler of fruit juice. "How did you find it?"

"I didn't, Hitler did. He sniffed it out in Padopolous' office. It's in the old guy's safe, but I got the combination."

"I don't think I want to know how you did that," she says as she sips her drink.

"No real problem there. Most people have their combination around somewhere. Safe cracking's the easiest job in the universe."

"Too bad it's him. You two have to work very closely on this project."

Regen takes a swig of bourbon before continuing. "Another thing, the food synthesizer's no good, and we can't afford a new one. We'll have to take enough food aboard to last the whole trip when we leave, and that's a lot of extra weight."

"Not to mention hoarding it up'll attract attention," Herion says.

"I don't care if Gilda sees us stockpiling food. She knows we're going to try an escape anyway. My only worries are the extra weight and the fact that it might give her some clue about when we plan to leave."

"Is the weight really a problem? Didn't the shuttlecraft carry some cargo besides a lot more passengers than you, me and Hitler?" Herion asks.

"I'll have to calculate how much we can take next time I see Padopolous, and I'll have to find something that doesn't have to be refrigerated." Regen sits back and muses on that problem, but Herion changes the subject

"I've been thinking about money. We'll need something that's negotiable for cash wherever we wind up, and jewelry might be a good trade item. I assume diamonds are as valuable elsewhere as they are here."

"Sure are, in fact, they're worth more in other places. You folks seem to have a lot of them, and they're cheap by my standards. But, like I told you, I got people who owe me favors if we can get to their planets."

"We can't count on being able to reach those planets in one hop. We may need to refuel, or something," Herion counters.

"You're right, I guess. It won't hurt to have a little extra, but don't overdo the jewelry buying."

"You can help there too, you know," Herion says as a wry smile spreads across her face.

"Is that a hint?" Regen asks.

"No, think of it as payment for services rendered," Herion says as she stands and lets her toga slip to the floor.

★ ★ ★ ★ ★

At the capital Selenia welcomes Gilda for cocktails and dinner. "Come in Lady. Aurora has cocktails for us on the terrace."

The women sit down on a balcony overlooking the capital. The artificial sky is beginning to show the marvelous sunset generated by the atmospheric computer each evening from a random selection of elements in its gigantic memory banks. They make themselves comfortable on chaise lounges as the servants pour wine and deliver hors d'oeuvres on silver platters.

"How's the restoration project going?" Gilda asks Selenia.

"According to schedule. They had to scrap the food synthesizer unit." A wicked smile brightens her face as takes a sip of wine.

"Won't that put a crimp in Regen's escape plans?" Gilda asks.

"Only a minor one. He can put enough food aboard to last until the PSF capture him," Selenia says. The ladies break into merry laughter at that remark, envisioning the eventual defeat of Regen.

"How is the Lady Herion doing? She's the key to all of this," Gilda asks.

"My sources say she's still doing well. It takes Bryllion's Syndrome a while to claim its victims. She'll be viable for another year, or so. After that no one knows," Selenia says. "She could be walking with assistance from a gravitational support unit or completely bed-ridden. It all depends upon which route the disease takes."

"I'm sure Regen will pull out as soon as she's no good in the bedroom," Gilda says. She pops a canapé into her mouth and follows it with a swig of wine.

"I'm not as sure as you are about that," Selenia says. "I think he really loves her, and I believe he'll stay with her until the end. In any case we'll have plenty of warning about his attempt to escape. Padopolous will tell us the moment Regen lays his hands on the Warp drive unit."

Gilda raises her glass in a toast. "To the eventual demise of Regen the Bremen," she says.

"Hear, hear," Selenia responds.

Chapter 11

On his next visit to the museum Regen is surprised by the progress. The hull is now polished to a high gleam, and new seals stand out in shining black contrast. He slaps the old scientist on the back nearly knocking him down.

"By Astarte, Doc, you're doing a good job. This thing looks ready to take off any minute."

Padopolous composes himself and catches his breath before responding. "Still a long way to go yet. We haven't even started installing your drive system. The water system's in and working as required, and you already know about the food synthesizer. Life support needed to be all new, but we'd calculated on that. The parts should be arriving next week."

"How about the navigation system?" Regen asks because he knows the original estimate did not include a new deep space system.

"All we need is an orbital system, but the odd thing is the original deep space system still works, even after all these years. Quite a tribute to those ancient engineers, I'd say."

"You got to be kidding?"

"Not at all. The star tracker unit's in first class shape, but its data base is over 5,000 years old. It wouldn't be much good if somebody tried to use it today. A lot of those stars don't even exist anymore, and none of them are where they were then."

"I don't know. 5,000 years isn't much time when it comes to galactic movement."

"I know, but that's a moot point anyway since we won't need

it."

Regen makes a mental note to do some research on galactic evolution and moves to another subject. "How about communication?"

"We put in all the standard PSF stuff. We ripped out the old deep space gear to save weight. This thing weighs a lot more than your old ship."

"You're right, but did the old stuff work?" Regen asks.

"No, it was shot, and the technology was ancient anyway. It's a good thing we could save some weight, the Council's only allowed us 30 fuel rods at a time."

"Thirty? It'll hold 75. Why only 30?"

"They say that's all the PSF can spare. You have to remember we only have two mines for fuel crystals on the entire planet. The PSF didn't want to give us 30, but Selenia had the Council authorize a step-up in mining to make 30 possible."

Selenia again. She's making sure I have enough to try an escape but not enough to outrun the PSF. She's a cagey bitch, that's for sure. "Well, we'll have to make do with 30. It'll just mean more trips to refuel."

"I figure we can go two weeks on 30 rods, and that's okay."

Yeah, okay for the tourists, but not enough to make a good run for it. "I guess you're right. Any thought of adding an artificial gravity system?"

"I priced it, and we can't afford it. Maybe if everything else stays in budget we can get one."

"The tourists won't think much of zero g if we don't get it, and I'm not too keen on cleaning out the cabin after a mass outbreak of space sickness."

"I know what you mean, but we'll just have to wait and see."

"Okay, I'll check with you on my next trip through. I have to get to Kamara and check on Herion now."

"How's she doing?"

Regen thinks he detects a genuine note of concern in the old man's voice even though he's sure of the source of the question.

"Not much happening right now. She has to take it easy, but she's still getting around good for the time being."

"Good to hear that. Give her my best."

"I'll do that. See ya, Doc."

★ ★ ★ ★ ★

Herion meets him at the station and takes control of Hitler's cage. "Welcome back. How's the shuttle coming?"

"Lookin' good, but Gilda and her harpies are making sure the PSF can catch us if we try anything. They're only letting me have 30 fuel rods."

"Is that bad?" Herion sets the cage controls to follow her, and the trio set off for the game preserve on foot.

"It isn't good. That's enough to try a run, but without stealth gear the PSF'd be all over us in no time."

"Looks like you're stuck here with me." She looks at him and smiles.

"Can't think of anybody I'd rather be stuck someplace with." He pulls her to him and kisses her gently. "How are you feeling lately?"

"No problems as long as I stay out of trees and off cliffs. I get a little woozy sometimes when I first stand up after sitting for a long time, but nothing to speak of."

When they reach their hut Regen opens his bag and hands a small case to Herion. "A little something to keep for our trip."

She opens the case and sucks in her breath. "Ohhh, this must have set you back a bundle." She lifts a sparkling necklace from the purple felt and lets the candlelight bring out its full brilliance.

"Believe me, we'll need all of this and more to get us where I want to be. Thirty fuel rods means I'll have to stop somewhere to refuel before we get to Terma, and they don't give that stuff away."

Herion finds a mirror and holds the necklace up to her throat. "It's so beautiful. I'd hate to have to sell it."

"Okay, I won't show you the next one in case you'd get too attached to it."

Herion puts the necklace back in its case and begins to cry. Regen moves to her side and takes her in his arms.

"What's wrong?"

She buries her face in his chest and sobs. "It isn't fair."

"What isn't fair? You sure as hell deserve a lot more than that necklace."

"Not that, this disease. By the time we're ready to go I may not be able to enjoy fine jewelry or anything else."

"It won't be long now. We should be ready to have a go at it before you get worse. I'm sure there's somebody out there that knows how to cure this bug, and I'll get you to him."

She regains her composure and pulls away from his embrace. "What if there isn't anybody? What if we don't even make it past the PSF? Even if we do, I'll die in a strange land away from all the people I love. Is it worth it?"

He turns her to face him and grips her shoulders. "Don't talk like that. You have to keep thinking positive about this."

"I know, but I doubt anyone out there can do any more than we can here."

"Look, the last time I talked to Lunna she said you should see a doctor in the capitol for a second opinion. Why don't you take a few days off and go see about it. She said you could stay with her."

Herion dries her eyes on a lace handkerchief she draws from inside her toga and shakes off Regens hands. "I should do that. I'll call her tonight."

"Okay, now let's have a glass of wine and think about something more pleasant."

"Sure, there's some good rosé in the cooler."

"I'll get it."

He opens the wine and pours two glasses. Herion smiles again and says, "What no bourbon?"

Regen sits next to her and hands her one of the glasses. He raises his in a toast. "Bourbon isn't good for toasting. Here's to only good thoughts from now on."

Herion raises her glass to touch his. "I'll do my best, but it won't be easy."

The next morning, Regen escorts Herion to the tunnel train station and sees her off to the capitol.

Chapter 11

Lunna's colorful toga is a welcome sight as Herion steps off the tunnel train.

"Herion! How good to see you," Lunna says as she embraces her life-long friend.

Herion exchanges friendly kisses with the bubbly and slightly plump Council member. "It's good to see you too, and good of you to put me up while I'm here."

They walk to the baggage claim area where Herion picks up one small suitcase.

"Is that all you have?" Lunna asks.

"I'm only going to be here a few days. I don't need any more than this." She hefts the case to show its light weight.

"If it was me, I'd have five times that much luggage. You don't even need a porter for that." Lunna's hand flies to her mouth. "I'm sorry, I forgot your condition. Do we need a porter?"

Herion laughs. "No, I can carry it. Did your limo bring you?"

"Yes, it's waiting outside the gate. This way."

Herion steps out of the terminal and basks a moment in the atmosphere of the planet's capitol city. It feels good to be back where so many happy moments of her life transpired. She remembers the feeling of awesome power she knew as a Councilwoman. She's glad to be rid of the burdens of authority, but being back in the seat of political power revives the lure of high office and the perks accompanying it.

Lunna notices the nostalgic look and says, "Do you miss it?"

Herion relaxes and smiles. "No, but I do have some very fond memories of this place."

"Next year is my last year on the Council. I don't know what I'll do after that. I do have one or two women who want me to join their businesses, but I'm not sure I want to tie up with either of them. You're lucky to have your situation, and Regen, of course."

"Yes, I always wanted to work with animals, and Regen is a bonus I hadn't planned on."

"Hey, a lover with an unusual animal for a pet, you kill two birds with one stone, so to speak." Luna nudges Herion with her elbow then recoils. "Oh my god, did I hurt you?"

Herion laughs. "Luna, it's not that kind of illness. Don't treat me as if I were made of glass."

"Sorry, I just don't want to make things worse. Here's my limo."

A pink limo with lavender trim stands at the curb. A driver in a powder blue jump suit opens the door, revealing a plush pink interior.

"Luna, are you sure my toga won't clash with your limo décor?"

They climb into the limo, and the driver gets underway without instructions.

"I assumed you'd want to rest a while after your trip," Lunna says.

"Yes, a nap before dinner sounds good. I have a full day tomorrow, though. The medics will be running a whole battery of tests."

"Will you need anyone with you?"

"No, I'll be fine, but thank you for asking."

"How are you, really?"

"I have spells of dizziness, but nothing serious yet. The doctor at the preserve says I've got a good 12-18 months of minor problems before the serious stuff kicks in."

Lunna decides it's time to change the subject. "Tell me, does Regen still have his horrible pet?"

"Oh yes, they're inseparable. He's still taking him out on jobs to control the runiga, but he's wrapped up in the restoration of one of the Ark's shuttlecraft right now."

"I heard about that project. I must have a ride when they get it finished."

"I think it'll be very popular. No one on Phoenicia has ever been off the planet's surface, except for the space force," Herion says.

The limo stops at an upscale apartment building, and the driver opens the door for his passengers. As they step out, he asks Lunna, "Will you need the car again before dinner, Lady?"

"No Dreppo. We have reservations at the Athena Room for 6:30, so you can bring the car around at six." She turns to Herion. "I hope that's okay with you."

"Oh yes, I haven't had a really elegant meal in years. You made a good choice."

"Good." She turns to Dreppo. "Just carry Lady Herion's bag up to the apartment, and you're free until then."

"Yes, Lady." He touches his cap and picks up the small bag.

They walks into the plush lobby and past the security guards to an elevator. Lunna's apartment is on the fourth floor, and Herion revels in the expensive aroma of the hallway. Lunna opens the door and leads Herion to her room. "This is your space while you're here. I'll leave you to nap and call you at four. Have a good rest."

Herion kisses her and directs Dreppo to place the bag next to the dresser. She falls on the bed and is soon asleep.

★ ★ ★ ★ ★

The next day at the hospital Herion is prodded, poked, run through a half-dozen machines, tapped for blood several times, hooked up to an assortment of beeping devices and spends over a half-hour entering data into a computer terminal. The final ordeal is studying the wallpaper pattern in an examination room while she waits for the doctor to tell her what it all means. She'd almost given up on finding the secret to life and the universe in the floral design when a short, stubby woman in a lab coat opens the door and approaches her.

"I'm doctor Valous, Lady Herion." She extends her hand.

Herion takes it without standing. "I'm pleased to meet you Dr. Valous, and I'm anxious to learn what you've discovered."

Valous pulls up a stool on coasters and sits down opposite Herion. "I'm afraid I don't have any good news. Your doctor on Kamara was correct in her diagnosis. It is Bryllion's Syndrome, but I'm afraid she was optimistic about the prognosis."

"How's that?" Herion feels her throat constrict a bit and her heart beat faster.

"You have Thalla's Variation. It's a particularly aggressive form of the disease. Where she said you probably had 18 months to two years before you become incapacitated, I would say you've only got a year or less to function independently. After that, you'll need to be in a facility providing constant care until your death."

Herion sags visibly, and her eyes grow moist with tears. "Only that long?"

"Yes, I'm sorry."

"And, there's nothing medicine can do to extend my usefulness?"

"There are medications which will help as the disease progresses, but none that will halt or reverse it. I'm sorry to be the one to give you the bad news."

"Don't be sorry. I've already resigned myself to my fate, but I thought I had longer."

"What will you do?"

"I'll go on as long as I can, then do whatever has to be done. I'm more worried about Regen than myself. He has a penchant for getting into trouble if I'm not around to advise him about customs on our planet."

"I've heard of him. He's quite rich, isn't he?"

"He has some money, but he doesn't have a tactful bone in his body, and he rubs people the wrong way at times."

"Well, I can't help much in that regard, but if there's anything else I can do for you, please call me."

"Thank you, Doctor. I'll do that."

The doctor rises, and Herion stands to shake her hand, but the doctor embraces her instead. "I wish you every happiness, Lady," she says, then turns and leaves the office with tears in her eyes.

Chapter 12

Regen's next job is on Logana Island. He'd plans on a hotel, but the Governor's limo is waiting for him at the station.

"Is that for me?" he asks the uniformed man holding a sign saying "Regen".

"Yes, sir. Governor Marana has requested you stay at the mansion while you're here unless you have other plans."

"Suits me fine. I'll cancel my hotel reservations."

"No need, Governor Marana has already done that."

The driver loads Regen's bag into the trunk of the limo, and Regen slaves Hitler's cage to the top of the limo. In only a half hour they reach the Governor's residence, a large mansion resting in the middle of a gated estate. Marana is there to meet him.

"Welcome to Logana Island, Regen. I've heard so much about you."

"All good, I hope," Regen says. He knows nothing about this woman but the tall, lithe redhead before him in the close-fitting toga is all the information he needs.

"Absolutely, come on inside."

She ushers him into the spacious entryway and up a flight of marble stairs to an ornately decorated room. "This is your room. Call me when you get settled in. I found some Gordian Bourbon you might like for cocktails."

"Sounds good. How do I get you?"

"There's a red button on the communicator console. It connects you to me directly. Just push it as many times as you like." She smiles as she leaves Regen to his unpacking.

He feeds Hitler but keeps him in his cage. The skeen will get plenty of exercise the next day hunting runiga. He pushes the red button and Marana's face fills the screen.

"Hey, Regen. You ready for some cocktails?"

"Sure, where are you?"

The picture changes to a view of a naked Marana lying on a silken-sheeted bed. "Two doors on the left down the hall. Don't be too long." The screen goes dark.

"I'll be right there," he whispers to himself before he moves to the bathroom and sprays some cologne on a few strategic areas.

★ ★ ★ ★ ★

The next day he takes Hitler to the first area of the surface called for in his contract. As the skeen hunts he relaxes under an umbrella-like tree and reads about the island on his portable console. At noon, he eats the fine picnic lunch Marana's staff sent with him, and two hours later Hitler pops into view carrying a dead runiga to his master.

Regen takes the varmint and throws it into the brush. "You know I don't eat those things, boy." Hitler looks after his catch, but makes no move to retrieve it. Regen loads him into his cage and returns to the Governor's mansion. Marana is waiting for him in her room.

★ ★ ★ ★ ★

The next morning Regen wraps his toga around his middle and pads back to his room.

Hitler lays in his cage not even attempting to move when Regen opens the door.

"What's the matter fellah? You off your feed, or something?"

He places his hand on the animal's nose and knows the answer. "You're cold as ice. What have you been eating?"

He checks the bottom of the cage where the skeen's stools fall and finds several recent examples. Breaking one apart, he sniffs at it tentatively. "Oh boy, you ain't right at all."

Regen scoops up two more stools into a sample container and closes the cage door. He carries them to a table and opens a case containing some diagnostic equipment. Now, Regen is no scientist, but since skeens are often killed with poisoned bait, he's accumulated some equipment to check for such chemicals in the animal's stools or blood. After several tests he pounds his fist on the table and rises with blood in his eyes. "Some no-good bastard's been putting out poisoned bait for the runiga around here, and it looks like quadzol."

A few quick tests confirm quadzol as the poison. "Yep, just as I figured. It's quadzol. They think it'll get rid of the varmints without hiring me, but those critters've almost developed an immunity to the stuff. Too bad it's just as bad for skeens as runiga." He fills a hypodermic with the antidote and injects Hitler. "Okay, fella, you should be okay in a couple of hours."

Regen makes sure the antidote is taking effect then enters the governor's sleeping room and shakes her awake.

"Get up, sweet cheeks."

Governor Marana pushes him away without opening her eyes. "Not now, Regen, it's too early for that."

"It's past seven, and besides, that's not what this is all about. We've got a problem."

Marana opens her eyes and glances at the clock. "Why didn't Boris wake me up? I should have been up an hour ago." She swings her feet to the floor and slips them into silver mules.

"If you remember, you told him to let you sleep this morning."

"Oh, yes, we were up quite late last night, but what's so drastic you've got to interrupt my beauty sleep?"

"Somebody's set out poisoned bait, and we have to find out where it is before I let Hitler out again."

Her face takes on a concerned expression as she rises and walks toward the shower. "Is he all right?" Without waiting for his answer, she steps into the enclosure and turns on the water.

Regen raises his voice to overcome the noise. "He's fine. I just gave him the antidote. He'll be okay in an hour or so. You need to put out a bulletin telling people to stop putting out poisoned bait."

She replies over the spatter of the shower, "I can't hear you. Wait 'til I'm out of the shower."

Regen sits patiently until the water spray stops then repeats, "You need to put out a bulletin to stop people putting out poisoned bait."

Marana wraps herself in a towel and returns to the bedroom. She sits at a mirror and begins to brush her hair. "I've already done that, but I'll get the police to check for anyone buying poison. Do you know what poison they should be looking for?"

"Yeah, it was quadzol," Regen answers

"Be a dear and call Boris for me, will you?"

"Sure." Regen punches up her communicator and finds her assistant.

"What's up, Regen?"

"Governor Marana's got a job for you."

Marana leans into the camera view and speaks. "Boris, darling, somebody's been putting out runiga bait poisoned with quadzol against my order. Have the police check the island over and arrest anyone who's purchased quadzol recently. We can't have that stuff out there while Regen and Hitler are here. They nearly killed his skeen."

"Yes, Lady. I'll get to it right away."

"Thank you." She blows a kiss at the screen as it goes dark.

★ ★ ★ ★ ★

By noon Hitler is himself again, and Boris calls to inform Regen they've found no one who purchased the poison Regen reported. "Where were you yesterday?" Boris asks.

"We were up on the surface checking out the air intakes near that big jungle area on the west side of the island," Regen replied.

"Hmmm, nobody up there but one old woman who lives by herself in the middle of that jungle. She never comes out for anything except when she needs a doctor. She doesn't even own a communicator. She's a real nut for environmental causes. I can't see her putting out poisoned bait. Hitler had to get it somewhere else."

"We haven't been anywhere else before he got sick. She must've set out the poison. Send some police up with me, and I'll show them where he was huntin'."

"Okay, I'll call the Chief and have her send Sergeant Damos and her squad with you. Damos knows the old bat, and can talk to her. Meet them at the elevator in an hour and show her where you were hunting."

"I'll be there."

★ ★ ★ ★ ★

Damos is not a typical cop. Regen figures the Phoenician dictionary has a picture of her next to the definition of the word "naturalist". She wears no make-up, and her hair hangs straight and unkempt down to her shoulders, but Regen knows the nerdy exterior hides a fit interior and a toughness not to be trifled with. The police wear jungle camouflage jump suits instead of their usual blue togas. He's anticipated this and wears his runiga hunting clothes. Damos greets him.

"Been a while since we saw you last."

"Yeah, not since runiga season last year. Come on, I'll show you where we were huntin' the other day."

Regen leads the group to the area and confers with Damos. "We were just east of here yesterday. I'll take that area. Have your people look around to the west. We'll meet back here."

"Sound good to me. Here, take one of these," she opens a container and hands Regen a sensor on a one-meter handle.

"Oh good, I was hoping you'd bring some 'sniffers'," Regen says.

"Not much use looking for poisoned bait without them. Do you know how they work?"

"Yup, I've used them once or twice."

"Good. I didn't think I'd need to train you. Let's get started," she replies and issues the orders to her squad.

Regen walks into the jungle. The summer sun blasts anyone in the open, but under the shade of the high canopy, the humidity makes breathing a chore. His clothes are wet before he's gone a few meters into the bush. He scans the ground for any sign of poisoned bait, lifting brush carefully in case he disturbs one of the many deadly snakes native to the island. He's quite surprised by the two men clad in black jump suits with ski masks over their faces. The tall one holds a laser pistol while the shorter one prods Regen with what looks like a short spear.

"Keep quiet, Regen, and put your hands up," he says as he

pokes the Bremen again.

"Easy with that thing." Regen drops his 'sniffer' and raises his hands. The tall man frisks him.

"He's not carrying," tall guy says.

"What's this all about?" Regen asks as he lowers his arms.

"It's about some people that want you dead."

"Take a number and wait your turn," Regen answers.

"We're crashin' the line, smart guy. Now follow him." The tall one walks into the jungle, and shorty prods Regen on from behind.

"Where are we going?" Regen asks.

"No questions, just keep walking." Shorty prods him again with the spear.

"If you're going to kill me, why not right here?" Regen stops walking and turns to face shorty.

"Now, if I do you here, we'd have to carry your body another stadia, or so. I really don't want to do that in this heat. If I kill you here, it'll be slow and painful, but if you walk on, I'll make it quick."

"Sounds like a bargain," Regen says as he resumes walking. *Okay, we've got a ways to go yet. Maybe I can think of some way to take these guys while we're on the way. I need to get them thinking about something else.* "What's so special about going deeper into the bush?"

"There's a crazy old woman who lives in this jungle. Nobody knows much about her except she doesn't have laser weapons and she hates strangers. You're just going to happen to run into her on a bad day, that's all."

"Is this Gilda's doing?" Regen asks.

"That ain't for you to know. Just keep walking."

"I know it's her. She's wanted me dead from day one, but I always thought she'd do it legal-like."

The tall one's jump suit shows the effects of the heat and humidity very quickly. Sweat soaks through the cloth and glistens even in the dim light below the treetops. Regen feels the salty dew sting his eyes and tastes the brine as it seeps into the corners of his mouth.

All I can hope for now is for one of Damos' boys to find us. I can't hear them anywhere close, though. I can take the guy with the spear, but the tall one with the laser pistol's a different story. If I take him first, the short one'll stick that spear in me before I could get hold of the laser pistol. Too bad Hitler isn't along. He could keep one of them busy while I took out the other one.

"You guys could save us all a lot of sweat by doing the job here," Regen says.

"That'd suit me fine, but we gotta get to the old woman's cave area before we take care of you. The people who sent us want it to look like she did the job. The story is that you came looking for her after she poisoned your animal, and she got you first."

"The cops with me won't go for that," Regen says.

"Sure they will. Everybody knows how you love that piece of shit lizard. Now that it's dead, they won't have to stretch their imagination any to believe you went after the old gal that killed it."

"What you guys don't know is Hitler's alive."

"Hold up a minute," the short one calls, and the tall guy stops and turns toward them.

"We need to get on with it. That old hag might find us any minute, and I don't want to have to deal with her too," the tall one says.

"Didn't you hear what he said? The skeen's still alive."

"Can't be. I put enough quadzol in that meat to kill five of them. He's lying."

"You guys aren't the first ones to try poisoning Hitler. I've been building up his tolerance for all kinds of poison, includin' quadzol. Herion told me a lot of folks use that to kill off runiga, and I started feeding him small doses two years ago. It still makes him sick, but it won't kill him if I get the antidote in him right away. Doesn't look like you have a motive now, does it?"

"Don't worry about that. The old woman'd kill him just for being around her cave. Come on."

At that moment a small dart lodges itself in the tall guy's neck. His eyes glaze over and his mouth flies open as he grasps for the missile. He only gets to look at it for a second before he falls to the ground.

Regen drops also and wrenches the laser pistol from the dead man's grip, but before he can fire, another dart finds the short one's neck with the same results as his partner. Regen sits still for a moment expecting to feel the pin prick of the lethal darts, but none come. Instead a voice comes from the deep brush.

"It's okay. I won't kill ya. Put down the pistol, and we'll talk."

Regen lays the weapon on the dead man's body and stands up.

"Looks like I owe you a big favor. Who are you?"

A woman older than any he's seen on Phoenicia steps onto the trail holding a long tube. Her hair is tangled where it isn't bound in various colored beads, and she wears what he could only describe as a poncho made from animal skins. Bony arms and legs extend from the folds of the garment. Soft leather moccasins cover her feet.

"I'm Karana, and this is my jungle. I saw you come up with those cops, and I saw those goons grab you. You're the guy that owns that lizard-rat thing, ain't ya?"

"Yeah, that's Hitler, he's my pet skeen. I use him to hunt runiga."

"I know, I don't like runiga any more'n anybody else, and I'm glad he thins 'em out a bit. Keeps people from puttin' out poison to kill 'em. The poison kills off animals I eat, and I can't eat 'em when they're full of poison. I saw those goons wanderin' around the other day, but I didn't know what they was up to 'til I found some of the bait. I figured they'd come back to put out more, so I waited for 'em here. I didn't know your…what'd you call it?"

"He's a skeen."

"Yeah, skeen…was the target. Anyway, I'm glad he's okay. Long as your skeen's around, people don't put out poison."

"Well, thanks again. Is there anything I can do for you?"

"Yeah, get them cops back down below. They're a trigger-happy bunch, and I ain't interested in getting' fried by no laser gun."

"Maybe you should take that one." Regen points to the one he's just dropped.

"Not me. I do just fine with my blow gun."

"I'd say so. That poison of yours works mighty fast." He starts to reach for one of the darts, but Karana stops him.

"Don't touch 'em. You don't know how to handle 'em, and just getting' the stuff on yer skin's enough. I'll do it." She takes some leaves from a pocket in her poncho and uses them like gloves to pluck the darts from her victims. She returns the darts to a small quiver hanging from her belt.

"Do you mind if I confiscate the pistol?" he asks.

"Help yerself."

He places the pistol in one of the large pockets in his jump suit. "Thanks again Karana. I'll round up the cops and leave you alone. By the way, how's Hitler doin' with the runiga population?"

"Give him another day or two and they'll be down to a manageable herd."

A call from nearby catches them both off guard. "Where are you, Regen?"

"That's Damos. I'll tell her we found the culprits and it ain't you. I'll have 'em get rid of the bodies for you too."

"Don't worry about that. I got a use for 'em." The old crone cackles ominously, and Regen figures he doesn't need to know what that use is.

"Let me search 'em first." He goes through the men's pockets finding nothing.

"Regen, where are you?" Another call from even nearer.

"I'll be there in a minute. Hang on," Regen calls back.

He turns back to Karana. "See ya later."

She only smiles and waves him away as she pulls a knife from a leather sheath and tests the blade with her thumb.

Regen rejoins the police.

"What happened to you? We never found any more poisoned bait, and we never saw the old hag," Damos says.

"It wasn't her. I talked to her, and she said two guys put out the bait a couple of days ago and left. She didn't get a good look at them, but she thinks she scared 'em off."

"You're quite a guy, Regen. It took me two years to even get her to come out in the open to talk to me," Damos says.

"Turns out she likes Hitler and wants me to tell her about him. She said she'd like to see him the next time we're up here."

"Well, if you're happy, we're happy.   Let's get back down where it's cooler."

Chapter 13

Elektra is not looking forward to her visit with Gilda. The terse note on her data file is far from a social invitation. She knows the reason for the meeting. Her agents halve not returned from their mission to dispose of Regen. The Bremen and his skeen are alive and well. Evidently, Gilda is not happy with her failure.

She steps out of her limo in front of Gilda's building and enters the lobby area, flashing her identity card at the reading station. The butch guard on duty waves her through with a smile portraying too much interest in Elektra's exposed legs. She takes the elevator to the fifth floor and steps into a busy outer office. The receptionist recognizes her immediately.

"Good morning, Lady Elektra. Lady Gilda is expecting you. Go on in." She nods toward an ornately grained wooden door Elektra knows only too well.

"Thank you, Rahma." Elektra opens the door on Gilda, busy with her computer.

"I got your message," Elektra says.

Gilda looks up and swivels the chair to face her guest. "Sit down, Elektra." She indicates a plush leather chair.

Elektra takes the seat and decides to get straight to the point. "I assume this is not a social visit."

Gilda's face grows more serious than Elektra thought possible, and she dreads the next exchange.

"I'm very angry with you, Elektra. You launched an action against Regen without my permission."

"Lady, I only wanted to surprise you with the results. I

thought you'd be pleased to see the Bremen and his pet dead."

"Pleased! Yes, I'd be pleased if I was watching his eyes bulge out and his nostrils flare for breath as they tighten the garrote collar around his neck. You would have deprived me of that pleasure by staging his murder to look like the evil deeds of an eccentric old woman. What were you thinking?"

Gilda's face glows a soft pink, and her neck shows rigid lines of tendons straining to clench her jaw. Elektra knows she has to do some serious groveling to avoid the powerful woman's wrath.

"I'm sorry, Lady. I knew he had a job on the island of Logana where that old woman lives, and I thought it would be an excellent opportunity to rid us of him and blame her for it. He's been avoiding anything that might bring him into conflict with the law on any level." She lowers her head and assumes what she hopes is a submissive demeanor.

Gilda's voice softens a bit, but it still holds the hard edge of a woman not used to being disobeyed. "I know you meant well, but leave Regen to me. Had you succeeded, I would have seen to it that you were prosecuted for his murder and assume his place at the execution post. Now go, and don't make any other attempt on his life. Do I make myself clear?"

"Yes, Lady, you certainly do. I had no idea you felt so strongly about seeing him die. I'm sincerely sorry for offending you. I value our friendship and my own life too highly."

"I'm glad to hear that. We'll say nothing more about this. As far as I'm concerned, the incident is forgotten."

"I'm glad, my lady. I will forget it also."

"Very well, but if you don't mind, I have urgent business to attend to."

Elektra takes the hint and leaves the building at once.

★ ★ ★ ★ ★

Regen stops off at Spara on his way back to Kamara to check on the progress of the shuttle craft restoration. As he walks into Padopolous' office the old man greets him warmly but closes the door and turns off his communication devices before taking a seat behind his desk.

"Why all the secrecy?" Regen asks.

"I'm curious, Regen. You've been around a lot. What's the rest of the universe like?"

Regen leans back in his chair and looks at his friend as if he'd just met him. "That's a strange question for a Phoenician. I thought you guys didn't care about the rest of the universe."

"I didn't until a few weeks ago. When we started this project, I just assumed it was what it appeared to be, but a lot of things have happened to change my mind."

Regen sits up as alarm bells go off inside his head. "What was that?"

"I had a visit from the Lady Selenia when we received the drive unit from your old ship. She gave me this." Padopolous reaches into his safe and pulls out the warp drive circuit board. He hands it to Regen.

Regen turns the board over in his hands and shrugs his shoulders before handing it back to Padopolous. "What is it? I don't know anything 'bout these gadgets." He lies, but he feels it is the correct way to handle the situation.

"Don't give me that innocent act. You know very well what it is, and you've known all along that I had it."

"Wait a minute. How would I know you had it?"

"I'm not a fool, Regen. I don't know how you found the combination, but when I put the circuit board in the safe, I activated the recording software. Shortly after one of your visits it showed someone opened the safe that wasn't me. I checked the rack for prints, and yours were all over it."

Regen you idiot! You should have known that safe kept a record of all openings. "Okay, so I was curious about it when it wasn't with the rest of the drive system. So what?"

"You can't get away from this planet without that rack. I wondered why a Councilwoman would give it to me when she could just as easily have the PSF recycle it. Then I thought about you and Herion. I know she's really sick, and I know you love her more than anything else in the universe, except maybe that skeen of yours. I also looked into the record of your trial before the Council. Gilda and her cronies wanted to do you in, but they lost that battle. Since then, you've kept your nose clean and proved to be an asset to the planet because of that skeen's love of runiga. Then it all began to fall into place. Gilda couldn't dispose of you at the trial, and you haven't given her any legal reason to come after you. That lady's determined, if nothing else. With Herion sick I think she saw a way to finally get her wish as far as you're concerned."

Regen thinks for a moment before he answers. *The old guy's figured it all out, but maybe it's just a way to trap me into opening up to him. This could be Gilda's work. I'd better play it cool.*

"You ain't making any sense. What does Herion being sick have to do with Gilda finally gettin' her wish to do me in?"

"It's simple, when the shuttle's finished, you play along until Herion dies. Then, you steal the warp board and take off for someplace else. Before you do that, I'm supposed to tip off the Council. The PSF catches you, and Gilda gets to watch you die."

"Even if what you say is true, why should you care about

what happens to me?"

"Let's suppose it is true. If I don't tip off the Council, you might have a slim chance of getting away from Phoenicia, but if I help you get out, I know you'll make it."

"Okay, I still don't know why you'd want to help me out. Gilda'd just get to schedule a double-header," Regen says.

Not if I go along with you."

Pretty cagey—thinks he can con me into trusting him so he can collect whatever reward Gilda's agreed to pay him. Regen stands and opens the office door. "Look here, Doc. I don't know why they gave you that circuit board, but I do know I ain't got no plans to leave this planet even after Herion's gone. I've come to love this place. There's nowhere else in the universe where a man can have all the women on the planet just for asking. This is a lover's paradise, and I got enough money to live high on the hog for a long time. Just forget about me trying to escape. You can throw that rack in the ocean for all I care." Regen leaves the museum and boards the tunnel train for home.

Chapter 15

The next day Regen is at the tunnel train station to meet Herion, but his hopes fall after seeing her. She walks less erect, and the confident smile is missing. He smiles as warmly as he can and pulls her into his arms.

"Welcome home, darling." He kisses her tenderly, but she doesn't return his optimism. He pushes her to arm's length and notices a hint of tears in her soft blue eyes. "That bad, eh?"

"Let's get home, Regen. I'll tell you all about it on the way."

He picks up her bag and leads her to the waiting skimmer. As they pull away, she begins to cry shamelessly.

"Here now! None of that. Remember we're going to stay positive about this thing,"

"It's worse than we thought. Doctor Valous told me I have an aggressive form of the disease. I'm afraid we don't have as much time as I thought." She buries her face in her hands and cries.

Regen stops the skimmer and takes her in his arms. "Hey, what happened to the courageous lady I fell in love with?"

"What's the use of being courageous when there's no hope left?" she sobs.

"You may be right. On my last visit Padopolous tried to trap me into admitting I wanted to escape by showing me the Warp Drive board. He said he wants to go with us when we leave."

Herion dries her tears and let her normal composure take over. "He did?"

"Yeah, and he's aware I knew it was in his safe all along. He had some kind of software built into the lock that told him each time it was opened, and he caught me from that. Of course, I denied I wanted to escape, but it was hard to explain why I had any other reason to crack his safe. At least he tipped his hand. He's part of Gilda's plan all right."

Herion sat in deep thought for a moment. "Maybe not, Regen."

"What? Why else would he confront me? Gilda's probably offered him a million Drachmas reward for my scalp."

"Money wouldn't buy Padopolous. I know what he really wants, and money isn't it. He's probably playing along with the Council out of fear, but I'm sure his heart isn't in it."

Regen never ceases to be amazed at Herion's ability to change focus instantly. Only a few seconds ago she was deep in self-pity, and now she's her confident self again.

"Why not?" Regen asks.

"He started out as a spaceship mechanic a long time ago. He had a natural talent for anything mechanical, and he invented a new tool for inspecting fuel rods that saved the PSF millions. He wanted to get an engineering degree, but the Council vetoed that. He tried again when I was on the Council, but I was outvoted by Gilda and her buddies. When I became Council Chair, I finally was able to at least let him study engineering. They still wouldn't let him get a formal degree, though. If he left Phoenicia for another planet, he might be able to get one elsewhere."

"Why do they call him 'Doc' if he ain't got no degree?"

"The PSF commander started calling him that after she promoted him into the R&D group. He owns over fifty patents on spaceship components."

"Phew," Regen whistles. "No wonder he wanted to restore a shuttlecraft."

"The Council wasn't giving him much support for that until you decided to help out. I think Gilda also saw a way to get both of you using that project. Maybe you should feel him out some more."

At that point Hitler jumps into the skimmer and lands on Regen's lap, carrying a dead runiga in its mouth. He drops the animal on the console.

"Aw damn!" Regen says as he lifts the runiga by its tail and throws it out of the skimmer.

Herion begins to laugh at the situation.

"Now that's the gal I came here to live with," Regen says.

"I can't help it. Your skeen is hilarious. It's such a vile animal, but around you it behaves just like a pet cat." She reaches over the console and strokes the skeen's neck. Hitler responds with a soft cooing sound.

"Well, looks like he thinks you're one of the family now," Regen says.

"Hitler amazes me sometimes with how intelligent he is."

Regen snaps his fingers and turns to Herion. "You just hit the nail on the head. I know how to find out if Padopolous really wants to leave with us."

"How's that?" Herion asks.

"I'll use a trick I used Hitler for a few years back. I helped the police break up a drug cartel on Petra VI by pretending Hitler could tell when somebody was lying. Those drug lords could fool any normal lie detector, but the thought of a skeen tearing their guts out was too much for 'em. They sang like canaries. It took me a while to train him, but he might remember some of it. I'll start on it tomorrow and go back to Padopolous when Hitler's ready."

"Wait a minute, Regen. If you were a drug smuggler, why would you cooperate with the police to snag other dope dealers?"

"Easy, I was eliminatin' competition." Regen's broad smile is infectious. The pair laugh all the way to their hut.

★ ★ ★ ★ ★

That evening Padopolous calls Regen. The face on the communicator screen seems very apprehensive. "Ah, Regen, I think we need to talk," Padopolous begins.

"I was just goin' to call you, Doc. I agree with you on that. Let's see, my next trip out is finished at the end of next week. How does your schedule look for that Friday?"

Padopolous breathes a sigh of relief. "I'm good all afternoon. When can you get here?"

"There's a tunnel train that'll get me to your place around 2:30. See you then." Regen ends the call and turns to Herion. "You heard?"

"Yes, I think he's sincere."

"I'll find out in a week if Hitler remembers how to be a lie detector."

★ ★ ★ ★ ★

Regen finds Hitler's retained a great deal of his training for the lie detector scam. It's Regen who has to ferret out the specific commands from the attic of his memory. Hitler hunts runiga all day and trains all night during the next job. By the time they board the tunnel train for the museum the skeen is performing admirably.

The train is a bit late arriving at Spara, but it's only a short taxi ride to the museum. Padopolous is waiting for him in the restoration project's office.

"Come on in, Regen." He notices Hitler by his master's side

on a leash. "Why is Hitler on a leash? You usually let him have the run of the shop."

"This time he's got a job to do."

Regen closes the door to the office, and Padopolous notices the Bremen's stern expression. "What kind of job?"

"I guess you don't know that skeens are great lie detectors or how they go about killing a man?" Regen unhooks Hitler's leash. "Detect, boy!" he commands. Hitler jumps on Padopolous' desk and fixes the man in a beady-eyed stare with his mouth hanging open to reveal the hideous teeth. The older man begins to sweat and starts to move away, but Hitler moves to block him.

"I don't know what kind of game you're playing, but I invited you to talk about our last conversation. The lie detector should be pointing your way."

"I know I pretended I wasn't interested in leaving Phoenicia, but I couldn't be sure you were being truthful about wanting to come along with us."

"Us?" Padopolous said.

"Yeah, me and Herion. Ya see, I want to take her somewhere they can cure what ails her."

"That puts a new twist on things. We'd have an extra mouth to feed, and I hadn't planned on that."

"We can handle that. Right now, I have to be sure you aren't in cahoots with Gilda and her cronies, and that's where Hitler comes in. I want you to tell me again how much you want to help me leave this planet, but first you got to know that Hitler's trained to attack a liar after I give him the command to detect. His usual first target is your guts. You'll still be alive but in a lot of pain. If you don't tell the truth after that, he goes after your throat, and you die quick. But you've got nothing to worry about as long as you tell the truth. You want to try him out, or do you want to admit you were lying right now and save yourself a lot of pain?"

"You wouldn't really let him kill me, would you?" Padopolous' voice grows shaky and beads of sweat form on his forehead.

"I couldn't stop him. Oh, I'd just explain that he got away from me and went berserk. The law'd probably kill him, and I'd hate to see that, but if you're lying, it'd be worth the price to eliminate a bad apple."

"O-o-okay, I'll t-tell you again. I-I-I want to leave Phoenicia with you and Herion. The Council's thwarted my ambitions from day one, and I figure another planet might be more grateful for my talent. I'm not interested in helping Gilda do you in. In fact, I can build something that will insure our escape if you take me along." The words come out in a staccato fashion. When he's finished, he stares at Hitler hoping he's convinced the animal. Hitler doesn't seem to change his expression, but hisses from deep inside his raptor-like chest. Regen notices Padopolous' right hand shaking almost uncontrollably.

"And, Gilda hasn't offered you an engineering degree if you play along with her?" Regen asks.

"Honest, Regen. She nor any of her friends have offered me anything—I swear."

"Cut, boy!" Regen commands, and Hitler jumps off the desk and moves to the office door.

"I think he wants out," Padopolous says with an air of relief in his voice. He produces a handkerchief from inside his lab coat and begins to mop the perspiration from his face.

"Yeah, I'll let him out, and he can run a bit while we talk about getting' out of here."

Regen lets Hitler out and returns to his seat.

"Okay, so why would you want to go along?"

"It's like I told you. I figure I can get a better deal somewhere else. On top of that I figured if you made it or didn't make it, Gilda would accuse me of helping you. My life wouldn't be worth a lead Drachma if I stayed behind. The Council already thinks I'm dangerous, and Gilda would have an easy time convincing them I was part of your plan. Going with you is the only thing that makes sense, but I'm worried about how I'd fit in outside of Phoenicia."

Regen sits back in a relaxed position. "I think you'd fit in real nice, Doc. In fact, with your brains and my connections we could do right well for ourselves."

"Do you trust me enough to tell me what you'd planned on doing?"

"I'd planned to try to make it to a planet called Terma. I have some connections there, and maybe some money."

Padopolous raises an eyebrow at this revelation. "I thought you were filthy rich now."

"I am, long as I stay on Phoenicia. The problem is I can't take Phoenician money anywhere even if they'd let me draw it all out of the bank—which they wouldn't. Your stuff's worthless on Terma, or anywhere else for that matter. If I converted it into gold, which they won't let me do either, I'd overload the shuttle with it. When I came back here to be with Herion I left most of my money with a woman I knew on Terma. Actually, I gave it to her, but I think she'd let me have some of it back if she knew I was broke and needed a grubstake. I'm buying lots of jewelry these days so we'll have something to tide us over until I can get back on my feet."

"How far is this Terma planet?"

"That's a good question, and one I have to know before we take off."

"You mean you don't know how to get there? I thought you were smarter than that."

"Herion's got the coordinates, but I haven't been able to check them out yet to see if we can get enough stuff aboard to do the job. I'd need her data and a decent navigation computer for that."

Padopolous sighs with relief. "If that's all you need, I got a unit at my office that'll do the job. I already plugged in the shuttle's information, and we can check it out any time. I'm just a bit edgy about striking out into the real universe."

Regen leans forward and smiles. "Doc, I been broke four times, in jail twice, damn near killed more often than I care to remember all because I'm not a smart guy. I've muscled my way out of trouble most of the time, and Hitler's saved my bacon when my muscles weren't enough. My main problem is I never had a lot of intelligence. Oh, I'm space smart, and I know my way around the low-life places on every planet there is, but you've got the intelligence it takes to make me see the traps before I fall into 'em. I think we'd make a great team." He stands and offers his hand, and Padopolous takes it in both of his.

"Here's to a new partnership," Regen says.

Chapter 15

Regen arrives back at Kamara just in time for the evening barbeque meal. Herion welcomes him with a kiss, a spit of roasted meat for him and another one for Hitler. The skeen runs into the bush with is meal while Regen sits down to fill Herion in on his visit to Padopolous.

"How did your lie detector escapade go?" Herion asks.

"He was scared to death. I'm sure he was sincere in wantin' to go with us. He wants to see if he can get a better deal somewhere else."

"Can he really help us?"

"He says he thinks he can help us get past the PSF. The shuttlecraft's almost ready, but I need to check out the coordinates pretty soon to make sure we can get to Terma okay. I'll need the data you've got to do that."

"I'll give you the chip as soon as we get home, but let's walk for a while after we eat. I need some tender, loving care right now."

"Oh, you mean more than my usual attentions?"

"I'm serious, Regen. I had a bad day today. I almost fell twice, and I wasn't doing anything dangerous. I'm beginning to worry I may not make it to wherever we're going."

"Don't talk like that. All we need is a few more days to figure out the details, and we're out of here. You'll be fine."

"I hope you're right," she says as she stares into the glowing embers of the communal cooking fire.

They walk along the beach until the moon sinks into the sea.

Regen stops from time to time to hold her close and tell her again what she means to him. Her mood seems to brighten a bit as they return to their hut and sleep.

★ ★ ★ ★ ★

"Aaaahhh!"

Herion's scream jars Regen awake. He jumps to his feet ready to defend against any invader then notices Hitler staring down at Herion from just above her head. She smiles as Regen swings a foot at his pet to send it scurrying for shelter.

"Sorry for the scream, but your skeen scared the life out of me. It's pretty un-nerving to open your eyes and see something that ugly looking at you like you're lunch."

"He does that to me all the time when we're traveling. He wouldn't hurt you for anything. He knows how I feel about you."

Hitler peers from his hiding place behind a chair, and Regen calls to him. "Come here, boy. I'm not mad at you."

The skeen runs to his master's side, and Regen reaches down to pet him.

Herion sits up and joins Regen in soothing the animal. "I'm sorry, Hitler. I'm not used to you doing that to me."

"He probably tried me first and moved to you when I didn't respond. He's definitely accepted you as a buddy. You should be flattered. I only knew one other person who could get close to him."

Herion stands and moves to a refrigerator. "Who was that?" she asks as she pours two glasses of juice. She returns to Regen and hands him one.

"A woman I met one time back on Gobra. She was a compeller, and she could make him do almost anything she wanted."

"I've heard of compellers, but you said, 'almost anything'. I thought they could even make a person do something they found disgusting or immoral."

"She tried to get Hitler to kill me, but he wouldn't do it. He attacked her instead."

"That's amazing. Your skeen has more willpower than a human." She takes a sip of her juice.

"Come to think of it, there was another guy who could get close to him. He was from some race that radiates a pheromone skeens like."

"Interesting, maybe some animals do the same thing."

Regen laughs. "I only ever saw one animal he wouldn't eat. Actually, he'd eat them, but he didn't like 'em. That fact saved my butt once and helped make me a rich man."

"That was on Agaam Valeem, right?"

"You remembered."

"That was a really gutsy adventure. How could I forget?"

They spend the rest of the day in routine and have dinner in their hut. That evening after dinner, Regen brings up the subject of the chip again.

"Would you mind if I took the chip to Padopolous tomorrow?" He opens a bottle of wine and pours two glasses, passing one to Herion.

"No, I think I'm okay now. The sooner we get going, the sooner we'll know if there's any hope someplace else."

"How do we get the chip?" he asks as he sips the wine.

Herion moves to a small table and removes the flowers from the vase with the chip. She dumps the water onto the grass outside their hut and sits down next to Regen.

"I figured the heat of firing the vase might damage the chip, so I made a small cavity in the base for it." She turns the vase over, but the chip's hiding place is not obvious.

"Hand me your pocketknife," she says.

Regen pulls a small folding knife from a pocket inside his toga and hands it to her.

She studies the base for a moment then begins to scrape away at a small area. The material is not ceramic. It carves away like wood or soft plaster. In a moment, a section falls away revealing a small cavity. She tips the vase, and a chip falls into her hand.

"There it is. Everything you need should be on there." She hands the chip to Regen.

He studies it for a moment before placing it in a pocket. "Tomorrow we'll know if we can make it or not. I sure hope Padopolous has got the brainpower to figure it all out. I know I'm no good at that kind of thing."

"Don't sell yourself short. I think you're quite bright in spite of your accent."

Regen recoils in mock anger. "Are you saying I talk like a hick?"

"Darling, if the overalls fit, put them on." She laughs merrily for the first time in weeks, and Regen smiles to see her somewhat normal again.

Chapter 17

Padopolous welcomes Regen with a broad grin. "Good news, partner. The Council's approved an artificial gravity unit."

Regen smiles as he embraces the older man. "How'd you get 'em to do that?"

"I just asked them if they were ready to answer a bunch of claims from space sick passengers. They figured the system was cheaper."

"Good man." He leans closer to Padopolous' ear and whispers. "I got the chip. Where's the computer?"

Padopolous nods his head to the right, and Regen follows him into a laboratory area of the museum. Padopolous locks the door behind them. "We don't want any visitors while we're doing this. I know the codes to erase any evidence of your visit after we're finished." He pulls a chip from his lab coat and places it in one of the drive slots.

"This is the data for the shuttlecraft. Give me the chip with the navigation data."

Regen hands him the chip which Padopolous places in another slot. The Doc sits down and begins to manipulate the device. "The first order of business is to find out where we're going. I take it this chip navigated you to some planet you're familiar with?"

"It took me to Terma, and that's where I want to go now. I've got contacts there that can help us."

A graphic display soon shows a star map with one star highlighted.

"This must be the system for Terma. Let's see how far it is."

Another screen appears showing rows of information. Padopolous scans down the list to one option.

"This is the shortest path as far as distance is concerned. It's 19.265 light years." He turns to Regen. "The life support system we have is good for up to two weeks for 38 people. With only three of us, we're good for at least eleven weeks. I figured Hitler for half a person."

"How long will the trip take?" Regen asks.

"We'll only have 30 fuel rods. That limits our speed or our range, one or the other. Let me do some calculating to see how long we've got on that fuel load."

A few more commands produces a graph. Padopolous uses the cursor to mark one point on the curve. "I could only beef up the shuttlecraft's structure so much. It'll take Warp 100 at most. That means the minimum travel time is a little over 70 days."

"What about weight? Could we put enough food aboard for 70 days, Doc?" Regen asks.

"Weight's not the problem. I loaded the shuttlecraft pretty heavy for these calculations. The limiting factor is the shuttle's structure. It'll only stand Warp 100. We don't dare go any faster or the ship might just break up."

Regen rubs his chin while he thinks about all the possible problems. He suddenly turns very serious. "What about the PSF, Doc? You forget we have to get away from them. How fast will those ships go?"

"They can do Warp 250. You can't outrun them. How were *you* planning to get away?"

"I was counting on surprise and guts and hoping to find some kind of edge beforehand."

Padopolous shakes his head in disgust. "You've got more gall than that skeen of yours. We may not have as much surprise as you think. Their long-range sensors all point out into space looking for incoming ships, but they're in the process of modifying the system to track ships in low orbits also. I think our little enterprise prompted that change, and I imagine Gilda also had some input into the decision. We'll have to blind them to get away."

"Don't count on the stealth gear from my ship. If it isn't at the bottom of the ocean, it's shot up too bad to be of any use to us."

"It *is* at the bottom of the ocean. I checked on that, but I can jam their sensors."

Regen eyes him suspiciously. "Just how do you plan to do that?"

"I spent 15 years in the PSF, and they asked me to help with the re-design of the sensor system to see low orbit. Because of that job, I had all the security clearances I needed to find out what types of sensors they're using these days. I've been secretly working on a jammer ever since I figured out you were planning an escape. It's crude, but it'll do the job."

"How much longer 'til it's done?" Regen asks.

"A couple of weeks. In the meantime, we can do a few test flights to check everything out. I told the PSF you'd do the flying since it's your drive system, and they've agreed. They think the whole idea is silly, and they don't want to risk any of their pilots."

"Good. When can we do that?"

"We'll be ready the first of next week. The artificial gravity system won't be in, but we can see if everything else works. That is, except the Warp drive system."

"I've got one job between now and then. I'll contact you when

I'm ready to come back."

Padopolous turns off the computer and removes the chips. He places them in his pocket. "I'll keep these in my safe for now if that's okay with you."

"Sure, go ahead. You need to work out a course for Terma anyway. See you next week."

Chapter 18

The shuttlecraft is ready for its first flight right on schedule. Regen meets Padopolous at the museum and watches as the craft is towed to the only elevator capable of lifting it to the surface. A crew of four technicians follow with several pieces of test gear and units for recording the telemetry.

On the surface, Regen and Padopolous enter the ship along with one of the technicians. Padopolous introduced him to Regen.

"Regen, this is Marcosia. She's going to monitor the on-board telemetry for us."

"Pleased to meet you," Regen says.

"Where's that skeen of yours?" Marcosia asks.

"I figured we didn't need him on this first flight. He likes to fly, but we'd better make sure of the life support system before we take him along. They don't make pressure suits for skeens."

"Speaking of that, we'd better suit-up for this flight. I've got suits aboard for us."

They board the shuttlecraft and don the pressure suits. Regen remarks on Marcosia.

"She's kinda on the small side, ain't she?"

Padopolous leans closer to Regen and whispers, "She's about Herion's size. I thought it might be good to have a suit aboard that fit her."

Regen smiles and takes the commander's chair.

Padopolous takes the co-pilot seat while Marcosia stations herself at a row of instruments connected to a computer readout. All three strap in.

Regen and Padopolous run through the pre-flight checklist, and Regen checks that Marcosia had cleared them through the PSF before beginning.

"Here goes," Regen says as he energizes the gravitational interaction drive. He places the gravity stick in the "up" position and twists the grip. The craft shudders heavily and leaps into the air before he can reduce the input.

"Easy, Regen. This isn't your ship," Padopolous says.

"I just found that out. I think I got the feel of it now. Next stop low orbit."

Regen's control is much smoother on the way to orbit. As the craft achieves zero gravity, he checks with Marcosia. "Anything weird on the telemetry?"

"Nothing so far. The life support system's holding up really well, and the structure seems to be fine. We need to spend some time in space vacuum to check everything out."

"Okay, you and the doc take a look around. I'll stay at the controls until you give me the okay to do the same," Regen says.

Padopolous leaves the co-pilot seat and floats to Marcosia at the telemetry. Regen tests the orbital controls and finds the ship responds well to the side-stick controller. Attitude control thrusters fire smoothly with little jolt, and the craft moves in direct proportion to the control input without need of correction on his part. He hears Padopolous in his earphones.

"Everything looks good. We need to check that engine stress bulkhead when we get back. I figured it was marginal for the drive we got, but the stress readouts are good. Do you think we need any more time on orbit?"

Marcosia responds. "Let's give it an hour, or so, to soak down to space temperature. Then we should do some rolls to see how it handles temperature transitions."

"You hear that Regen?" Padopolous asks.

"I got it. Tell me when to roll it."

Regen busies himself scanning the instruments and familiarizing himself with the auxiliary controls until Marcosia calls for a roll. After several moves, she pronounces herself satisfied the craft can handle the temperature differences without over-stressing.

Padopolous joins Regen at the controls. "I haven't been weightless in a long time. Feels good," he says.

"I never cared much for zero g. I'll have to take some stomach pills when we get back. I brought some along just in case," Regen says.

"Don't tell me the tough Bremen gets space sick?" Padopolous says as he grins from ear to ear.

"Well, you're lucky I don't mess up the inside of this suit."

"There's a barf port just to the left of your mouth if you need it."

"I think I'll be okay for a short flight like this, but I couldn't do much more without tossing my cookies. Ready to land?"

"Okay by me."

The shuttle settles smoothly on the landing site, and Regen is glad to feel gravity again. The trio step out of their pressure suits and leave the ship. They follow as the crew loads it on the elevator and return it to the museum.

"Come on in the office. I got some Gordian Bourbon there for you," Padopolous says.

"I could us some of that to wash down these stomach pills," Regen says as he produces a small container and shakes two small tablets into his hand.

Once below, the men settle into chairs, and Padopolous speaks. "How are you coming with food and jewelry?"

"A few more trips and I'll have all the gems I can manage. I'm still workin' on the food. When will the artificial gravity system be installed?" Regen pops the pills into his mouth and takes a healthy swig of his bourbon.

"That'll be in by the weekend. We should also be finished analyzing the telemetry by then. If that looks good, we could start giving the customers rides in two weeks. We could go any time after that."

"What about your plan to jam the PSF sensors?"

"I'll have all that ready in two weeks. I think we need to do a few rides to keep Gilda off guard, if you and Herion don't mind."

Regen studies the liquid in his glass for a moment before answering. "I think we could use the suckers as a cover for the escape."

"How's that?" Padopolous leans forward in his chair.

"We have to go to Kamara to load the food and jewels. That'd be a sure tip-off to Gilda something's going on. What if we had a load of tourists aboard and developed engine trouble? We could time it so we had no choice but to abort to Kamara. Once we get there, we get the customers off and load on the other stuff. We take off from there, and you jam the sensors on our way out."

It is Padopolous' turn to think. He leans back in his chair and rubs his short beard a moment. "It might be a good plan. Let me think about it for a while. Kamara might just be an ideal location for the escape attempt. Check back with me next week. We'll be ready to start the rides by then, and I'll have it all figured out." He raises his glass to Regen. "Here's to a new life on a new planet."

Regen responds in kind. "I'll drink to that."

Chapter 19

Herion is on a trip when Regen returns from the test flight. He releases Hitler from his cage and lets him hunt while he decides a nap is in order. His stomach is still recovering from his first zero-g flight in years.

★ ★ ★ ★ ★

The setting sun bursts from behind a cloud and floods into the sleeping area of Herion's hut, awakening Regen. He rises on one elbow and notices Herion asleep on her futon. His cot shades her from the effects of the sun's rays, and she still sleeps soundly. A smile spreads across his face as he studies the woman he loves so dearly. He sits on the side of his cot and begins to pray.

*You gods know I ain't no religious man, but whichever one of you has any control over people and their fates, I'm appealin' to you to take this woman's illness away. I've dropped money in every temple of every god in every city I've ever been in since she came down with this curse. I've even built a temple to Astarte at one place, so she should be on my side. I've screwed the brains out of a half dozen priestesses who assured me they had some kind of "in" with **Her Godship**. I think I done my part to win your help, whoever you are. If that ain't enough, just hit me with a flash of lightnin' and tell me what I need to do.*

At that point Herion opens her eyes and sees Regen sitting in deep thought, his eyes closed and his face pointed toward the ceiling.

"Don't tell me you're praying?" she says.

Regen opens his eyes and smiles at her. "Yep, that's what I was doin'. I was prayin' for you."

"I'm really amazed…and flattered. I've never known you to pray before."

"I never did. I always figured what happened to me was my own fault and not some god's. I was pretty young when I noticed everything in the universe lives by eatin' somethin' else. I thought that if that's the way whatever gods there are made it, why should I be any different? I watched other people pray and sacrifice and all that, and I never saw much come from it. I figured we're no different from skeens or runiga."

"What made you change your mind?" Herion sits up and takes one of Regen's hands. She looks at him as if for the first time.

"Your situation. Besides Hitler, you're the only thing in this universe I give a damn for. Prayin' was the only base I didn't have covered, so I did what everybody thinks you should do to get the gods on your side."

She sits down next to him on the cot and puts her arms around him. "For a tough guy you've got a very soft heart, and I love you for it." She kisses him then suddenly becomes serious. "Regen, I got a communication from Lunna while you were on the test flight, and we need to talk about it." She rises and finds a toga before returning to Regen.

"What's on Lunna's mind these days?"

"Lunna said she heard a rumor that Padopolous is cooperating with Gilda and her bunch."

Regen looks at her with a scowl. "I can't believe that. How could he pass the skeen test if he was rotten?"

"I don't know, but Lunna said her source is reliable."

"Did you tell Lunna anything about our plans?"

"No, she thinks Gilda's going to sabotage the shuttlecraft

some way to get rid of you, and Padopolous is going to do the job."

"If he is working for them, he's a pretty good liar. He's even made sure we'll have a pressure suit aboard for you. I've dealt with some pretty devious characters in my life, and I wouldn't rank Padopolous up with even the most inept of that class of rat." Regen rises and dresses.

"I still think you'd better keep an eye on him. I'll try to think of some way to catch him out. Lunna's said she'll keep her ear to the ground for us. By the way, I forgot to ask you how the test flight went."

"It was fine. Looks like we'll be ready to go in a couple of weeks. Padopolous has got the vectors all figured out, and he says he'll have the jammer ready by then too."

"Maybe you're right about him, but we need to be careful just in case. The only reason I'm agreeing to this is because you're so sure there's someone out there who can help me. Otherwise, I think it's suicide."

Regen wraps his arms around her and kisses her cheek. "Then at least we'll die together."

Chapter 20

The next week Regen stops off to check on the status of the shuttlecraft. He releases Hitler to wander the working area before entering Padopolous' office.

"Well, how's the telemetry look?" he asks.

"Hey, Regen, glad you're here. The telemetry looks great. I think we're ready to start flights." He rises from behind his desk and shakes the big Bremen's hand. "All we need now are provisions for the trip."

"Herion's workin' on that, but it'll take her a while to..."

The screams of a group of schoolgirls interrupts their conversation. Both men run from the office to investigate and find ten teen-aged girls cowering in a corner staring at Hitler.

"How'd he get out of the work enclosure?" Regen asks.

Padopolous slaps a hand to his forehead. "Damn! I forgot about that overhead door in back. It got stuck a few inches off the floor, and we haven't fixed it yet."

"That's all he needs to get out. I'd better go get him." Regen leaves the work area and walks up to his pet, who seems to be enjoying the reaction of the girls. He feigns attacks and hisses in his most horrible manner before backing off to observe the effect.

"Come here, boy!" Regen calls. Hitler turns and looks at his master with a pleading expression as if to say, 'Can't I do this a bit longer?'

A snap of the Bremen's fingers tells Hitler his fun is over. He scuttles to his usual position at Regen's feet.

"It's okay, ladies. He won't hurt you. Go on about your

business."

The girls edge out of the exhibit room and vanish around the corner. Hitler takes this as his cue to explore other areas of the museum. Before Regen can stop him, he runs off through another door. Regen follows on the run, but he lags behind considerably. He reaches for the ultra-sound whistle that seems to make the skeen obey just as Hitler vanishes into an open doorway.

Regen enters the room and finds he is in a warehouse. Cases stacked half-way to the ceiling hide the skeen from view. He blows the whistle but gets no response. Walking down an aisle between the rows of cases, he soon hears Hitler scratching at something. He follows the sound until he spots his pet busily consuming some kind of dried meat.

"So that's what you're up to," he says as he studies the ripped open case. The label indicates its contents consist of various dried meats from a supplier named Mythras Restaurant Supplies. While Hitler eats, Regen checks the other cases. They all contain food items of one kind or another.

Hmmm, this could be the solution to our food problem. He produces his palm unit and records the various suppliers' data from the codes on the boxes. He could buy what they needed and have it shipped here. His purchases will probably alert Gilda, but he know she's already planning to trap him. A woman dressed in a chef's outfit opens the door opposite Hitler and shrieks her surprise. Hitler barely looks up from his stolen meal.

"Don't worry. He won't hurt you. I'm sorry for the mess, and I'll pay for whatever he eats."

"He scared me half to death. What is that horrible thing?" She composes herself and wipes her hands on her apron before offering one. "You must be Regen. I'm Norma, the head cook in the museum restaurant."

"Pleased to meet you, Norma. If you've heard of me, you should know about Hitler. He's a skeen, the only one on this here planet. You got quite a stash of food here." Regen sweeps an arm across the rows of cases.

"We keep about 10 days of supplies on hand. Bread products are delivered daily, of course, as are any dairy products, but we use mostly dried meat and canned vegetables."

"I'll have to eat in your restaurant sometime. Hitler seems to like your meat selection, and he's a pretty good judge of quality."

"Any time. We're open from noon to nine—an hour before the museum closes."

Regen studies the woman. She's short and a bit on the round side, but she has a lovely face and soft brown hair held back in a hairnet topped with a chef's toque. He decides not to press for any further information.

"I'll go get his cage while he's eatin', and get him corralled. You can figure out how much I owe you, and we'll settle when he's under control."

"Fine, I'll wait for you."

Regen retrieves Hitler's cage and coaxes the skeen inside with a packet of dried pork.

"Come inside, and I'll figure the damages," Norma says.

He follows her into the kitchen to a computer station where she punches up his bill. "Looks like your skeen ate about 100D_p worth."

Regen steps to the machine and swipes his credit card. The display of his credit standing impresses Norma. "Phew, you could buy this whole place if you took a mind to."

"I ain't in the restaurant business, darlin', but it was a

pleasure talkin' to you."

He adds a generous tip before signing off.

"Thanks a lot," Norma says.

A great idea suddenly hits him.

"Say, darlin', you know we're restorin' a shuttle, don't you?"

"Everybody knows that."

"Yeah, and we need something to use for cargo to make it look all authentic like. I was just thinkin', we could use some o' that stuff you got in your storage area when we start givin' rides. I'd pay you for it and throw in a few Drachma for you in the bargain."

She looks up at him with a wry smile. "I see. How much would you need?"

"I gotta figure that out. I'll let you know real soon. Meantime, keep this under your hat, eh?"

She runs a finger across her lips. "My lips are sealed."

He smiles at her and leads a caged Hitler back to Padopolous' office.

★ ★ ★ ★ ★

"You got Hitler under control? The curator's been calling every five minutes," Padopolous says.

"Yeah, he's back in his cage. Everybody can relax."

"I'll call Marga and give her the good news." Padopolous turns to his communicator and assures the curator all is well before turning back to Regen.

"I think I've figured out a way to get aboard what food Herion can't stock up in time," Regen says.

"How's that?"

"We stock the cargo area with canned stuff and dried meat from the museum restaurant's supplies. We make it look like fake cargo to give the shuttlecraft a more authentic appearance. What do you think?"

Padopolous thinks for a moment before responding. "That's a great idea."

"We'll have the stuff delivered here to the museum restaurant then re-marked as shuttle cargo."

Once more Padopolous grows thoughtful. "We'd need some way to heat up the food. I'm not interested in a diet of cold asparagus for 70 days."

"I figure that's somethin' you can take care of. I'll tell Herion to store up some fresh fruit and enough rats for Hitler. We can pick that stuff up when we get her. You got the jammer ready yet?"

"All set, but I can't test it without tipping off the PSF. We'll just have to keep our fingers crossed that it works." Padopolous notices the look of concern on his partner's face and adds, "Don't worry, I've built dozens of racks like this and never had one fail yet."

"Okay, I'll trust your expertise."

"I thought of something else that will give us an edge. Selenia thinks I'm her man on the inside on this caper. I've been feeding her accurate data on the progress of the restoration since she dropped off the warp drive rack. She's ready to believe anything I tell her about your escape plans, and she has no inkling I'm going with you. As soon as we're ready, I'll give her a date two days later than our actual escape date. The PSF won't be looking for us to make a break. The only thing I'm worried about is using Kamara as our abort site. That's sure to arouse suspicions."

Regen rubs his stubble beard and sits pensive for a moment. "I got it. We'll use Logana. I did a job there a while back, and there's a good landing area close to the capital city. Herion can use the excuse of a trip into the jungle there to get some new species for her game preserve." He doesn't think Padopolous needs to know about the attempt on his life there.

"But, don't we still have to get to Kamara to pick up the fresh fruit and Hitler's food?"

"That's easy too. Herion can buy fresh fruit on Logana as provisions for her crew, and I'll have the old hermit lady there trap the runiga for Hitler. I met her on my last trip there, and I think she'd help us out. She hates the Council and all government people."

"Looks like we may have to delay our departure while you set this all up."

"It shouldn't take too long. I got an 'in' with the Governor there. When do you want to start givin' the tourists space rides?"

"We can start tomorrow, if you like. Everything's go for that."

"Okay, have Marga start the publicity for rides beginnin' in two days." Regen rises to leave. "I'll see you then."

Chapter 21

Herion meets Regen at the tunnel train station and drives the skimmer back to their hut. Once inside, Regen opens a bottle of wine and pours two glasses. He carries them outside to where Herion is relaxing on the porch.

"I think I've found another way to feed us on the trip," he says.

"I was going to ask you about that. I can't order too much extra food without the Council becoming suspicious." She takes the glass and raises it to Regen. "A toast to our eventual success."

"I'll drink to that," Regen says as he takes a sip.

Herion continues, "What did you think of?"

"The cafeteria at the Ark Museum uses a lot of dried meat and canned goods. I can get enough stuff there to take care of our meat and canned goods needs. We can load it on the shuttlecraft right there at the museum."

"A good idea, but that's not a very balanced diet. I can provide some fruit from the local sources. When do you think we can make a break for it?"

"That's somethin' we need to talk about. Padopolous thinks aborting to Kamara would arouse suspicion at the PSF, and I agree with him. We have to go somewhere they won't suspect, and I suggested Logana."

Herion reacts with surprise. "What? Why there?"

"There's a good landing site there, and I think the old woman hermit there'd help us out. 'Sides, I got an 'in' with the island's governor."

Regen's smug expression tells Herion all she needs to know about his "in" with Marana. She's very familiar with the Governor's taste in men, and Regen would be at the top of her list. "So, what do we do?"

"I figure you could set up a research operation there on some pretext. While you're doin' your research, you could gather some of the local fruit. The old hermit could trap runiga for Hitler."

"I'd need Marana's permission to set up a research station, and we don't know where she stands vis-à-vis Gilda and her gang," Herion warns.

"I'll feel her out on that before I do anything."

Herion laughs, "I'm sure you'll do a wonderful job of 'feeling her out'. Just be sure of your ground before you say anything incriminating."

"You can count on me, darlin'."

Herion feels she'd exhausted that subject and changes topics. "When will you start the tourist trips?"

"We're startin' in two days. I'll have to spend the weekends at the museum until we're ready to leave."

"I'll miss you, but we'll be ready to try an escape soon, won't we?" Herion asks.

"Yep, the first time I have to refuel everything should be ready."

They finish their wine and retire for the night.

★ ★ ★ ★ ★

The next day Regen leaves for Logana. As he expected, Marana is very open to his visit. Her limo meets him at the station and whisks him to her private apartment. She greets him at the door in a very filmy negligée.

"Regen, how good to see you again. Come in." She looks

behind him and asks, "Where's Hitler?"

"I left him with the security guys in the lobby. I figured he'd be too much of a distraction while we did business."

"You said you wanted to talk business, but I've got some 'business' for you first."

He calculates taking care of her carnal demands is the first item on the agenda and follows her lead to the bedroom.

★ ★ ★ ★ ★

As they lay together afterward, he broaches the subject of the real purpose of his visit. "I need your help with somethin', darlin'."

"What's that?" She rolls over and begins to trace a pattern in the hair on his chest.

"Herion thinks there's some kind of exotic frog livin' in your jungle, and she wants to set up a temporary operation here to look for it. Do…"

Marana interrupts him. "That's easy, I'd do anything for Herion anyway, but it's also a way I can get to see you more often." She begins to nibble on his ear.

"Now how can I think with you doin' that?"

She stops nibbling and moves out of the bed, taking the sheet with her as an improvised toga. "Well, if you want to get that serious, we'd better get dressed."

Regen rolls out on his side and begins to dress as he talks. "Is there any kind of paperwork she needs to send you?"

Marana calls from the bathroom, "You'll have to wait until after my shower, darling." She turns on the water, and Regen finishes dressing. She emerges from the bathroom wrapped in a towel and moves to her closet to select an appropriate toga. She selects a gray print with red floral patterns. As she models it in her full-length mirror, she speaks, "She knows all of the procedures. Just let her know I'll approve whatever she wants. Of course, it would be nice if you could slip a small gratuity into my personal account."

"How grateful do I need to be, darlin'?"

"For you only D_{p}10,000 and some time with me when you come to visit Herion between jobs."

He kisses her tenderly. "It's a deal."

★ ★ ★ ★ ★

Regen picks up Hitler from the security guards, much to their relief, and takes the elevator to the same area where he was ambushed. He opens the cage and lets the skeen run off into the bush. It isn't long before he hears a familiar voice.

"You alone, Regen?"

"Yup, just me an' Hitler."

"I seen yer lizard and figured you'd be around some'eres. You lookin' fer me?"

"He ain't no lizard, he's a skeen, and you're right again. I got a proposition for you."

The old woman cackles merrily. "Been a long time since I been propositioned by a hunk like you."

"Not that kind, a business kind," Regen corrects her.

"Don't git yer balls in a uproar. I was only kiddin' ya. What you want?"

"I'm gonna need about 300 live runiga in three weeks. What would it cost me for you to trap 'em and keep 'em alive until I pick 'em up?"

The old hag eyes him suspiciously. "I thought you made yer livin' getting' rid o' runigas. What the hell you want with 300 of 'em?"

"They're for Herion. She's going to set up a research operation here on Logana pretty soon and she says she needs 'em for her project."

"Why from here? Runigas is all over her own island."

Regen has to think fast. The old bag is even more suspicious than he thought, but he knows there is little risk of her contacting the authorities, given her hatred of all government officials. "She says the runiga from here have a special gene mutation she wants to study. I'm no scientist, so I got no idea what she's tryin' to do."

The dumb act seems to work. The woman relaxes a bit and lapses into a pensive mood. "Well, I could use a new set o' knives. The ones I got've been sharpened so many times they'z only a shadow o' their former selves." Her eyes brighten a bit as she snaps her fingers. "Say, could ya throw in a meat cleaver? That'd sure come in handy fer butcherin' game."

"Whatever you want, darlin'. Anything else you need?"

"Course, I'd need cages fer them runiga and somethin' ta feed 'em."

"No problem, Herion'll take care of all of that. Anything else? Need any cash?"

"I got no use fer money, but I could use a 20 kilo bag o' sugar."

"Sugar?"

"Yep, sugar's the only thing I can't get from th' jungle."

Regen cocks his head to one side and gives her a curious look. "I'd have thought you could grow some sugar cane in there somewhere." He points into the jungle.

"Nope, tried once, and the damned runiga ate it all up 'fore it could get a foot high. You get me some knives and some sugar, and you'll have yer runiga in a couple of weeks, or so."

"Okay, I'll get that stuff and be back here next week."   Regen turns to leave, but the old hag speaks again.

"I just thought o' somethin' else."

"What's that?"

"You're workin' on that spaceship at the Ark Museum, ain't ya?"

"Yeah, what about it?"

"They got somethin' I really want."

"Oh, they take something from you?"

"Yeah, I found a bunch of stuff in a cave three years back—a lot of necklaces and pins made out of seashells and bone. Two o' them necklaces had a pretty green stone in 'em, and I thought they might be worth somethin'. I needed some new boots, so I took one of 'em into th' city to a gal I knew who bought things, figurin' I could get enough out of it to buy some good ones. She traded me two good pairs o' boots fer it, but when she tried to sell it, some do-gooder had a fit and sicked the locals on me. They made me show 'em where I got it and took everything fer that damned museum. I'd sure like t' have one of them necklaces back."

Regen thinks for a moment. *I've seen those things in the museum. They're pretty primitive and can't be worth that much. They aren't even under very tight security. I think I'll pay 'em a visit.*

"Tell you what, I'll bring you that necklace when I visit Herion's operation sometime. I can probably buy one of 'em from the museum, but it may take me a while."

"That's okay, but I'd be mighty grateful if you could do that."

"You can count on me, darlin'." He bends and kisses her on the cheek, making sure to hold his breath while he does so. "See you later with the knives and the cages."

★ ★ ★ ★ ★

A quick call to Marana confirms she's willing to see him at her office in an hour. He takes the elevator down to the city then a cab to the capitol building. He only has a short wait for Marana. She almost drags him into her office and closes the door behind them. As she begins to undo Regen's toga, she asks, "Is this urgent business, or can we mix some pleasure with it?"

He pulls her into his arms. "There ain't nothin' that urgent."

★ ★ ★ ★ ★

As they enjoy a glass of wine afterwards, Regen says. "I'm interested in some primitive jewelry for Herion, and I understand your museum here has some stuff that's pretty old. Do you suppose they'd be willing to sell one of their collection pieces?"

Marana turns to her communication console. "I'll find out fast."

In a moment a bookish woman in a beige toga appears on the screen. "How may I help you, Lady Marana?"

"I have a big donor in my office who's willing to make a large contribution to the museum in return for a piece of primitive jewelry for his private collection. Are you interested?"

"I might be. What size contribution are we talking about?"

Marana turns to Regen who holds up two fingers.

"I think he'd do two hundred thousand," Marana says.

Regen shakes his head vigorously and moves his cupped hands toward each other in a minimizing gesture. Marana only smiles at him.

"What kind of piece would Regen want?" the curator says.

"You guessed who the donor is, I see," Marana laughs.

"He's the only man in Phoenicia who has that kind of money. Send him over, and we'll talk."

"He's on his way," Marana says as the screen goes dark.

"Her name's Livia, and you heard what she said. My limo will take you over there and bring you back here. I have plans for you this evening."

"I was plannin' on goin' back to Kamara, but considering the circumstances, I guess I could spend another night here. See you later."

The limo drops Regen off at an impressive structure with marble columns and a frieze showing women studying scrolls and engaging in various scientific exploits. He walks up the broad stairs and finds the curator's office easily. Livia's secretary tells him the curator is waiting for him. He walks into the office and Livia rises to greet him.

"It's a pleasure to meet you, Regen." She extends her hand, and Regen kisses it gently.

She has a bookish face, but her figure is slim and lithe. She's tall, almost 170 centimeters, and attractive legs show below her mid-thigh toga.

"You're much more attractive than your image on a communicator screen," Regen says.

"Thank you. I understand you're interested in some primitive jewelry."

"Yes, it's a gift for the Lady Herion."

"Follow me, and I'll show you some artifacts we confiscated from the old woman who lives in the jungle. They're old, but we have a lot of items from that period."

As they walk through the exhibits, Regen asks, "I didn't think there were any people here when your ark arrived. Who made these things?"

"You're right. There were no people here when we arrived,

but we did find evidence humans once existed here. We're not sure what happened to them, but most scientists think there was some sort of volcanic eruption that snuffed out most surface life over 250,000 years ago. Only marine life survived, and some species evolved into air-breathing animals. We have an exhibit showing all of that if you're interested."

"No thanks, I'm only interested in a necklace."

Livia leads him to a room featuring dioramas of primitive humans engaged in various activities with a dozen display cases in the center of the room. Regen is interested in the depiction of the people.

"How do you know what those people looked like?" he asks.

"We found many skeletons in burial sites, and our scientists were able to reconstruct the people from those remains. As you can see, they were quite short and very robust. Who knows what they would have evolved into? They might have become a beautiful race. The necklaces are over here." She shows him a case containing several items of jewelry, and Regen recognizes the one Karana is interested in.

"I like that one," he says, pointing to the one with the green stone.

"You're in luck. We have two of those in our collection. The other one is in our vault downstairs. I think Marana mentioned a contribution of D_p200,000?"

"She did. We hadn't discussed a figure before she called you, but I'm willing to do that." *It's highway robbery, but I'll have to leave a lot more than that behind when we go. Might as well have something to show for it.*

"Good. We can go back to my office, and I'll have the item brought up while we complete the transaction."

Regen leaves the museum D_p200,000 poorer, but carrying a box containing the necklace. A detour to a cutlery shop produces the rest of Karana's needs before he returns to Marana.

★ ★ ★ ★ ★

The joy rides to space are a great success. The shuttlecraft is crowded for each trip as the people gladly lay down 100D_p to see their planet from 300 kilometers high. Even with a full load of food and passengers, Regen finds the craft handles easily. No serious problems arise. It seems the restoration crew did their job well.

Data from the flights shows the life support system easily capable of handling the requirements of the 70-day trip to Terma. The only unknown left is the shuttlecraft's performance at Warp speeds and fuel economy under deep space conditions. The fuel requirements demanded by the gravity interaction drive are favorable, however, and Padopolous guesses the consumption at Warp speed might be less than he'd calculated. He's re-running the simulations based upon the orbital data as Regen returns to the office after the last flight of the day.

"You look happy," Regen says as he hangs up his jump suit and changes into a toga.

Padopolous turns from his computer. "Hey, Regen. Just running my latest simulation, and it looks like good news."

"How's that?" Regen finds Padopolous' stash of Gordian Bourbon and pours himself a glass before taking over the scientist's swivel chair.

"We may be able to do Warp 200, or better, for a short burst to get past the PSF and still have enough fuel to make Terma, but just barely."

"I thought you had a way to jam those guy's sensors."

"I do, but it doesn't hurt to have a back-up plan."

Regen downs a healthy slug of the bourbon. "It also don't hurt to have a fuel reserve when you land. Besides, I thought you said the shuttlecraft couldn't stand Warp 200."

"It can't for the long haul, but it'll probably take a short burst at that speed."

"How short? The PSF isn't gonna give up easy with Gilda eggin' 'em on."

"I got another trick up my sleeve if they hang on too long. I'm not worried about Warp speed, but I thought you were fearless. Are you telling me you always had a fuel reserve on all the adventures you told me about?"

"Most of 'em. I only got caught short on one or two."

"Well, I hope we don't have to use a speed burst, but I think it's there if we do. When do you want to make a try?" Padopolous asks.

Regen finishes his bourbon and sits up in the chair. "I'll need to refuel tomorrow, and we won't have any trips for two days. Herion's got some fruit stockpiled for us and plenty of rats for Hitler. Maybe we should go as soon as I'm refueled."

Padopolous takes on a pensive mood and rubs his chin. "I don't know. Gilda'll expect us to try a run on a full fuel load, but your idea of having engine trouble might fool her. She's also waiting on me to tip her off."

It's Regen's turn to think. "Sounds like a plan to me. You could slip Gilda the word we were planning on going after the next refueling following this one to throw her off guard, and the PSF would think we were grounded and relax some."

"Okay, it's all set, then. We go in three days."

★ ★ ★ ★ ★

The day comes, and Regen takes on a full load of tourists except for one seat occupied by Padopolous. The scientist already informed Gilda of the phony escape plans and made sure the Warp drive unit was in place. His belongings are aboard in a box labeled furga root extract.

Regen lifts off after the usual briefing but cuts power a bit and returns to the intercom.

"Ladies and gentlemen, we're experiencing some technical problems. It isn't serious, and there's no danger of a crash, but we'll have to land to make repairs. Unfortunately, we won't be able to get back to the museum. We'll land at Logana Island where the museum will provide for your return trip on the tunnel train. Please hold on to your ticket stubs as they will be good on any future flight. Thank you for your patience. We should be landing safely on Logana in a few minutes."

There is little panic, and everyone breathes a sigh of relief as the craft settles down in the clearing as pre-arranged with Herion. Some of her people are there to escort the passengers to the elevator for a trip to the underground city where they will await transportation back to the museum. When they are clear of the shuttle, Herion embraces Regen.

"I'm really nervous about this, darling," she says.

"Piece of cake. Is all the stuff here from Karana?"

"Yes, she's already delivered it, and we have plenty of runiga for Hitler."

"You got him too?" he asks.

"You know I do. How could we leave him behind? It's all rigged as a baggage train controlled by this remote." She hands

Regen a remote. "All you have to do is get Hitler in his cage and aboard. His cage is over there."

Regen hands the remote to Padopolous. "You load all the stuff aboard, and I'll get Hitler. See you in a few minutes." He moves to the edge of the jungle and blows the whistle only dogs and Hitler can hear. There is no response.

Damn it boy, you picked a lousy time to get out of range. He blows the whistle several more times to no avail.

Padopolous comes up behind him. "We're all loaded and ready to go. The PSF's getting antsy about us, but I told them we could do the repairs in an hour or two with spares we had aboard. We gotta get going, though, before they send somebody to check us out."

"I gotta get Hitler aboard. I ain't leavin' here without him." He blows the whistle again, but this time the sound of brush crashing tells him the skeen hears it. Soon an ugly head appears from a fern with a dead runiga in its mouth.

"There you are. Come on, we gotta get goin'."

Hitler drops the runiga at Regen's feet, and he uses the carcass to lure his pet into its cage. The shuttle's radio is alive when they enter the ship. Herion buckles into a passenger seat while Regen and Padopolous answer the calls from the PSF.

"PSF station 23 to shuttlecraft. Are you still okay?"

Padopolous signals Regen he would respond and dons a headset. "We're fine. We'll have repairs made in just a few minutes. It was only a glitch in the gravity field sensor system. Luckily, we had a spare unit aboard. It just takes a while to get it changed. Regen's working on it now."

"Does he have video back in the engine compartment? You don't have any for the flight deck or passenger area."

Regen smiles as he pointed to the circuit breakers for the video system.

"No, we've also got a problem with that system, but we can get home without that. We'll be ready to leave soon, and we'll go right back to the museum. You don't have to keep tabs on us."

"Okay, I could use a coffee break right now anyway. Call when you're ready to take off."

"Will do." Padopolous removes the headset and turns to Regen. "Good job turning off the video early. I'll go back and get the jammer set up now."

"Hurry it up," Regen says. "I'm anxious to get started on this game."

Padopolous returns in a few minutes and signals Regen to start the escape. "The jammer's set to start as soon as we're out of the atmosphere. Let's go."

Regen turns to Herion. "You ready, love?"

"I've got my fingers crossed." She holds up both hands to show it's true.

The whine of the engines drowns out conversation, but there is nothing to say at this point. Each of them is busy with their own thoughts. Regen is concentrating on milking every drop of performance from the ship. Padopolous is monitoring the jammer, hoping he has the right parameters for the current sensors. Herion is praying, and Hitler's asleep.

The shuttle lifts from the clearing and rises through the atmosphere. The black velvet curtain of space soon envelopes the craft, and Regen turns to Padopolous.

"That jammer workin'?"

"It only works on their Warp speed sensors. I can't jam their radars."

"Then they'll see us goin' into orbit."

"No problem, just tell 'em we got it fixed, and we're making a test run."

The communicator comes alive with the PSF duty officer. "Shuttlecraft, what's happening?"

Regen answers. "No problem, we got our malfunction fixed, and this is just a test flight."

"Roger that, we'll keep an eye on you in case you need any help."

The craft grows quiet as the main engines stop and they settle into an established orbit. Only the sound of the auxiliary generator powering the controls and the artificial gravity system hums steadily in the background.

"There goes our surprise," Regen says.

"Don't worry, they'll be surprised enough when we engage Warp drive. Here's the program for departure." He hands Regen a chip, and the Bremen plugs it into his console.

As the display changes to show the program's details, Regen reacts with surprise. "This ain't the program for Terma. You got the wrong chip, Doc."

"No, I didn't. Just let it go," Padopolous says.

Herion chimes in. "Do you two know what you're doing?"

Regen turns to her. "I do, but the Doc, here's, got us set up for god knows where."

"Let me explain before we have to make another orbit," Padopolous says.

"Go ahead, but I ain't engagin' Warp 'til I know what's happenin'," Regen replies.

"Look, we need to throw the PSF off our trail. When they see us engage Warp drive, they'll check for our last bearing. They'll think we can't change course once we make that move, so they'll follow on that vector. Their ships can outrun us easily. They'll just run until they overtake us and pull us out of Warp with their tractor beam so they can board and take us over."

"But we can't change course at Warp speed. It'd take up too much fuel, and we barely got enough to get to Terma as it is," Regen protests.

"It's okay, Regen. I figured this maneuver into my calculations. We can do it, trust me."

Regen gives the scientist a wary look. "The last person what said that to me took me for 100,000 credits."

"You forget I'm in this up to my neck. If they catch us, we're all going to the garrote post. Believe me, it'll work."

Herion breaks in. "I believe him, Regen. Do as he says." She places one hand on the Bremen's arm to emphasize her point.

Regen looks at her, and his expression seems to soften a bit. "Okay, If she says go, I'm ready." He activates the departure program.

The shuttle begins to re-orient for Warp firing, and the countdown clock begins. A mechanical female voice intones the remaining seconds. "Warp drive engaging in 30 seconds."

"The fat's in the fire now," Regen says. "Everybody buckle in. Warp engagement creates quite a jolt."

Herion and Padopolous do as he asks. This will be a new experience for both of them, though it's old hat for Regen and Hitler.

"Twenty seconds."

The trio sits in silence as the seconds tick by.

"Ten seconds, nine, eight, seven, six, five, four, three, two, one, engage."

The ship shudders heavily as the system pushes space itself out of the way and the engine noise changes from a whine to a low frequency hum almost louder than they can stand. The headsets on Regen and Padopolous help, but Regen turns to see Herion holding her palms over her ears. He reaches into a drawer and throws her some ear covers. Hitler is now wide awake and clawing at his head.

"Your skeen doesn't like this. I thought he was used to Warp speed," Padopolous says.

"He is, but my old ship was better insulated in the engine area. This won't last long."

The radio comes alive again. "Shuttlecraft, you're gaining too much speed. What's wrong?"

Padopolous activates his Jammer, and Regen reaches to the console and shuts down the communications system.

Chapter 22

Gilda's communicator chimes steadily on her direct channel as she reaches across her console to check the caller. It's General Regna, and she decides to take the call.

"Yes, General."

"Lady, the shuttlecraft is making a run for it. We know they have Regen and Padopolous aboard, and we suspect they have the Lady Herion with them."

A wicked smile creases Gilda's face as she contemplates watching Regen die. "How long before you catch them?"

"We estimate the shuttlecraft is only capable of Warp 100, at most. They won't have much of a head start before our interceptors launch, and they can reach Warp 250. We should have them in an hour, or so."

"Wonderful. Instruct your pilots not to fire on the shuttlecraft. I want those people alive. I want to be there when you bring them in. Keep me posted."

"It will be as you wish, Lady. Are there any further instructions?"

"No, just call me so I can be there when they arrive. That's all."

"Yes, lady."

The screen goes blank, and Gilda punches in Selenia's code. The screen comes alive again with her face.

"Yes, Lady," Selenia answers.

"Regen's made his move ahead of schedule. Padopolous said he'd do it next week, but he and Herion are with Regen. The PSF expects to have them in custody in an hour. I thought you might want to be with me when they arrive back here."

Selenia's face changes from business to pure hatred. "I'd like nothing better, Lady."

"Good, it shouldn't be long now until we have his wealth and his life. Why don't you come to my office so we can go to the PSF Headquarters together?"

"I'll be right over, Lady."

Gilda signs off and sits back in her chair smiling. *What a pleasure it will be to watch you gasp for breath, Regen.*

★ ★ ★ ★ ★

The Warp drive grows quieter as the ship begins to coast at 100 times the speed of light. Regen switches his display from system to system to check the ship's status while Herion and Padopolous remove their headsets and unbuckle their harnesses. Herion heads for the lavatory while Padopolous begins scanning the exterior sensors

"We must have fooled them," Padopolous says.

"Don't count on it. This ship's got no Warp communication. There's a good chance they're commin' after us right now. We won't know it 'til they start shootin'. They got weapons that can operate between two Warp speed ships, I'm sure. If they get that close, we're dead meat unless Gilda's told 'em not to blow us into space dust."

"If she did, the only way they can talk to us at Warp is by a parasite communicator. We'll hear that hit the hull before they try talking us back to Phoenicia. If that fails, they'll hit us with a tractor beam and pull us out of Warp to board," Padopolous says.

"There ain't no Warp indicator on the panel. The only one's back on the engine. Take a headset back there and tell me what we're doin'," Regen says.

"Right." Padopolous leaves the flight deck and moves past a nervous Herion and a sleeping Hitler to the engine room. Inside the noise is deafening, but he manages to find the Warp gage.

"We're doing Warp 105, Regen," he reports.

"Well, we'll know pretty soon if that jammer thing's workin'. When do we make the vector change?"

"I'll be right back with the chip for that."

While Padopolous is in the engine room Herion joins Regen at the control console.

"Why can't I see any stars, darling?" she asks.

"We're in Warp drive now. You don't see nothin' when you're in Warp. I don't know why that is. I ain't no scientist, all I know is it always happens. Padopolous might know."

The scientist soon joins Regen and Herion at the flight controls. Herion asks her question at once.

"Doc, why aren't there any stars?" She points to the view screen to emphasize her point.

"We're at Warp speed, Lady. You can't see anything because we're outside of space. The warp drive clears space itself from around our ship, and since light must have the medium of space for its transmittal, we see nothing."

Herion goes pensive for a moment, then her face turns sour. "But, what if there's something ahead of us, like another planet or an asteroid? Won't we crash into it?"

"No, Lady. You see when we travel at this speed, we pass through matter as if it wasn't there. The particles we call neutrinos travel slightly faster than light. They pass through even the largest star unhindered. We learned about Warp speeds by studying neutrinos."

"That's amazing," she says.

"Thanks, Doc. I always wondered how that all worked," Regen says.

"Here's the chip for the next maneuver." Padopolous hands Regen another navigation chip, and the Bremen inserts it in the console.

Regen calls up the new program and swears as he points to the screen. "Damn, Doc. Look at that. This program takes us out of Warp speed in a half hour. If the PSF's still on our tail, they're sure to get us then."

"I don't think so. They'll be doing Warp 200 or better to catch up to us. They'll buzz right by us. I'm going to drop the jammer pod before we come out of Warp. It'll continue on it for another 3 hours before it quits working. They'll come out of Warp then thinking it quit because we left Warp speed. By that time, we'll be too far away for them to detect us."

"I sure hope so. This program says we coast for another 3.4 hours at .8 Warp before we resume Warp speed. If that jammer only works for three, they'll come out and start scannin' for us. They'll have almost a half hour to find us, and that's plenty of time to do the job," Regen says.

"You gotta trust me, Regen. I know what I'm doing. The PSF won't be expecting us to change course. That, and the jammer will lose them completely. You'll notice the course change at sub-Warp takes no fuel." Padopolous points to the screen.

"Yeah, how do we do that?"

"This course takes us to a huge planet in the Morna system. We use the gravitation of the planet to divert us to the right course for Terma." Padopolous sits back in his chair smiling proudly.

"Doc, I gotta hand it to you. We use gravity to make the course change then we go back to Warp for the rest of the trip." Regen fast-forwards to the final stage of the program. "Making a landing on Terma'll be a close thing on fuel, but I think we may have enough."

"I've got a plan for that contingency too. If we do this right, we'll have plenty of fuel left to make a safe landing. But you have to activate this program now or we won't make it."

"Okay, strap in again," Regen orders.

Herion and Padopolous resume their seats, and Regen activates the program. His displays show the jammer pod separating, and once more, the ship shudders so much Herion is sure it will fall apart at any moment. Alarm claxons begin to sound, and red lights appear on Regen's control panel. The Bremen moves as if he had four arms to silence the sounds and eliminate the danger signals. The ship grows quiet again, and he breathes a sigh of relief as the stars reappear.

Padopolous has the best view of the control console. His face shows the concern of someone who fully understands the prospects for total failure they've just endured. "Great job, Regen." He slaps the Bremen on the back as the big man relaxes in his command chair.

Regen pushes out a huge breath of air and wipes the sweat from his forehead with his sleeve. "That was a near thing, Doc. This boat ain't made for many Warp transitions."

"Look at the fuel status." Padopolous points to the display.

Regen shakes his head in disbelief. "I guess you were right. There's still enough to get us to Terma, but we ain't on the right vector yet. I sure hope that big planet's where you think it is."

"It'll be there, trust me."

"It'd better be. I figure this crate's got one or two more Warp transitions left in it before it comes apart at the seams."

"Relax, I got it all figured out," Padopolous says with a grin from ear to ear.

★ ★ ★ ★ ★

Once more Gilda's communicator chimes with General Regna's call. She answers immediately.

"Do you have them?"

"No, Lady. They've jammed our sensors, and we don't know if they've changed course, but..."

Gilda interrupts the General, "You incompetent fools. Does this mean Regen is making good his escape?"

"No, Lady, it's only a minor problem. Our engineers estimate the shuttlecraft can survive only a few course changes at Warp speed, and they only have enough fuel aboard for one, at the most. The jammer signal is dying out, and we should be able to pick them up again very soon. I'll call you, personally, when we have them in our sensors."

Gilda finds it hard to control her anger. This is Padopolous' doing. Regen isn't smart enough to rig a jammer, and Herion knows nothing of technical things. She'd relish seeing both the men die even if she decided to spare Herion. After all, the lady doesn't have that long to live anyway.

"I need not remind you, General, that if Regen gets away, you will answer for it."

"We're doing our best, Lady. They won't escape us."

"Keep me posted," Gilda shouts as she cuts off the conversation.

★ ★ ★ ★ ★

The shuttlecraft drops to Warp .8, and the coasting period

begins. Regen points to a bright point ahead.

"Is that our planet, Doc?"

"I think so. We'll know in three hours."

Herion joins the men and views the magnificent sight before her. "It's so beautiful. I never imagined it could be so grand. You two are so fortunate to have witnessed this many times in your careers."

"Mostly, you don't see nothin'," Regen says. "You can't get anywhere at sub-light speeds, so you don't get this view until you're ready to land."

"The PSF operates mostly at sub-light, so I've seen the universe from our planet, but this is the first time I've seen this part of space. I would have thought it would look much the same, but it's quite different," Padopolous says.

While Herion marvels at the grandeur of space, Regen is busy checking his meager sensor array for any indication their pursuers are nearby.

"Damn, Doc, it's too bad we couldn't afford more gear than this. They'll be on us before I get any warning from this stuff."

"I'm sure my calculations are right, Regen. We'll be well out of their range if we can hold out until we get our course change from that planet. Once we go to Warp speed after that, they can't go after us and get back to Phoenicia."

"Looks like we'll know pretty soon," Regen says as he set the console clock to count down the time for resuming Warp speed. "Did we bring any bourbon along? I could use a final drink in case they grab us."

Herion smiles and pats Regen on the shoulder. "I'll be right back."

In a few moments she returns carrying a bottle and three

plastic cups. "Here you go, boys. Pour one for me too." She places the bottle and cups on the console.

Regen opens the bourbon and pours a healthy shot in each glass. Padopolous takes his and sips at it. Herion cradles hers in both hands as she stares into the amber liquid.

"It won't kill ya," Regen says.

"I know, I just haven't tried the stuff before, but I guess it's the right way to begin our adventure." She raises her cup in a toast. "Here's to making it to safety."

"Hear, hear," Padopolous says as he raises his cup to Herion's.

"Likewise," Regen says as they touched cups.

Regen downs his cup in one gulp, but Padopolous just takes another sip. Herion takes one sip and begins to cough. She sets the cup on the console and moves a hand to her throat.

"How do you stand that stuff? It's liquid fire," Herion says.

"If you don't want it, don't throw it away. I'll drink what you don't," Regen answers.

"You're welcome to it," Herion pushes her cup toward Regen.

The trio sit in silence for a while watching the clock count down the time. Padopolous breaks the mood. "We have to do something besides sit here and watch this clock."

"We got more'n three hours to kill. I usually take a nap, look at a video, read a book or eat something," Regen says.

"I could fix us something to eat," Padopolous says. "What would you like?"

"I don't care. I'm not really hungry," Herion answers.

"Me neither," Regen agrees.

"We don't have any videos, do we?" Padopolous asks.

"I've got a few on my personal computer," Herion says.

"I got a whole bunch back there in the cargo area. The box is marked 'Dried Prunes'," Regen says.

"I've also got a deck of cards in my bag," Padopolous offers.

"I don't know any three-handed games," Regen says.

"I never played cards much. Didn't have the time," Herion says.

"If the PSF don't get us, we'll have plenty of time to kill on the way to Terma," Regen says.

"In the PSF we used to play Eula when we stood alert. Any number can play. I'll get the cards," Padopolous says.

In a few moments he returns with the cards. They use the console for a table, and learn the inane game that keeps their minds busy while they wait for either capture or escape. For the first few hands Padopolous wins easily, but Herion soon claims her share of wins while Regen doesn't seem to have his mind in the game. After two hours Regen excuses himself to feed Hitler.

He releases Hitler to run around the ship. The skeen welcomes freedom and heads for the runiga cages. Regen releases two of the hapless creatures and watches while Hitler pursues each one. He catches one before it can find a hiding place and consumes it fur and all in short order. The other one finds shelter among the food cases stacked high at the rear of the shuttlecraft.

"Well boy, that one'll keep you busy for a while 'til we find out what's gonna happen to us," Regen says as he strokes the leathery head of his pet.

Hitler is soon in search of the hidden runiga, and Regen returns to the flight deck.

"Want to play another game?" Padopolous asks.

"Nah, I can't concentrate while the PSF still has a chance of catchin' us," he replies.

Once more the three sit for several moments watching the console clock click down the minutes. Herion breaks the spell.

"I'm hungry now. Can I fix something for us?" she asks.

"You know you can't boil water," Regen says. "What's this 'fix somethin'' talk?"

"No need to get testy," Herion says. "I was only trying to suggest a way to kill the rest of the time, and I can cook a bit. I used to cook for Apalon and me sometimes."

"I'll make us something," Padopolous says. He rises and moves to the food cartons.

"I ain't really hungry," Regen says.

"Eat something anyway. It may be our last meal," Herion scolds.

They continue to stare at the clock.

Padopolous returns a half hour later with a tray. He sets it down on the console with a flourish. "There you go. Lamb stew like mother used to make."

Three steaming plastic bowls waft a delicious aroma toward the travelers. Herion picks one up and selects a plastic spoon. She takes a tentative bite and savors it a moment.

"Not bad, Doc. If the rest of the stuff's this good, we won't go hungry on this trip."

"Easy as pie. You just open the can and heat it in the microwave," Padopolous says as he joins Herion in devouring the stew.

Regen looks at his bowl, picks up a spoon and stirs it a bit. "I guess it's better'n the space food I usually eat on long trips. Got any bread?"

"Yeah, I'll get some." Padopolous leaves and returns with a whole loaf of bread. He passes it to Regen who breaks off a chunk before starting on the stew.

"How long will this bread last?" Herion asks.

"We'd better eat it up this week. We can nuke it for a couple of days after that, but it'll turn green pretty quick," Padopolous says.

They eat in silence always watching the clock count down.

"Only another minute," Herion announces.

"That's an eternity in the space biz, darlin'," Regen says.

"Look at that," Padopolous says and points to the forward viewing screen.

A large orange planet begins to fill the display. Regen changes the magnification, and it shrinks to smaller size.

"Looks like you figured this part right, Doc," Regen says.

"That's our planet. Once we get past it, we go back to Warp speed, and we're home free," Padopolous says.

A beeping sound causes them to turn back to the console. The clock reads all zeroes.

★ ★ ★ ★ ★

Selenia checks the clock in Gilda's office. "The PSF should have them by now."

"Yes, it's been over an hour since I heard from General Regna. Are you ready to see the end of our Bremen friend?"

"I can't wait to see his face when they bring him in, and Padopolous too. I've been suspicious of him ever since he made senior rank in the PSF," Selenia says.

The signal of the communicator sounds, and Gilda smiles broadly at Selenia. "This should be our good news now."

Gilda activates the communicator, and General Regna's face appears. It is not a happy face. Gilda turns suddenly sober. "What is it, General?"

"Lady Gilda, I'm afraid we've lost the shuttlecraft. After...," Regna begins, but Gilda interrupts.

"What! You'll pay for this clumsy operation, I'll see to that," Gilda shouts.

"Lady, you didn't let me finish. When I say we've lost the shuttlecraft, I mean it is destroyed," Regna said.

Selenia breaks in. "You mean your interceptors fired on it?"

"No, Lady, it disintegrated when it tried to transition from Warp speed. After it left orbit, it began to jam our sensors immediately, but we tracked the jammer signal, and we were overtaking it in good order. They must have calculated we were close to an intercept and attempted to transition to sub-light speed, hoping we would overrun them so they could take up a new vector undiscovered. When their jammer signal stopped, our ships left Warp speed and searched for them, but all we found was a debris cloud. We knew the shuttlecraft was only capable of a limited number of Warp transitions, and it looks like two was the limit—once in and once out."

"Did you find any bodies?" Gilda asks.

"No, Lady, they had no space suits aboard that we know of. They would have evaporated into space dust when the ship broke up," Regna says.

"Damn! I was really looking forward to their executions, but I understand it was no fault of yours I'm deprived of that pleasure. Please forgive my initial outburst," Gilda says.

"No need to apologize, Lady. I'm sorry we couldn't take them alive."

"Well, you did your best. Thank you and goodbye." Gilda switches off the communicator and turns to Selenia. "Disappointing, but it can't be helped. We'll drink to the demise of the traitors anyway." She pours two glasses of wine for the toast.

★ ★ ★ ★ ★

At PSF headquarters General Regna breathes a sigh of relief. Her Chief of Staff shakes her head. "Do you think she'll find out about our little deception?"

"How could she? The interceptor crews think that's what happened. The fact that they seemed to pick up the shuttlecraft at sub-light speed for a moment before a large planet obscured their sensors can be explained as an anomaly. They're not even sure themselves it was them."

"But there was no debris field in their report?"

"We'll make sure that mistake is corrected in the official records, won't we?"

"Yes, Ma'am. I'll take care of that oversight."

Chapter 23

"We made it!" Padopolous shouts as the huge gaseous planet obscures the view behind them.

"Good job Doc," Herion says as she bends to kiss him on the cheek.

"I guess you do know what you're doin', Doc," Regen says.

"Okay, now we'd better all strap in for the transition back to Warp speed," Padopolous says.

They take their seats and fasten the harnesses, remembering the jolt of their first transition. Herion finds her ear protectors and puts them on. Hitler is nowhere to be seen.

"Everybody in? This thing's goin' Warp in ten seconds." Regen says as the delicate female voice in the navigation computer calls out the count.

Once more, the ship shudders and the console comes alive with warnings. Regen listens for the tell-tale sounds of a ship breaking up but only hears the moans and groans of an old structure protesting the demands on its design. The view screens go black as the ship settled into Warp speed. One by one Regen silences the warning claxons and extinguishes the blinking red and yellow lights.

"Well, we're still in one piece," Regen says.

Padopolous pats the console affectionately. "I knew you could do it."

Herion joins the men at the control console. "Now all we have to do is keep from murdering each other for another 70 days."

"That won't be easy. I'm used to this routine, but you two are doin' this for the first time," Regen says.

"Do you have any tips for us first timers?" Padopolous asks.

"You gotta sleep a lot and stay busy when you're awake. Ain't no exercise stuff aboard, so you'll just hafta do with runnin' around the main cabin and exercisin' on the deck. I got three boxes of movies and computer games tied down back there," he points to the cargo area, "There's also a storage disc with a couple of thousand books I downloaded from the Astartia library. Each one of us has a tablet we can read and game on. Other than watchin' Hitler eat his runiga, that's all there is for entertainment."

Herion yawns and stretches. "I think I'll take your advice on sleeping a lot. Where do we bed down?"

Padopolous answers, "The seats fold into beds. I'll show you." He leads Herion to the passenger compartment and changes a row of seats into a passable bed. "The blankets and a pillow are in the compartments under the seats. I made sure we had five sections restored once I decided to go with you two."

Herion looks around the compartment. "There's 36 seats, but they only make up 5 beds," she says.

"Right. Remember, this thing was a lifeboat not a luxury liner," Padopolous says.

"Good thing there's only three of us," Herion says.

Padopolous points to the makeshift bed. "I guess you and Regen'll have to sleep separately. I can't see two of you fitting in that."

"Doc, we've never slept together. He can't stand futons, but we manage to compromise from time to time." They both laughed over the picture of Regen on a futon.

"I guess this won't be an inconvenience for you two, then," he says.

"Doc, out of courtesy to you, I think we'll abstain from any intimate activity during this trip. There isn't much privacy here, and as nice a person as you are, I'm not really interested in servicing both of you," Herion says.

Padopolous blushes. "Lady, I was not hinting at anything."

Herion places one hand on his cheek and looks at him tenderly. "Doc, I didn't take it that way. I just don't want to put you in an awkward position, that's all."

"Thank you, Herion. I understand." They embrace, and Herion busies herself making up a bed. Padopolous returns to the flight deck.

Regen is pouring himself a large cup of bourbon as Padopolous takes the co-pilot's chair.

"I'll take a little of that," Padopolous says.

Regen pours him a cup and sits back in his chair. "Herion all settled in?"

"Yes, I think the stress of this escapade was a bit much for her."

"Poor kid. I know it's been hard on her lately, but I feel confident we can find a medic who'll get her over this disease, or I wouldn't have gone to all this trouble to get away from Phoenicia." Regen knocks back his bourbon and throws the cup in a disposal chute.

Padopolous changes the subject. "Do we need to man the console on a 24/7 basis?"

"Naw, the alarms'll sound if anything goes wrong. In fact, I was just about to do some readin' myself. You can stay here as long as you like."

"I think I'll take advantage of one of your videos," Padopolous says. He starts to leave the flight deck just as Hitler jumps into Regen's lap.

"I guess he's hungry," Padopolous says.

"I don't think so. I just fed him a while ago. He likes to watch the lights on the console. Kinda soothes him on the long runs. I'll join you later."

Chapter 24

Herion soon settles into a routine. After a sparse breakfast of reconstituted fruit juice and microwave oven oatmeal, she walks 25 laps around the main compartment. The water system is adequate for a sponge bath each day, though Regen only bathes every other day. Reading takes up her time until lunch, consisting of some kind of canned vegetable or reconstituted dried meat with microwave gravy. She occupies her afternoons with a movie or a video game then joins the men for a "family" meal Regen prepares from whatever he can find in their cache of storable food. He often says he misses his food synthesizer, but Herion has no experience with such a unit and cannot appreciate the difference. Evenings are consumed in various card and board games until time to retire. She often envies the men who seem to have some duty to perform associated with keeping their ship in working order.

Padopolous helps Regen with maintenance on the ship. Something seems to go wrong every day, though none of the incidents are life-threatening so far. He fills any idle time with technical books and videos. He often thinks this must be the way prisoners feel doing long sentences.

Regen seems to take it all in stride. He's the only one used to long, inter-galactic journeys. He sleeps a lot, but never misses a feeding for Hitler. The skeen amuses himself by exploring the ship or chasing the light displays on the console. It loves feeding time, chasing down the runiga Regen shakes from their cages.

One evening Herion declines any card game. "Tell me about

this Terma planet," she asks Regen.

"It ain't much—mostly desert except for some places near the oceans. Only two civilized nations on the planet. One of them's Ausland, and that's where we're going. The other countries are all run by tin-horn dictators who mostly make war on each other for entertainment. Ausland has a mighty fine research hospital in the capital city, Daq Vinas, and if they can't whip your disease, nobody can," Regen says.

"I can only hope you're right, Darling." Herion sighs.

★ ★ ★ ★ ★

The days drag on in monotonous routine, but the early morning of their 51st day brings the first serious problem. Regen awakens to the sound of alarm claxons and rushes to the console to find an array of flashing red warning lights. Padopolous joins him shortly followed by a bleary-eyed Herion.

"What's up?" Padopolous asks.

"I'll know in a minute if we're still alive," Regen says. He moves swiftly and methodically across the console controls, extinguishing one light after another until only one remains.

"Damn!" Padopolous shouts.

"Yep, we got a bad fuel rod," Regen says.

"What does that mean?" Herion asks.

"It means we're screwed," Regen says as he works the computer keyboard at a furious pace.

Herion looks to Padopolous for a clearer answer.

"A bad fuel rod reduces our range considerably. Regen's bypassed it, so it can't impact the other rods, but we'll have to come out of Warp speed before we get to Terma," he replies.

"And that means we'll never make it to Terma before we run out of food, water and oxygen," Regen inserts. "It's all right here," he points to the computer display then stands and begins to walk away.

Herion stops him. "I don't understand this, Regen. Please explain it in layman's terms."

Padopolous answers for him. "We can still get to Terma, but at sub-light speed the journey will take 10 days longer than we anticipated. Our survival was a near thing at Warp speed—there's no hope now."

Herion's face falls, and she throws her arms around Regen and begins to sob. "It's all my fault. You should have let me die on Phoenicia. Now I've killed you and Padopolous for nothing."

Regen pushes her away. "Listen, the Doc and I knew the odds when we took off. Nothing's your fault. It's just bad luck. I had to try. I couldn't just watch you die. Besides, what would my life be worth without you?"

"Gilda wouldn't dare go after you even with me gone. You've managed to steer clear of her this long, haven't you?"

"I wasn't talkin' about Gilda." Regen's eyes begin to cloud over as he turns away from her.

Herion stands rooted to the deck with a wide-open mouth. Padopolous sits quietly taking in the emotional situation.

Herion recovers first. She throws her arms around the big Bremen. "Oh, Darling, I love you so much. I guess I never realized how much you love me."

Regen turns and takes her in his arms. "I'd kill Hitler for you." He kisses her passionately as Padopolous busies himself at the computer console.

While Regen and Herion blubber in each other's arms, Padopolous works the keyboard at a fast pace. He finally slams a fist on the console in disgust. "Damn, there's nothing in that chip's data base besides Terma."

Regen wipes away Herion's tears with his fingers. "Can't you see we're having a tender moment?" he says.

"He's right, Darling. We need to find some way out of this mess," Herion says.

Regen sets her in a passenger seat and plops down beside Padopolous at the console. "Ain't there anything in the PSF data about this part of the galaxy?" Regen asks.

"No, PSF data doesn't go beyond 10 light years," Padopolous answers. "Do you remember anything about the planets in the vicinity of Terma?"

"All the planets I remember are on the other side of Terma from this vector, and that don't do us no good," Regen answers.

"Well, all that leaves is the universal emergency frequency," Padopolous says.

"You mean the PSF knows about that?" Regen says. "I thought you guys didn't give a damn about the rest of the universe."

"We don't, but we monitor that frequency in case there's a ship too close to us for comfort. When that happens, the Council has to decide whether to help it or blow it away," Padopolous answers.

"I remember several decisions I had to vote on while I was a member of the Council," Herion says. "You were lucky, Regen. You landed before the PSF could shoot you down, and the Council decided they could safely send you back where you came from because we could erase all evidence you'd ever been here."

"That's why all the hullabaloo when I came back, then," Regen says.

"Exactly. You put your neck in the garrote band, and you were lucky I was on your side at the trial."

"I know I owe you for that one, but we're still deep in the boondocks of this galaxy. Who's going to hear a distress signal from way out here?" Regen asks.

"It's our only chance. We've got no other options," Padopolous says. "You know the languages, Regen. Record a call for help in as many as you know, and I'll put them on a loop feed to the transmitter. We'll have to drop out of Warp speed to transmit then wait for a response, but it's all we can do."

Chapter 25

They coast for ten days, only using the engine to maintain Warp .8. Regen and Padopolous take turns monitoring the communications console. Regen checks the visual fields for anything that might look familiar, but finds nothing. One evening as Padopolous sleeps, Herion comes to Regen.

"Hold me for a moment, darling. I'm a little depressed right now."

He wraps his arms around her as she sits down on his lap. "What's this stuff about bein' depressed?"

"Is there any hope for us at all?" she asks as tears begin to roll down her cheeks.

"We ain't dead yet, and somebody may hear us any time now." He brushes the tears from her face with a tissue.

"I still feel badly. I know my time is limited, but you've got years and years ahead of you, or you did until you decided to try to help me."

Hitler jumps on the console and begins chasing the flashing system status lights. Herion points to the skeen. "Poor Hitler, he doesn't know anything about this. He's happy as long as he gets his runiga on time. He's condemned to a slow death by suffocation just like we are."

"If it comes to that, I promise you it won't be a slow death. I've got that laser pistol I confiscated from the goons Gilda sent to kill me. I had it handy while the PSF was chasing us. If they'd caught us, I planned to shoot you and Padopolous then turn it on Hitler then me. I wasn't about to give Gilda the satisfaction of seeing us all garroted. I'll do the same thing if it looks like there's no hope left."

Herion sobers considerably. "Promise me you won't act too hastily, that's all I ask."

"Don't worry. I don't want to check out as long as I think there's a way to salvage this mess."

At that moment, the communications console comes alive, and a male voice begins speaking. Hitler turns to the speaker and sits up as if listening intently.

"What's he saying? I don't understand him, but it looks like Hitler does," Herion says.

Regen's face changes from gloom to elation. "He's speakin' Bremen. Maybe this is the chance we've been looking for." He dumps Herion unceremoniously, pushes Hitler off the console and jumps to the pilot's seat and a headset.

"This is Regen aboard a shuttlecraft. Who is this?"

"This is the freighter Heracles. We heard your distress call. What's the problem?"

"We need fuel, and our navigation software for this sector is outdated. We're bound for Terma, but I'll take the closest place we can buy fuel rods."

"You're one lucky guy. We're heading for Quada III, but we had to drop to sub-light speed to make some repairs. We'd never have heard you otherwise. The closest refueling stop from here is Bandio 491. I'll send you the coordinates, and you can see if you have enough fuel left to make it there. You'll have to be able to do Warp 60 or better to get there in any reasonable time."

"We can do 100. Send 'em over."

The console comes alive with lights and displays as the data piles in. The noise awakens Padopolous, and he joins Regen.

"What's up?" he asks.

"We got an answer to our distress call, and they're sendin' over coordinates to the nearest fueling station. It's a Bandio store, and they're a bit on the pricey side, but we can't be choosers."

"That's it. You got 'em," the Heracles says. "I'll stay with you until you check it out."

"Thanks, it should only take a minute," Regen replies.

Padopolous is already busy doing the calculations. In only a moment he claps Regen on the back. "We can get there with two rods to spare," he shouts.

"You get that, Heracles?" Regen says.

The laughter on the other end tells him they did, but the man responds. "Yeah, we didn't understand a word of it, but the feeling was unmistakable. Glad we could help out. Have a safe trip. Bye."

Regen sets the new course and computes the fuel needed to reach Terma from the fueling station. "We'll need to buy four rods to make it, Doc. I'm sure I got enough diamonds for that with some to spare. If I had my old credit account, we could fill up."

Herion joins them looking in at the cabin door. "Is it good news?" she asks.

"Sure is. We've got it made now thanks to the Heracles," Regen says.

Herion smiles at the name. "Heracles is one of the heroes of Phoenicia. How appropriate."

"He's a hero in my book now," Regen says. "Strap in. We're going to Warp 100 again if this old bucket holds together for it."

Once more the console goes crazy with warning lights as the ship accelerates, but there is no serious problem. The exterior displays go dark again, but the trio celebrate by opening the last bottle of wine aboard.

★ ★ ★ ★ ★

The shuttlecraft can't dock at the fueling station since none of the docking ports match the shuttle's construction. Regen is forced to don a pressure suit and traverse a cable between the ship and the station. Once inside, he's met by the station manager.

"Welcome aboard. What kind of ship is that? I've never seen one like it," the manager asks.

"And you're not likely to see another one. It's from a planet that ain't part of the normal galactic commerce system," Regen replies.

"What kind of fuel does it take?"

"It's got a modern propulsion system in it, and it'll take the standard rods. We'll need four rods to make it home. How much is that?"

The manager consults a wall calculator. "₵20,000 credits, tax included," he answers.

"Look, I don't have a credit account right now, but I got some trade goods I could give you."

The manager's face takes on a disgusted look. "Another one of you bums. I got all the rations and petro I can use. No deal." He is about to turn away when Regen opens his case to reveal a diamond necklace. The man's eyes grow wide as he studies the gems. "Are those real?"

"Every one of 'em. I figure this piece is worth ₵40,000 credits anywhere. What do you say to a trade now?"

"Look, I got no way to prove these gems are real and nowhere to sell this stuff anyway. I know what petro's worth, and I can test it out for purity, but diamonds are over my head. I like the idea if they're real, but how will I know you're not scammin' me?"

Regen lays the case on the deck and picks up the necklace. He takes it to a porthole and scratches his name in the glass. "How about that?"

Regen points to another ship docked at the station. "That's a Valerian battle cruiser. They've got a lab aboard that can tell you all about these stones. See if they'll check 'em out for you."

The manager finds a communication panel and hails the ship. They aren't scheduled to leave for another half hour, and the DO gets the Captain's permission to do the tests. Regen meets him at the port for the warship and passes the case with the necklace to the young Ensign.

"The science officer says it won't take but a few minutes to check these out," he says. "You can wait here if you like."

"I ain't movin' as long as you've got that necklace."

The DO laughs as he vanishes inside the big ship, and Regen and the manager stand waiting in silence. True to his word, the DO returns with the case and passes it to Regen who opens it to make sure the necklace is still there.

"The Science Officer says, they're real and worth a ton. He said he'd love to have this as a present for his wife on their 25th wedding anniversary."

"Well, well," Regen says. "Ask him if he'll give me ₵35,000 for it."

The DO looks at Regen half in shock. "I'll tell him right away. That's a helluva price."

He moves to a communicator panel and informs the Science officer of the offer. "I'll be right there. Don't let him get away," is the reply.

Very soon a somewhat ruffled officer appears with his bank card in his hand. "Who do I pay?" he asks.

"Well, I ain't got a credit account right now, so you have to pay this guy, and he'll give me credit," Regen said.

The officer hands his card to the manager who inserts it into his hand-held terminal. "Your Space Force must pay pretty good," the manager says, "You got enough credit on this card to buy the station."

"I've made some good investments," the officer answers.

The transaction complete, Regen and the manager move back to the shuttlecraft.

"Okay now, load me four fuel rods and send a weld-bot out to check my ship's structure, and I'll call it square for the ₡35,000," Regen says.

"You got a deal, mister. Just open your fueling port for the load."

Regen returns to the shuttlecraft to be met by an anxious Herion and a bored Padopolous.

"That took you long enough," Padopolous says.

"I had to convince the manager the stones were real, and that took a while."

"How did you manage that? I'm sure the guy running this place is no expert on gems," Herion says.

"That big Space Cruiser docked on the other side had a science officer aboard, and he verified the gems. He offered me ₡35,000 for it, and I let him have it," Regen says.

"35,000?" Herion says. "That necklace had to cost ₯150,000."

"Shows you what the Drachma's worth outside of Phoenicia," Regen says.

"Just the same, I think you gave it away," Herion protests.

"I probably did, but we needed the fuel rods, and there weren't no jewelry appraiser handy."

"Regen's right," Padopolous says. "We can't be picky right now. Once we make it to Terma, we can get a fair price for the stuff, but right now we need the fuel."

The noise of the fuel loader and the weld-bot stops all further conversation. Padopolous checks the computer after the fuel load and confirms they have enough to reach Terma before they run out of food and the life support system needs servicing. The weld-bot report confirms Regen's suspicions that the transitions to and from Warp speed took a toll on the small craft, but they only need two more jumps.

★ ★ ★ ★ ★

The orbital station at Terma is a welcome sight, but the prospect of some real food is even more welcome. Though the docking port on the shuttlecraft is not any standard size, they manage to jury-rig a portal from the ship to the station. The reception at immigration is one of pure puzzlement.

"What kind of papers are these?" the immigration officer asks as he scans the trio's documents into his computer.

Regen has to speak for the group as neither Herion nor Padopolous speak any Auslish.

"They're from a planet nobody ever heard of and you'll never see anything like this again. I had Terman citizenship a few years back. Maybe you can find me, but these two are new to the system."

The officer punches in some data on Regen and finds his papers. "What happened to your papers?" he asks.

"That's a long story. Let's just say I lost 'em, okay?"

"I can handle that," he says as the machine spits out a new set of documents for Regen. "These two'll have to come in as aliens on temporary visas. You can get permanent status for them at the office in Daq Vinas."

"No problem, I've been through that routine before," Regen says.

"Okay, can you translate these documents for me so I can print out their visas?"

"Sure, let's start with Padopolous." Regen translates the information, and the immigration officer soon produces entry visas.

"The only thing left is the entry fee for your friends. You're cleared without a fee, but I'll need ₡2,000 each for them."

Regen doesn't translate for Herion and Padopolous. He feels it's better they don't know about the problem. "Can't you let them go now and send a bill later?" he asks.

"Sorry, I have to have the fee now or they have to stay here until it's paid."

"Can I take the ship to the surface? I can get money there and bring it back here in a few hours."

The officer thinks for a moment before answering. "I guess they could stay in the quarantine area for that long. Yeah, go ahead."

"Thanks, let me explain all this to them, and I'll be on my way." Regen turns to his friends and tells them about the problem.

"Where will you get the money?" Padopolous asks.

"Mariva'd probably give me that much, but I know she'd let me hoc a piece of our jewelry. She's a fair woman, and I trust her."

"What do we do while you're gone?" Herion asks.

"This guy says you can wait in the quarantine area. I won't be gone long. I know she'll be willing to help us out for a while."

He starts to leave, but Herion stops him. "That jump suit's pretty gamey. You can't go in that." She emphasizes her point by waving a hand in front of her face.

"I ain't got nothin' else except those damned togas, and I don't think the Velvet Saddle's quite ready for a guy in a bed sheet. Besides, I'd have every gay guy in the place climbing all over me once they saw that."

Herion sighs in resignation, "Okay, but see if her help will extend to a shower and a new set of clothes."

After a perfunctory customs check of his ship and an explanation about Hitler, Regen uses the gravity interaction drive to land close to the Velvet Saddle.

Chapter 26

Regen walks to the entrance of the Velvet Saddle, barely disturbing the crowd in the lobby. The desk clerk recognizes him at once.

"Regen! I thought you were gone forever. Where's Hitler?" He reaches over the counter and shakes the Bremen's hand vigorously.

"He's back at the ship. Good to see you too, Titus, is Mariva around?"

"Sure is. You know where her office is. She'll fall over in a dead faint when she sees you. If not when she sees you, when she smells you. Phew."

Regen walks behind the desk and down the hallway to Mariva's outer office. A new woman sits behind the administrative assistant's desk. She rises as Regen tries to walk past her.

"Excuse me, sir. Is Mariva expecting you?"

"No, it's a surprise, but she's probably been hoping I'd walk through that door for the last three years." He brushes past the woman and opens the door on Mariva studying the display on a computer.

"Not now, Glenna, I need to go over these casino figures," she says without turning around.

"This aint Glenna," Regen says.

A startled Mariva turns her chair to face the man she kissed goodbye forever long ago. "Regen! Why are you here?" She rises from the desk, steps around it and throws her arms around

Regen, planting a sensuous kiss on his lips.

Regen returns her ardor, but she soon pushed him away.

"Phew, you could use a shower. Where have you been?"

"Sit down, and I'll tell you all about it." He gives Mariva the whole story and his need for money to bail out Herion and Padopolous.

"So, you're here to find someone to help Herion, and you can't go back to Phoenicia, is that right?"

"That sums it up."

"I can't say I'm happy to see you under these circumstances. I thought you were gone forever, but I never stopped hoping that someday my door would open, and you'd be standing there. Now you're back, but in love with another woman. As far as I'm concerned, you're still light years away. I think you've got a lot of nerve asking me for help, but you were never short-changed in that category. Why should I help you?'

"I was hoping you'd do it for old time's sake, but if you remember, I signed over my part of the Velvet Saddle to you along with more than six million credits when I left. If I'm not welcome on a personal basis, I'd think I wouldn't be off base too far expecting a bit of consideration for that."

Her expression softens a bit, but she's still upset. "I can put you up for a while, but what will you do for money?" she asks.

"I got a lot of jewelry I brought from Phoenicia. All I have to do is find someone who'll give me a fair price for it. I reckon there's a couple million there." He reaches into a pocket in the jump suit and produces a diamond bracelet. "This here's a sample." He passes it to Mariva.

She studies it carefully under her desk lamp before speaking. "If the rest of the stuff's this good, you should have no problem getting top price. I've never seen such quality workmanship, and the stones look to be perfect."

"That's a gift for you, darlin'," he says.

Mariva slips it on her wrist and admires it for a moment.

"That's a good start. How much do you need right now?"

"I need ₵4,000 to bail out Herion and Padopolous, and then a few thousand for new clothes. I gotta see if there's a translator rig for Phoenician. If there is, that'll set me back a few thousand. Let's say ₵20,000 to tide me over until I can set up a credit account and sell some jewelry."

"Okay, I can do that for an old friend who helped make me a rich woman." She smiles at Regen and punches her communicator. "Titus."

"Yes, ma'am."

"Cut a cash card for Regen for ₵20,000 right away, please."

"Right away, ma'am."

"Thanks, darlin'. I knew I could count on you. What about two rooms? We'll need a single and a suite."

"Titus'll have them by the time you get back. I know I'm a sucker for doing this. The best I can hope for is that there's no cure for this Herion you brought along." Her smile tells Regen she isn't serious in wishing Herion dead.

★ ★ ★ ★ ★

At the hotel, they all select new clothes. Herion is awed by the selection of styles available and has a hard time choosing. Regen helps as best he can, and the salesclerk does the rest with him interpreting. He also helps Padopolous select new clothes, but he is an easier task than Herion. They find their rooms, and Herion heads straight for the shower with Regen joining her.

She uses the things she'd brought along on the shuttlecraft to do her hair and makeup, and there are no surprises there. The big change is when she dons the new clothes. A dark blue dress trimmed in silver compliments her silver hair. She has some trouble with the bra as she didn't use them on Phoenicia. Regen is awed by the result.

"You look like a million credits," he says as he sweeps her into his arms and kisses her tenderly.

The communicator signal sounds, and Regen answers to find Mariva. "Regen, I want you and your friends to join me for dinner this evening. Can you make it?"

"Got nothin' else on the calendar for tonight."

"Good, seven sharp in my private dining room. You remember where that is, don't you?"

"Sure, see you at seven."

The screen goes dark and Herion comments. "Mariva's a nice-looking lady."

"I was pretty taken with her at one time. I always wanted to retire on Terma. They got some beautiful villas on the seacoast, and I was gonna buy one."

"What stopped you?"

"I checked in to this place and found Mariva runnin' it. She made me a good deal on a place here, so I decided to stay. I would have too, but I found you."

"And you left all of this behind for me. I'm flattered. I noticed all the ladies in the lobby. You must have enjoyed your time here very much."

"I can't say I didn't, but I think you Phoenicians have got it right when it comes to male/female relations. Things are a lot different in the rest of the galaxy. Women here tend to get attached to you too easy. They have a hard time acceptin' a man having anything to do with other women. It don't seem to make any difference if they're married to you or not. Once you get in bed with 'em, they think you're theirs forever."

"Kind of like you and me?"

"Not the same thing at all."

"Maybe our relationship is the other way around."

"What do you mean by that?"

"I mean, you felt so strongly attached to me you couldn't leave me on Phoenicia when you thought I could be cured somewhere else. I'd say you were pretty attached to me to do that."

"Well, you came along and left everything you loved behind to be with me."

"I guess that just proves we're pretty attached to each other," Herion says as she throws her arms around Regen and kisses him.

"Okay, okay, you win, but we need to get down to more practical matters. First, we gotta see if we can find you a translator thing."

"How do we do that?"

"Over here at the computer." Regen moves her to the computer console and calls up the proper program. An attractive brunette appears and asks for the language to be translated.

"No known language," Regen responds.

"Is a person or computer familiar with the unknown language available?"

"I'm here," Regen responds.

"Thank you. Now, please have the person speak these words into the microphone in their native language." A text appears, and Regen translates for Herion who repeats the words.

"Thank you.   Please wait while we attempt to create a translation program."

The computer goes into a standard waiting mode. After a few moments, Regen says, "I think you got 'em stumped, darlin'."

Just then the woman comes back. "This language is related to the ancient Earth language of Mycenaean Greek. I will now show a text in that language. Please ask the translator recipient to speak these words to the translator to see if they convey the message shown in the Auslish text below."

Herion laughs at the display.

"What's so funny?" Regen asks.

"That text is a bit garbled, but I can read it. It's like one we use in our children's books. I'll read it to you in Phoenician."

★ ★ ★ ★ ★

It was a sunny day. Nancy wanted to play outside. Mother said she could. Dress warmly, her mother said. I will wear my warm coat, Nancy said.

Nancy went outside. She played in the snow with her dog, spot. Spot ran all over the yard. Spot plowed the snow with his nose. Nancy laughed at Spot.

Tom came over to Nancy. Spot is funny, he said. Spot is funny, Nancy said. They both laughed at Spot.

Regen laughs now.

"So you agree it's ridiculous?" Herion said.

"No, that's just exactly what it says in Auslish."

They both laugh as the woman continues.   "Did the unit recipient understand the text?"

"Yes," Regen manages between fits of laughter.

"I'm sorry, I didn't understand your answer. Please repeat

it," the woman says.

Regen calms down and repeats his answer, "Yes."

"Very good. I think we're on the right track. Now let's do a few more exercises."

They wind through texts that become more complex with each step. As Herion is about to call it quits, the woman says, "I think we have enough information now to produce a translator unit. How many would you like to receive?"

Regen inputs for two units, and the woman continues. "Your total cost will be ₡3,000 credits. Please use your account card to make payment."

Regen swipes his card through the slot and waits while the transaction is approved. Then a soft thumping sound tells him the items have been delivered. He opens the delivery door and takes out two translator units. Each unit consisted of a small box with a speaker connected to a combined earpiece and miniature microphone. Regen shows her how to wear it.

"Okay, ready for a test?" he asks.

"Let's go," she answers.

"You turn it on by pressing here." He shows her the tiny red button on the speaker unit.

"How do I sound?" she says.

"You gotta wait a second on the translation," he says.

"How do I sound?" A mechanical voice comes from the speaker unit in Auslish.

"Looks like it's workin' good. "You're ready to face the world now until you learn Auslish."

"I think I'll study really hard at that."

"I'll buy the course. It's only ₡500 more."

Chapter 27

That night at dinner Mariva and a male companion are seated in the private area of the large hotel dining room when Regen, Herion and Padopolous arrive. She introduces the man as Dr. Morova, the head of the large research hospital at Daq Vinas. They order drinks. Regen asks for Gordian Bourbon while Mariva and the doctor introduce Herion and Padopolous to Ausland whiskey.

"You're just the man we need to see," Regen says.

"Mariva's filled me in on the problem." He turns to Herion. "Tell me what the doctors on your home planet know about this disease and what treatments they've ordered for you."

"The disease is known as Bryllion's Syndrome. They told me it's a genetic disorder with no known cure. They've been treating it symptomatically with shots and medicines."

"I see, did you bring any of the serums and medicines with you?" he asks.

"Yes, I only have a week's supply left now, so I hope you can determine what they are in your world and prescribe more," Herion says.

"I'm sure we can do that. Would you be willing to spend a few days at our clinic in Daq Vinas for some tests?"

"Yes, certainly," Herion answers.

"When could you take her, Doc?" Regen asks.

"If you could come the day after tomorrow, we could start our testing immediately," the doctor says.

"We'll be there by noon. I need to find someone who's

interested in buying some fine jewelry, so I can combine some business with Herion's testing," Regen says.

Mariva turns to Padopolous. "And what is your specialty?"

"I am an engineer, ma'am. I specialize in spacecraft," Padopolous answers.

"There's a big spaceport in Daq Vinas. You should be able to find something there," the doctor offers.

"I'd like to get fluent in Auslish first so I can get rid of this." Padopolous fingers his translator unit.

"I don't blame you," Mariva says. "It's been hard to keep from laughing at the voice it projects."

"Don't feel badly, Mariva," Herion says. "I think it's hilarious myself."

"Did Mariva invite you here just for us?" Regen asks the doctor.

"Not quite. I use the Velvet Saddle as my R&R site from time to time, and I just happened to be here," he replies.

"The head of the spaceport will be arriving in a few days," Mariva says. "I'll see you get to meet him Dr. Padopolous."

"Thank you, I'd appreciate that," Padopolous says.

Mariva turns to Herion. "Are you and Regen married?"

"No, we don't have marriage on Phoenicia. The planet is governed by women, as was our original home planet thousands of years ago," Herion answers.

"So you and Regen have been living in sin these last few years," Mariva says.

"There is no such concept as a sinful relationship between a man and a woman in our culture. I'd assumed you shared our views on that subject, considering the main business of the Velvet Saddle," Herion replies acidly.

The men react with a sly snicker, but they are quickly sobered by one look at Mariva's indignant expression.

"Touché. And, what's wrong with my business? It's perfectly legal here in Ausland," Mariva says.

"I didn't think we were discussing the legal aspects of male/female relationships. You gave me the impression we were talking about the *morality* of those relationships," Herion says.

"It's the morals of the men that are in question as far as I'm concerned," Mariva says.

"At least on Phoenicia men could have sex with women as often as they like and free of charge," Herion says.

Regen thinks Mariva is about to come across the table and start a brawl. He decides it's time for some male intervention. "Okay ladies, let's switch to a different subject, please."

"Mariva, you have to understand Phoenicia is ruled by women, and we worship the female god Astarte, the creator of the universe," Herion says.

"What a wonderful idea," Mariva says. "I think Ausland would be a much better country if it were run by women. Maybe you and I can start a movement for female government, Herion."

"Judging by what I know of Regen and what he's told me about this planet, we'd have a very hard time doing that," Herion says.

They order dinner with Regen giving the two Phoenicians help with the menu. Another round of drinks arrives before the conversation continues.

"I understand you have an unusual pet," the doctor asks Regen.

"Yeah, I got a pet skeen," Regen answers.

"You should see the thing," Mariva says. "It's the most

hideous creature you can imagine, but it follows Regen around like a lap dog."

"I'd like to see it," Dr. Morova says.

"I don't bring him to fancy places like this," Regen says.

"He's really quite tame," Herion says. "He obeys Regen without question."

"I used to be able to pet him," Mariva says. "Go get him, Regen."

"If you insist," Regen says as he rises from the table and leaves the dining room. In a few moments he returns with Hitler following close behind. The skeen's presence draws a few gasps from Morova, but Hitler settles into a ball next to Regen's chair as the Bremen sits down.

Regen calls Hitler up to his lap and says, "This here's Hitler."

"What an odd name," Dr. Morova says as he reaches toward the animal.

Regen grasps the doctor's wrist before it can get too close to Hitler's jaws. "I wouldn't do that, Doc. He likes to take off fingers."

"I've seen him do it," Mariva says. "It's quite a shock to the wise guys who try to tease him."

"He snaps at anything that comes close to him," Regen says. "It's a natural reaction for skeens."

"What does he eat?" Dr. Morova asks.

"Whatever he can catch outside. He ain't particular about his diet, except when I have to feed him dog food. He'll only eat a few kinds, and sometimes he gets picky 'bout that," Regen says.

"An interesting specimen. I don't believe we have them on Terma," Dr. Morova says.

"We had them at one time, but none of them were that large.

Hitler's a real monster as far as skeens go. They were worse than rats, so we killed them off with traps, poison, whatever," Mariva says.

At that point dinner is served. Regen relegates Hitler to a spot under the table by his feet. The conversation dies down then picks up again after dinner as a variety of liqueurs appear for the diner's selection. Padopolous finds several to his liking and quickly becomes a bit on the tipsy side. He excuses himself to take to his bed and recover. The party breaks up shortly afterward.

Chapter 28

The next day is spent checking out places to turn the jewelry into cash. The leads Mariva provides prove most profitable. Since they are all in Daq Vinas, they decide to take about a third of the items from the hotel safe when they accompany Herion into the capitol the next day.

That evening Regen and Padopolous discuss possible business ventures.

"Anything we do off planet will require a ship, and that shuttlecraft ain't much good for that," Regen says.

"No, I think we've got all it has to give," Padopolous agrees.

"I can't think of nothin' legit we could do here on Terma that wouldn't bore us to tears," Regen says.

"You don't want to go back to drug smuggling?" Padopolous asks.

"Naw, lots of money in it, but too dangerous for my likes these days. Plain old smugglin' might not be bad, but we'd need a ship for that too."

"I'm too old for that kind of thing anyway," Padopolous says.

Regen thinks for a moment then his face brightens. "Say, we need to talk to my old gun runnin' partner Amalek. I'll bet the Zunids know of something we could get into that's not boring. I think we ought to pay him a visit."

"Tell me about this guy Amalek," Padopolous asks.

"He's a Prince of the Zunids. He traveled with me on the gun runnin' trips to Bardour. I'm sure he'll remember me. Let's go right now."

"Wait a minute. How do we know where this guy'll be?"

"We'll go to the main camp. If he ain't there, somebody'll know where he is. Come on."

Regen rises and Padopolous follows him to the desk in the lobby renting skimmers. Regen makes the deal, and they're soon on their way with Hitler riding happily in the back seat.

"Shouldn't he be in his cage?" Padopolous asks.

"I got his cage in the boot. He likes the fresh air and the wind in his face. Just like a dog."

They ride on through the dessert country, and Padopolous remarks on it. "There's only three places on Phoenicia like this. They're just as desolate and just as hot. No wonder nobody goes there."

"This place is different. Lots of people think this is home sweet home here on Terma. The Zunids rule most of the dessert, but there's another tribe that claims a big hunk of it. They used to go to war a lot, but Amalek married one of their princesses, and I guess that calmed things down. I didn't see anything on the news about a war in this area."

"Then what's that smoke coming from?" Padopolous points to a black column rising into the air just beyond the next row of hills.

"Beats me. Let's go have a look." Regen speeds up and is soon in a narrow pass between two hills. As they are about to reach the plain beyond the hills, four Bedouins on horseback move into position blocking their path.

"Who are those guys?" Padopolous asks.

"I think they're Zunids, but we'll soon find out."

One of the men signals Regen to stop, and Regen halts the skimmer just short of them.

186 M. L. Hollinger

"Who are you, and what are you doing here?" the apparent leader asks.

"Yeah, they're speaking Zunid all right," Regen says. "I don't know much Zunid, but most of 'em know some Auslish. "I'll ask him."

Regen uses most of the Zunid he knows to pose the question. The leader switches to Auslish. "I said, who are you, and what are you doing here?"

At that moment another of the men points to the skimmer and babbles to the leader in Zunid. The leader smiles and says, "He says you are Regen. He recognizes your skeen. Are you Regen?"

"Sure am. We come to see Prince Amalek if he's around."

The leader turns to his men and speaks hurriedly in Zunid. The men begin to ululate and fire their laser rifles at the rocks on the hillsides.

"Come, Regen, we will escort you to Prince Amalek. The Wamani are raiding our caravans again, and this is dangerous country. You probably saw the smoke."

"Yes, that's what drew us this way," Regen says.

"They managed to destroy one of our escorting armored cars, but we drove them off. This way." The leader turns and gallops off with Regen following close behind.

"Good thing that guy recognized Hitler," Padopolous says.

"I don't think they'd have hurt us anyway. We don't look much like Wamani to them," Regen says.

The skimmer speeds past several bodies in Bedouin dress as they join the convoy.

"Looks like the Zunids did a pretty good job defendin' the convoy. Those are all Wamani bodies," Regen says.

"I'm going to have to get used to human brutality. We didn't have this on Phoenicia," Padopolous says.

"It gets worse," Regen replies.

★ ★ ★ ★ ★

The caravan must have sent word ahead for Amalek rushes to greet Regen as soon as the skimmer stops.

"Regen, I thought you were never coming back."

Regen leaves the skimmer and embraces his friend. "I'd still be there, but Herion got sick, and I think somebody somewhere else may be able to help her. The medics there gave up on her."

"I'm sorry to hear that. Why didn't you bring her along? I'd like to meet the woman who could tame you."

"I'll bring her around when she can speak some Auslish. She's self-conscious about her translator device."

"Come into my tent. I want to hear about everything that's happened to you."

"Is your daddy around? I'd like to see him too."

"No, he's over in Rugistan visiting Yussah. He's trying to get him to reign in his bandits. They've been attacking our caravans lately, and that's a breach of our treaty."

"I noticed that on the way over here. Didn't look like they made out very good."

"No, we guard our caravans very well. We don't trust the Wamani any more than they trust us."

The joy of seeing Amalek again makes Regen forget about Padopolous for a moment, but he quickly remedies the problem.

"I almost forgot about the guy who made all of this possible. Prince Amalek, meet Dr. Padopolous, the best damned spaceman in the galaxy."

"Coming from Regen, that's quite a compliment," Amalek says as he embraces the Doc. "It's a pleasure to meet you. Any friend of Regen's is welcome in Zunid territory."

"Thank you, Prince. Regen told me all about your adventures during the long journey from Phoenicia. I'm quite impressed."

"Enough of this small talk. There's Gordian Bourbon waiting in the tent. Follow me." He leads them into the luxurious interior of the air-conditioned tent and seats them around a table laden with food. Regen helps himself to the Gordian Bourbon while Padopolous takes some of the red wine. Amalek also pours himself a glass of Bourbon.

"I thought you guys didn't drink alcohol," Regen says.

"As Crown Prince I'm also head of our religion, and I can grant exemptions to anyone. I decided to grant myself an exemption in the case of alcohol. You left some Gordian Bourbon behind when you went to Phoenicia, and I sampled it one day out of curiosity. I thought it might be the elixir that gave you such good luck and daring. I found it very tasty, so I had to use my religious powers to drink it without sinning."

Regen and Padopolous laugh at the explanation, and Padopolous says, "At least we on Phoenicia had no problem with alcohol as a sin. It certainly creates some criminals, but the justice system deals with that problem."

"A wise land, Padopolous," Amalek says. "What do you consider 'sinful'?"

"Actually, almost nothing in human behavior. On Phoenicia the only sin is blasphemy against the goddess Astarte. That can be remedied by an appropriate sacrifice. All other human acts are covered by our legal code, things like murder, robbery, assault that kind of thing."

"What about adultery?" Amalek asks.

"We do not have marriage, so there is no such thing on

Phoenicia."

Amalek turns to Regen, "No wonder you sacrificed your wealth to go to such a planet."

"I gotta admit it was hard leavin', but I had to find somebody to help Herion."

"Well, it's good to see you alive and well and Hitler looking fine as ever." The skeen is curled up asleep near Regen's feet, and the servants give him a wide berth as they do their jobs.

"Actually, we came here to see if you had any ideas about how a guy like me could make some money. I brought all I could with me in the form of jewelry, but it won't last forever," Regen says.

"Jewelry? Don't go selling that off at wholesale until my father and I have had a chance to look at it. We're both very fond of the stuff."

"That's good to know, but with the Wamani on the rampage, we'd need an escort from the border to your place when we bring it."

"You'll have it. Just let me know when you want to come over. Now, as far as some lucrative business goes, I've got two ideas. First, there's still a market for petro all over the galaxy, and some of your old sources are probably still in business. Second, they've found tricentium ore on Saros II, and the prospectors are paying anything to get there quickly. I assume you have some kind of ship, so you could make a bundle bringing in the eager beavers and hauling out the losers."

"That's the big problem, The ship we used to get here is all worn out, and it'll only do Warp 100 anyway. That ain't fast enough for either one of your ideas."

"What would it take to get it back in shape?" Amalek asks.

"It would take a miracle," Padopolous says. "I've beefed up

the structure as much as possible, but the Warp transitions coming here were pretty hard on it. I don't think it'll take many more. It could come apart at the seams any time."

Amalek thinks for a moment before speaking again, and both Regen and Padopolous wait for him.

"I know. There must be a dozen hulks out in the desert. Maybe one of them could be salvaged," Amalek says.

"Why so many?" Padopolous asks.

"The Ausland Space Force have a test center on the other side of the border near the great desert. They use the desert for weapons testing, including aircraft and spaceships. They pay the Bedouin tribes well for the privilege. When an airplane or spaceship goes down, we try to get to the site first. Of course, we rescue the crew and give them medical treatment, but we also strip the ship of anything useful."

"Don't they object to that?" Padopolous asks.

"Oh yes, but they're usually willing to pay to get the most critical pieces back. The others they let us keep."

"I'd like to take a look at them," Padopolous says.

"Good. I'll have my men send out some drones to find the wrecks and take some pictures. They should have something for you to look at by tomorrow afternoon. Can you stay tonight?" Amalek asks.

"I can't stay, as much as I'd like to," Regen says. "I gotta take Herion into Daq Vinas tomorrow to see the medics there, but the Doc could stay, if he wants to."

"Please stay, Dr. Padopolous?" Amalek says. "I'm sure you'll find it worth your time." He claps his hands, and several lovely women appear. "You may have your pick of my harem for tonight."

"I thank you very much, your highness. I'll accept your kind offer," Padopolous says.

Amalek dismisses the women and summons another servant. "Tell Captain Jahal I want to find all the wrecks in the desert. I'll need locations and as many pictures as he thinks important."

"Yes, your highness," the servant replies and leaves the tent.

"Now that's settled, I'll head back for the Velvet Saddle," Regen says.

"Come back soon, and bring the jewelry and your lady," Amalek says.

Chapter 29

The next day Regen takes Herion to the big research hospital in Daq Vinas. Dr. Morova meets then after Regen checks her in.

"It's good to see you again Lady Herion," he says as he embraces her. Regen has already clued him in on her title.

She speaks through the translator. "Please know that I don't expect you to be of any help, Doctor. Our medicine on Phoenicia is quite advanced and used to dealing with my race and its ailments. I welcome your attempt, but I won't be disappointed if you find you can't help me."

"You're a brave woman Lady Herion. I will be honest with you after we've run our tests. I won't hold out any false hopes."

"Thank you, I'm ready to proceed."

"I'll wait here in the lobby while you're doing that," Regen says.

Herion counters quickly. "On no you don't. I want you along to be sure this *thing* says what I want it to say." She points to her translator unit.

"Okay, I'll be there."

Various tests, scans and inspections consume the morning. Regen needs to interpret several times when the translator doesn't catch the subtle aspects of Herion's statements. Dr. Morova tells them the results will be ready after lunch and shows them to the executive dining room of the hospital. He excuses himself since he will be busy going over the test results while they eat.

Regen translates the menu and describes several of the items Herion is not familiar with. They order and sip some wine while they wait.

"Now I know how you felt after landing on Phoenicia," she says. "A stranger in everything, including the food."

Regen laughs. "I got used to it, and you will too. What did you think of the medics here?"

"They ran most of those tests back on Phoenicia."

"Were there any new ones?"

"There were two relating to my brain that I wasn't familiar with. I'm anxious to know what they show. You could be right about finding help here."

★ ★ ★ ★ ★

After lunch they meet with Dr. Morova. They sit in front of computer screens while Morova sits behind the same kind of screen facing them.

"These are the results of your body chemistry tests." The screens changed to show numbers and letters in various shades of green. "All of the results would be highly unusual for a woman of 67, if I compared you to a woman of that age on this planet, but look at this." He changes the screen again and the numbers are still mostly green, but quite a few are yellow or red. "This is what your numbers should look like considering your present condition, but they correspond to those of a woman half your age."

"I told you we have long life expectancy on Phoenicia," Herion says.

"I know, but this is remarkable. You haven't even experienced menopause."

"I can vouch for that, Doc," Regen inserts.

"Darling, the doctor is not interested in our sex life," Herion says.

"That's good to know too," Dr. Morova says.

"So, what do these figures show us?" Herion asks.

"Only the basics. The most interesting results are connected to your genome." The screens change to show two dozen, or so, items resembling jellybeans with bright tails on each end. "These are you chromosomes. The bright objects on each end are your telomeres. Notice their length. They are twice as long as any I've ever seen, regardless of race."

"Yes, that helps explain our long life," Herion says. "I could have told you all of this, Doctor."

"I thought as much, but your chromosomes are different in a number of ways. It's hard for us to determine exactly what is causing the damage to your vestibular system. I'm afraid it would take years of research to determine which gene on which chromosome is causing the mutations we see in those cells."

"I can help you there too," Herion says. She points to one chromosome. "The gene is on this one, but I don't remember which gene it is."

"I see, there are 1300 genes on that chromosome. Testing to determine which of those 1300 cause the mutation could take months, and it would be quite an expensive process. Are you prepared to pay that much?"

"How much are we talkin' about, Doc?" Regen asks.

"I'd say something in the area of ₵3 million."

"Phew, that's a pretty expensive area, and it's more than we've got right now," Regen says.

Herion turns off her translator and says this in Phoenician so that Morova will not be offended, "Regen, this is useless. Even if they find the gene, they'll still have to develop a means of correcting it. That could take even longer and cost even more. Let's go home."

Regen responds in Phoenician, "Listen, I had ten times that much when I left this place for Phoenicia. I've been broke a lot of times before, and I always bounced back."

"That was from drug smuggling. I don't want you to go back to that. What if you're caught and sent to prison? What would I do then?"

Morova interrupts their conversation. "Excuse me, but there may be a way to reduce the cost or possibly eliminate it altogether."

Regen responds, "How's that, Doc?"

"The Medical Research Ministry may be interested in studying Lady Herion's genome. I could apply for a grant to pursue that research. It's worth a try."

Herion turns on her translator. "What did he say?"

Morova repeats his statement.

"How long will that take?" Herion asks.

"The committee meets in two weeks. I can put together a grant request in time to meet their deadline, and we should have a decision in a month, at the most."

"Then go ahead and give it a try," Herion says.

"Good. In the meantime, I've managed to analyze the medications you brought with you, and I've transmitted prescriptions for them to the hospital pharmacy. You can pick them up on your way out. Do you have any questions, Lady Herion?"

"No, though you've only confirmed what the doctors on Phoenicia already told me, you, at least, have some hope of finding a remedy. Thank you Dr. Morova." Herion stands and offers her hand to Morova. He takes it and raises it to his lips.

"It's the least I could do for a lovely lady."

Regen offers his hand as substitute for Herion's, which the doctor seems to be holding a bit too long. "Yeah, thanks, Doc."

Morova releases Herion and grips Regen's hand. "You're entirely welcome."

Regen picks up Herion's prescriptions, and they leave for the Velvet Saddle. On the way they discuss the situation.

Herion's first action is to remove her translator device. "I hate this thing. Is there any way to learn some l language than using this?"

"You can learn any language in a few hours, but it costs an arm and a leg, and we gotta watch our money 'til I can turn our jewelry into cash."

"How much were my prescriptions?"

"A ton. I gotta get back to workin' soon, or we'll run out of money pretty quick."

"You haven't sold even a fraction of the jewelry we brought with us yet. Won't we have plenty of money after we sell it all?"

"If I'm goin' back to work, I'll need a spaceship, and they ain't cheap. It'll take all we got and a little more to buy a ship I can use to run drugs."

Herion looks at him with an expression of disgust. "I told you, you're not getting back into that business. It's too dangerous. Besides, we've only talked with one doctor so far, and you were so sure we'd find somebody who could cure me."

"I know, I know. I'll hold off doin' anything rash until we find out how much the stuff's worth here. I was gonna check some places Mariva suggested on this trip, but Amalek said his father'd buy the stuff. By the way, he really wants to meet you."

"I'm not meeting anyone that important with this thing on." She holds up the translator with two fingers as if it were something loathsome.

"Okay, we'll get you a session with the language school guys soon as I can sell another piece of bling."

They talk about the scenery the rest of the way back to the Velvet Saddle.

Padopolous meets them in the hotel lobby with Hitler by his heels.

"Welcome back," he says as Hitler runs to his master and leaps into his arms.

Herion excuses herself pleading a need for a nap after the medical ordeal. Regen leads Padopolous to the coffee shop.

"Let's have some coffee while you tell me what you found out with the desert wrecks."

The waitress seats them and both order beer.

"Well, they've got all the parts to make a fine ship. They had to find a guy to explain some of the more modern stuff, but I understood it all. The only thing missing is an airframe. They showed me some wrecks the military abandoned, but none of them were good enough to restore by themselves. We hauled three back to the Zunid camp, and I want you to look at them with me. I think I can cobble a ship together using parts from all three."

"Sounds great. We can go as soon as I get Heroin some basic Auslich training. I'll also take some jewelry for Jahallah to look at. Let's say by the end of the week."

"Sounds good. Can I get in on the Auslich training?" He fingers his translator device.

"Don't see why not. I'll get it set up."

Chapter 30

Herion and Padopolous are basic in Auslich after only three sessions in the trainer. Regen contacts Amalek for an escort, and they board a rented skimmer for the trip. The Zunid escort meets them at the border, and the trip to Jahallah's camp is uneventful.

When they arrive, two brawny guards take command of the jewelry chest and another guard ushers them into Jahallah's tent. The Zunid Chief rises and rushes to his old friend. "Regen, it's good to see you again." He embraces the big Bremen then turns to Heroin.

"And this must be the Lady Herion." He bends to kiss her hand.

"It's a pleasure to meet you, your excellency," Herion responds. "Regen has told me so much about you."

Jahallah casts a wary glance at Regen. "I'm sure he's exaggerated, as usual, but he could not have exaggerated about your beauty, Lady."

Jahallah pushes Herion out to arm's length. "Even a woman as lovely as you must be formidable indeed to tame Regen the Bremen."

"She's all that, I guarantee," Regen adds.

Amalek joins the group, and Regen introduces him to Herion.

"Come, sit," Jahallah commands as he sweeps an arm to indicate a row of divans. "We will have some lunch."

They dine on typical Zunid fare. Regen explains the dishes to Herion and Padopolous, and Herion passes on one or two, but

Padopolous consumes everything. After the meal and a fine liqueur, the jewelry chest appears. Jahallah inspects each piece, laying aside the ones he favors. When he's finished, he calls over the jeweler Regen remembers from a previous incident involving jewelry and Hitler.

"Behgin, come tell me what these are worth."

An older man steps forward and bows to Jahallah. "Your excellency, I am at your service." He produces a small device and passes each piece through it. With each one, his smile broadens. "Excellency, this is some of the finest work I've ever seen. There is nothing in this galaxy to compare with them. The items you've selected have a total value of ₵5,000,000, but my evaluator is incapable of rendering a true price for such fine pieces. I'd say these items would easily bring ₵7,500,000 at any auction house."

Jahallah's jaw drops a bit, but he recovers quickly. "This is only a fraction of what Regen brought us. Look at the rest."

Behgin pulls item after item from the chest and uses his machine as well as his practiced eye to evaluate each one. When he's finished, he shakes his head in amazement.

"Excellency, this chest minus the items you selected is worth over ₵20,000,000 at wholesale, but over ₵30,000,000 at auction."

"By the gods, Regen, you have nearly ₵40,000,000 here. I'll give you ₵30,000,000 for the whole batch here and now. What do you say?"

"Yer man said it was worth nearly forty," Regen counters.

Jahallah waves a hand in the air. "That was at auction. If I had to sell them in a hurry, I'd only get what the evaluator says they're worth less a percentage I'd lose to haggling. I'm giving you ₵5,000,000 more than that."

Regen turns do Herion, "What do you say, darlin'?"

Herion muses for a moment before answering then rises and moves to the chest. She searches the contents for a moment before holding up the first piece Regen purchased back on Phoenicia.

"I think it's a fair price as long as I can keep this necklace."

Jahallah bursts out laughing. "It's yours, Lady. Regen, I'll transfer the funds to your account now. Is it the same as last time?"

"Nope, everything's new this trip." Regen produces his account card and hands it to Behgin who signals to an assistant. The assistant brings an accounting machine and hands it to Behgin. In a moment, the machine shows the full credit in Regen's account.

"Thanks a bunch, Jahallah. I think we can start gettin' things done now."

"Wonderful, now that business is over, why don't you three relax until dinner," Jahallah says.

"I'd like to show Regen the wrecks we brought in," Padopolous says.

Herion speaks, "You go with the Doc, Regen. I'll take his excellency up on some rest."

Regen kisses her softly. "Okay, darlin'. I'll see you later."

A servant leads Herion to her tent while Padopolous, Regen and Amalek leave to inspect the wrecks.

Amalek shows Regen six sections of spacecraft hull which once comprised two military transports of different types and one battle cruiser. "There they are, Regen. Padopolous thinks we can get one good hull out of this mess."

Regen walks around the hulks before speaking. "I like the idea of combinin' a battle cruiser and a cargo ship, but I don't see no guns on the cruiser."

"We have a few that might work," Amalek says, "The space force boys got to the cruiser too fast for us to get those guns."

Regen turns to Padopolous, "What's yer idea?"

Padopolous points to a bulkhead on the battle cruiser, "This bulkhead comes close to matching one on that cargo ship. I'll show you."

He leads the group to another hulk. "This one matches almost exactly. We'd only have to make a short adapter section to match the longerons."

Regen rubs his chin. "How much is all this gonna cost?"

Amalek breaks in, "Padopolous gave me a good idea of the work to be done, but he doesn't know what that is in Credits. From what he told me about the structural work and what I know about the installation of the systems, I figured it at around ₵10,000,000."

"Phew," Regen reacts. "That'll blow a big hole in what your dad paid for the jewelry."

Amalek responds, "Look at it this way. A new ZHS 2200 will run you over ₵20,000,000. You save ten, and you can buy 10,000 kilos of petro for one million, leaving you nineteen left over for expenses."

"Yeah, and somethin' that size takes 300 fuel rods for starters. It'll take five trips to sell that much petro, and that's another ₵1,000,000 for fuel plus, let's say, ₵1,000,000 for other expenses. Herion has big medical expenses besides having to live while I'm gone. That's cuttin' it pretty fine, but 1 don't see any other way to get back on my feet. I used to get ₵1,000 a kilo for petro. That means ₵7,000,000 profit. I'd recover the cost of the ship in less than ten trips."

Padopolous breaks in, "Herion doesn't want you back in the drug business, if you remember."

"You guys are sworn to secrecy about this. I'd have to sell ₵70,000,000 in regular goods to make ₵7,000,000 even through regular smugglin'. As far as Herion's concerned, that's what I'd be doin', ya hear?"

"I got you," Amalek says.

"Me too," Padopolous echoes.

"Okay, start as soon as you can and keep me posted on progress. I got to take care of Herion before I can start workin' anyway."

The next morning, Regen, Herion and Hitler return to the Velvet Saddle. Padopolous stays with the Zunid to begin work on the construction of a new spaceship for Regen.

Chapter 31

On the way back to the Velvet Saddle, Regen explains the situation to Herion.

"Doc thinks he can cobble together a spaceship from the wrecks the Zunids salvaged. The cost is okay, but it'll take a good chunk out of our dough. Once it's done, I can get back in business."

Herion turns to him with a stern expression. "Not the dope business, I hope."

"Naw, none of that. I'll get into something legitimate, but I can begin makin' money again."

"Do we have enough left to cover my medical expenses?"

"Sure, and a lot left over to live on comfortably," he lies.

Conversation turns to future plans the rest of the way back.

★ ★ ★ ★ ★

A message from Dr. Morova awaits them back at their room. The Research Committee is considering his grant proposal, but if Regen can afford ₵500,000, he can begin his work now in anticipation of approval. Regen calls him back and confirmes transfer of that amount to Morova's research account.

★ ★ ★ ★ ★

Two weeks go by with Herion's illness getting no worse. It seems the medications are holding it in check. Her only problem is worrying about approval of Morova's grant request. Regen is hard pressed to keep her from calling the doctor every day. The next week Morova calls to tell them the grant for ₵3,000,000 was approved, and he hopes to have some positive results by the end of the month.

Padopolous is also making some progress on the spaceship. The adapter section is complete, and work continues on the rehab of the two wreck sections. Thanks to the dry desert, there is very little corrosion to contend with. He expects to have the two pieces together in six weeks or less.

Herion is biting her nails waiting on Morova's call. It comes early the next month when he asks them to meet with him at the hospital. They rent a skimmer and make the trip the next day.

"I've got some good and bad news," Morova begins.

"Tell us the good news first, Doc," Regen says.

Herion leans forward in her chair.

"Thanks to the information Lady Herion provided, we've mapped the chromosome she indicated. We found one gene which appears to be the culprit. It codes for a protein which attacks the neurons in her central nervous system dealing with balance and muscular control. It's not like anything we know of. I've named it Herion's protein." Morova pauses a moment, and Herion breaks in.

"Thank you, Doctor. What's the bad news?"

"The bad news is that we have no way of testing possible treatments. We can replicate the protein, but it has no effect on any laboratory animal available in our galaxy. Our body chemistry is that much different from yours, Lady."

Herion sits in deep thought for a moment as the room falls silent, then she speaks, "Our scientists and doctors on Phoenicia knew all of this. It's why we have no cure only palliative treatment. I'm afraid you've reached the same dead end we did several years ago."

"That's true, but we've also studied your medications, and

they suggest some other approaches to treatment. The problem is we have no way to test them except on yourself. Would you be willing to serve as a test subject for us?"

Herion turns pensive and studies the doctor's face before responding, "I don't know. What are the risks?"

"We don't know what kind of side effects the experiments may produce, but I'm confident none would be fatal. Some may be very uncomfortable. We just don't know. This is an entirely new field for us."

Regen breaks in, "You've treated lots of people from other planets, Doc. Is Herion so unusual?"

"She's an entirely new genome. Most of the other races I've helped have only a small deviation from the normal human genome, but hers is over 10% different, and her problem stems from that 10%."

Regen turns to Herion, "It's up to you. You know I'll be with you whatever you decide."

Herion grasps the big Bremen's hand and smiles at him. "I think I'll do it. The only other way is to just wait around to die. I'd rather do something even if it doesn't work."

Morova gives a relaxed sigh. "Thank you, Lady. I'm confident we'll find something to help you. The only requirement I have is that you stay in the hospital during the treatments. We need to keep you under close observation to evaluate the treatments."

Regen interrupts. "That's okay as long as I can stay with her."

"Of course. We have a suite for just such situations."

"When do you want to start?" Herion asks.

"I'll call you as soon as we have something. Meanwhile, stay on your medications and get as much rest as possible."

★ ★ ★ ★ ★

It's one week before Morova calls again. Regen helps Herion check in and get settled while moving into the guest room next to hers.

Morova comes in later to explain the procedure. "We've found a chemical that seems to attack the protein produced by the faulty gene. Your current medications attempt to do that, but they are only effective against a particular fold of that protein. We think this chemical will combat nearly all the variations, but it may have some side effects. We'll begin the infusion this afternoon. Is everything else alright?"

"Yes, Doctor. I'm ready to try anything."

Just before the evening meal, the nurses set up a port in Herion's arm and begin to feed the chemical into her bloodstream. There are no adverse effects until that evening when she becomes violently ill.

Dr. Morova checks the devices hooked up to her and gives orders for other injections. These ease the vomiting but do little to control the headaches. A heavy dose of pain killers finally ease the situation enough to allow for sleep. Regen stays by her bedside all through the night.

The next morning Morova runs more tests before he meets with Herion and Regen.

"The treatment seems to be effective in reducing the amount of that protein in your bloodstream, but I don't like the severity of the side effects. We'll need some more time to find a way to lessen the impact, but I'd like to continue the treatment. How do you feel about it?"

"It was pretty bad, but if it's working, I don't mind continuing."

Regen chimes in, "Are you sure about that? You were in pretty bad shape last night."

"Last night didn't kill me. Bryllion's Syndrome will. Keep going Dr. Morova."

After four days, Regen begs Herion to stop until Morova finds a way to lessen the side effects, but she insists on continuing.

Regen brings a hand mirror to her bed. "Look at yourself. You've lost a good ten kilos and your hair is starting to fall out. Stop now."

"Morova says I'll get back the weight and my hair." She pushes the mirror away.

At that moment, Morova walks in. "How are you today?"

"Very tired," Herion replies.

"I know. Your tests show some troubling factors. I'm discontinuing treatment for a few days."

Regen sighs heavily. "I've been tryin' to have her stop, but she won't listen to me."

"What about Herion's protein?" Herion asks.

"We've managed to reduce it to a trace amount, but the gene responsible has mutated and now produces a different version. I need to stop treatment for your own health, but I really need a hiatus in treatment to see what this new strain does."

"Very well, Doctor. Let's give it some time," Herion says.

In the next several days, Herion's condition improves steadily, but batteries of tests each day continue. Her hair is now gone, prompting Regen to purchase a wig. He takes it out of the box and presents it to her. "Here you go, darlin'. I just couldn't get used to a bald Herion."

A nurse helps Herion don the wig and holds up a mirror for her to see the results.

Herion primps the curls a moment before speaking, "I like it. Why did you select this color?"

"I always wanted to see what you'd look like as a redhead," Regen replies.

"I think I'll star shaving my head and wearing wigs. I could have one for every color, and you'd never be bored."

They both laugh at the remark, but Herion suddenly turns serious. She pushes the mirror away. "That is, if I live that long."

Regen takes her in his arms. "Don't talk like that. The Doc says they're lickin' this thing."

"I don't think so. The medics back on Phoenicia told me there were 72 different strains of Bryllion's Syndrome. He's only licked one, so far."

"Okay, so he has to fight one at a time. We'll still lick it, eventually."

Herion begins to cry. "I don't know if I can survive 71 more sessions like the last one."

Regen holds her close and whispers, "It's your call. Do you want to give up now?"

She shakes her head. "No, I can go on a while longer."

★ ★ ★ ★ ★

The next two weeks are every bit as harrowing as the first week. Herion is now only a shell of herself. Dr. Morova meets with the couple as soon as Herion is capable of understanding.

"Lady Herion, I'm sad to admit your suspicions are correct. Every time we manage to conquer one strain of the disease, it mutates into another variation. We have been able to develop medications to combat each strain, but the treatments are taking too high a toll on your system. Our only course of action now is to stop and allow you to recover before we go on. I'm sending you home with a small staff to care for you until we can resume."

Herion pats Morova on the shoulder. "You've done all that can be expected of you, Doctor. I am ready to discontinue treatment. I'll let you know if I ever decide to resume." She falls back into the bed exhausted.

Morova leans forward and speaks excitedly, "Lady, don't give up now. We're working night and day to develop drugs with fewer side effects. I'm sure we will find something soon."

Regen speaks, "It's okay, Doc. I'm sure she'll change her mind once she's back on an even keel." He looks toward Herion who is sound asleep.

"Do your best to convince her to carry on, Regen."

"I'll sure do that, Doc. Right now, she needs to get back to normal before she can make any decision."

★ ★ ★ ★ ★

Three weeks later, Herion is almost back to her normal self. Ever since leaving the hospital, Herion refuses to discuss the matter, but Regen is losing patience.

"You look great this mornin'. How do you feel?" he asks one morning after breakfast.

Herion gives him a sly look before answering, "I feel pretty good today. Why?"

Are you ready to go back to Morova now?"

She sighs and turns away from him. "I told you several times, I don't want to discuss it."

"We have to talk about it. Morova keeps calling. He says they've got a new medicine for this strain, and he thinks they've managed to cut down on the side effects."

"Okay, I'll talk to Morova, but he better be encouraging as hades."

★ ★ ★ ★ ★

Two days later, Herion is back in the hospital undergoing Morova's latest chemotherapy. This time, the side effects are worse.

Regen sits by her bed listening to the machines whir and beep and watching her fade away. What little hair had grown back falls out quickly, and her skin becomes even paler and more shrunken than before. Morova comes up beside him.

"I'm sorry, Regen. I thought sure we had this licked with the new chemical."

"Not your fault, Doc. You did your best, and you got nothin' to test the stuff on but her."

"I'm afraid we really screwed up this time. She seems to be reacting much more violently to this one."

"Just tell me she'll pull through."

"I wish I could. I don't know what will happen. We're doing the best we can with her symptoms, but I don't like how she's responding."

Regen sits back in his chair and sighs heavily. "I never should've taken her off Phoenicia."

Morova puts a hand on Regen's shoulder. "Don't talk that way. You said they weren't doing anything for her there. At least we're trying here, and we may yet succeed."

At that point, Herion opens her eyes and smiles at Regen. He moves to her side.

"How you doin', darlin'?"

Her voice is weak. He leans closer to her.

"I'm not doing very well. Is Morova here?"

Regen looks to Morova. "She wants you, Doc."

Morova moves closer to Herion. "What is it, Lady?"

Her voice is barely a whisper, "How much longer?"

"You've had the last infusion. The effects should be wearing off soon."

"Thank you, I don't think I can make it much longer. The pain is too great."

Herion falls back on her pillow and closes her eyes.

Regen buries his face in his hands. "By the gods, Doc. I'm sure I never should have brought her here. I was so confident our medicine was superior to hers, but I was dead wrong. I hate to see her suffer like this."

Morova moves closer to Regen. "Listen, she's still alive, and we've beaten seven mutations. We've learned how to minimize most of the side effects. This time, it's hit her hard, but it will get easier for her in the future. You did the right thing bringing her to me. The whole galaxy is watching our progress and making contributions to our treatment protocols. She will get better, believe me."

Regen sighs and rises to his feet. He moves to the bed and takes Herion's hand. "I want to believe you, Doc, but it's hard when she's like this."

★ ★ ★ ★ ★

The next morning, Herion is much better but still very weak. She glances around her room and sees Regen asleep in a chair. The stubble of beard on his face tells her he's been there all night. She debates about how to awaken him and decides calling for the nurse will do it easily. She presses the call button.

The nurse arrives, and Herion informs her she needs the bedpan. The activity soon arouses Regen who moves to her bedside.

"Good mornin'," he offers as he leans to kiss her.

Herion pulls back from the kiss. "Phew, you need a shower."

"I know, but you were pretty bad last night, and I couldn't leave you."

"I'm okay now. Go get cleaned up," she commands.

"Be right back."

Dr. Morova is with Herion when Regen returns, freshly shaved and smelling of cologne.

"Good morning, Regen," Morova says.

"How's she doin', Doc?"

"She's weak, but it looks like she survived the latest treatment."

Herion shifts slightly on her pillows. "It was a close call, Doctor. I think I need a lot of rest before we try another session."

"I agree. We'll release you tomorrow if all the tests look good. I'm sorry it has to be this way. The approach we're using reminds me of when we studied ancient medicine in medical school. We used to treat cancer this way before we had modern methods of dealing with it. I understand some patients declined the treatments, feeling they were worse than the disease."

Herion thinks about Morova's remarks. She's beginning to feel that way herself. Another treatment with side effects like the last one will stand a good chance of killing her. Morova will have to assure her they have such things under control before she'll agree to another round of infusions. She decides it's not something to bring up now. She'll discuss it with Regen later.

Chapter 32

Back at the Velvet Saddle, Herion is still too weak for any activity. Regen sees to it she's comfortable in their rooms before contacting Padopolous.

"Hey Doc, how's the spaceship comin' along?"

"It'll be ready for a test flight next week. How's Herion doing?"

"Not that good. Every new procedure seems to kill one version of the disease, but a new bug crops up soon as we kill the old one. It's all takin' a heavy toll on her. I don't think she'll do any more treatments no matter how hard I beg her."

Padopolous goes pensive for a moment. "You know, men on Phoenicia don't get Bryllion's Syndrome. Maybe there's something in my genetic material that might help the doc?"

"That's an idea. I'll talk to Morova the next time he calls. By the way, I'll do the test flight when you're ready."

"Okay, I'll let you know when. Give Herion my love."

"I'll do that. Talk to you later."

Regen signs off and goes to Herion's bedside. The nurse is serving her dinner, or trying to.

"You must try to get some of this soup down Lady," the nurse implores, but Herion only turns her head away from the spoon.

"You givin' this lovely nurse a hard time?" Regen says.

"I'm not hungry. Besides, it won't stay down if I eat it."

Regen nods toward the door, and the nurse takes the hint. On her way past Regen she whispers, "Try to get her to eat something. She needs to build her strength."

Regen nods his understanding and moves to Herion's bedside. "Padopolous had an idea today."

Herion moves in the bed to face Regen. "What's that?"

"He thinks there might be something in his genome that could help Morova since men on Phoenicia don't get Bryllion's Syndrome."

Herion turns away. "He's wrong. Our scientists investigated that possibility years ago. There's no hope there."

"Maybe Morova's next treatment'll be the one. Won't you try some soup before it gets cold?"

He takes a spoonful of the soup and tastes it. "Mmmm, pretty good stuff. I think you'd like it."

Herion turns back to him. "I'll try some."

Regen holds the bowl close to her mouth and feeds her a sip.

Herion smacks her lips. "It is good. I'll try some more."

She gets down half the bowl before pushing it away.

"That's all for now," she says and drops back into bed, closing her eyes.

Regen watches her as she drifts off to sleep. He reaches out to her and brushes what strands of hair she has left from her forehead as gently as he knows how.

I made a big mistake taking you away from Phoenicia and subjecting you to this ordeal. Look what I've done to you. My heart breaks for you. If you decide to quit, I'll go along with it. Whatever time we have left together, I want it to be good time. I don't want to see you suffer like this. I love you too much.

He leans back in his chair and falls asleep himself.

★ ★ ★ ★ ★

Regen's awakened by the communicator signal, but Herion doesn't stir. He answers before another ring can disturb her. It's

Padopolous.

"Hang on. Doc. I'm takin' this into the next room so's I don't wake up Herion," he whispers.

Once safely away from her, he raises his voice. "What's up?"

"I think the ship's ready for a test flight. When can you come over?"

"Herion's not doin' too well right now. I need to stay with her 'til she recovers some."

"Sorry to hear that. Did the last treatment do any good?"

"Morova seems to think he's lickin' it, but the side effects are 'bout to kill her. I don't think she'll go for any more treatments."

"She's a brave lady for going through what she has. I don't think Bryllion's Syndrome's any worse than that."

"I'll keep you posted. Maybe next week we can do a test flight."

"Okay, talk to you later."

He moves back to Herion's bedside, and she stirs.

"How're you feelin'?" he asks.

"No better than the last time you asked."

Regen decides he needs to change the subject. "Padopolous called. He says the ship's ready for a test flight, but I don't want to leave you like this."

Herion sits up and takes a drink from the water bottle by her bed. "Go ahead. The nurse will take care of me. I'm not dying now, just worn out. All I need is rest."

Regen mulls over the situation. She doesn't look well at all, but if she says he can go, he'd just as soon get the ship flying.

"Okay, I should only be gone a couple of days, and I'll call you every day." He kisses her on the forehead and leaves the room to call Padopolous.

★ ★ ★ ★ ★

The cobbled together ship is a welcome sight to Regen. He performs a thorough inspection of the outside and turns to a smiling Padopolous. "She looks great. You'd think it just came out of the factory."

"The Zunids have some pretty good sheet metal men and welders. Had to bring in some electrical and electronic people from Ausland, but that was about all they couldn't do. Working through this translator unit was a pain in the butt, though. Sometimes they just laughed out loud at what I said, and Amalek had to translate for me."

"Well, let's have a look at the inside," Regen says as he moves to the cargo hatch. "Wow, this is spacious," is his reaction to the rather large cargo compartment.

"I figured it should be this big if you're going to pretend you're doing honest work. I know you don't need this much space for drugs."

"Maybe I'll mix some honest work in if I got this much space. Let's see the flight deck."

They move to the flight deck, and Regen takes the command chair. He scans the consoles and fingers the controls. "This one's th' gravity reaction lever?" he asks.

"Yes, the military system uses a different shape for their controls than the civilian world." Padopolous points to another lever. "This is the throttle."

Regen moves the control to get the feel. "Yeah, this is a little weird, but I'll get used to it. Is it ready to fly?"

"Sure is. The Zunids even set up some target in the desert for you to practice on. Let's strap in and get going."

Padopolous points out the proper switches, and the craft

comes to life. Regen lifts his new ship into the air and puts it into a low orbit after clearing with orbital control. He's a bit wobbly, but soon smooths things out. Padopolous stays busy monitoring a bank of instrumentation readouts, and pronounces all is going well.

"Okay, let's try it out at Warp speed," Regen says.

"I've put in a course for the planet Ruba in this system. It's only .5 light years away. All you need is clearance," Padopolous answers.

Regen receives his clearance and waits for Padopolous to give him the go signal. The ship moves smoothly into Warp drive, and Regen whistles as he scans the Warp meter.

"Wow! Warp 300. My old ship would barely hit that figure, and this baby seems to be doing it with lots to spare."

"It's a military drive system. The Zunids tell me it's capable of Warp 450."

In a few hours they arrive at the planet, and the ship drops to sub-light speed and goes into orbit around Ruba. Regen scans the surface.

"Pretty desolate place."

"The Zunids tell me smugglers use this planet for storing their stuff. It's riddled with caves. I thought you might like to check it out."

"Any atmosphere?"

"Very weak. You need suits, and they have several poisonous lizards according to the Zunids."

"I'll leave those to Hitler. He's pretty good at killin' that kind o' varmint. Let's go shoot up some targets."

They clear Terman orbital control and begin to blast away at the targets in the desert.

"These laser guns are pretty powerful," Regen says.

"Yes, but look at the energy level," Padopolous says as he points to the readout.

"Phew, that little session o' target practice cost us nearly a whole fuel rod. We can't afford much o' that."

"Keep that in mind if you have to use the cannons in the future."

They land and conduct a thorough post-flight check.

"Looks like it came through everything okay," Regen says.

"I'll go over the data in detail, but nothing rang any alarm bells."

They encounter Amalek on their way back to his tent.

"How did it go?" Amalek asks.

"All ship shape," Regen answers. "I'm ready to start makin' money."

"Good, I got a guy you need to talk to. He's waiting back at my tent."

"What's his angle?" Regen asks.

"I'll let him tell you all about it, but it sounds pretty good to me. Otherwise, I'd have thrown him out before now," Amalek answers.

They enter the tent, and a middle-aged man in a conservative suit rises to meet them. He's not tall, no more than 170 centimeters and a bit on the portly side. His round face is smooth shaved, and a fringe of salt and pepper hair rings his bald head. Soft brown eyes twinkle behind circular glasses.

Amalek makes the introductions. "Regen this is Mallan. Mallan, this is Regen and the man with him is Dr. Padopolous, the man who built the spacecraft."

Mallan wears a translator, and its mechanical voice says,

"Pleased to meet you both. You must excuse the translator. I'm from Istria, and I speck no Auslish."

"That's okay. I don't mind," Regen says.

Amalek motions to divans, and they all sit while Amalek orders drinks and snacks.

Mallan turns to Regen. "I heard you were building a spaceship, and that you were a man who didn't mind a bit of adventure."

"Normally, I'd jump at a chance for an adventure, but I got a real sick lady right now, and I ain't interested in any adventures."

"I understand, but before you refuse me, I'd like you to try some of this." Mallan produces a small chest. He opens it revealing a light brown powder.

Regen inspects the contents, taking a pinch and tasting it. "Tastes terrible. What do you do with it?"

Mallan picks up a glass full of water and drops a small spoonful of the powder into it. As he stirs the mixture, it turns a light blue color. "Drink this," he says as he hands the glass to Regen.

"You sure this is safe?" Regen says as he sniffs the glass.

"I've used it, and I'm still here," Mallan says.

Regen takes a tentative sip. "Hmmm, doesn't taste as bad when it's mixed with water."

He downs the concoction and shrugs his shoulders. "Don't feel nothin' yet."

"It takes a moment to work," Mallan says.

Regen's eyes glaze over and he falls back on the divan. Padopolous rushes to check Regen's pulse.

"He's still alive, but out cold." He closes the big Bremen's eyes.

"Is this normal?" Amalek asks.

"No problem, he'll come out of it in a few minutes. I only gave him a light dose," Mallan assures them.

The tent falls silent as the others stare at Regen. A broad smile suddenly creases the Bremen's face as a sudden tremor convulses his body.

Amalek turns to a servant. "Get Doctor Zindah in here right away," he orders.

"It's okay. He's not in any danger. He's just having an orgasm," Mallan says.

"A what?" Amalek says.

"An orgasm. I'll explain it all when he wakes up," Mallan says.

In a few moments Regen opens his eyes and sits up shaking his head. "That stuff's better'n petro. I just had a great dream. I was screwin' the most beautiful woman I've ever seen, and..." He stops talking and feels his crotch. "Holy Astarte! I just had a wet dream. I ain't done that since I was a kid."

Mallan is laughing heartily, and the others stare at him. He stops laughing. "It happens to everyone the first time. Let me explain."

"Have at it," Regen says.

"I was part of a scientific expedition to the planet KCC 1257. It's a primitive planet, not even out of the stone age yet. We were there to study a people we called the Q Tribe. They were long-lived and very healthy for primitives, and we wanted to find out why. We landed well outside their territory and approached what we decided was their chief village. We'd had microphones and cameras planted secretly for several months to study their customs and language, and we managed to develop translator modules. We also donned clothing similar to theirs but more colorful, and we didn't dye our skins to match their bronze color. The villagers were wary of us, but we explained we'd travelled a long way to trade with them and showed them steel knives and colorful fabrics. When they saw the superiority of our knives over their stone tools, they welcomed us. They offered furs and some kind of gemstone for trade, and we accepted them while we also took blood and DNA samples. They balked at the blood draws at first, but we managed to get them past that with offers of pots and pans in return. The head man was the first to let us draw blood. He said he had plenty of blood and his people needed the cooking stuff.

"All was going well. Then they showed us this stuff." Mallan points to the drug. "We were afraid to try it until our lab back at the ship told us it wasn't harmful. Once we did try it, we couldn't stop using it. We began trading for it. They called it Xeno, their word for dream stuff. After the first erotic dream, the dreams got more bizarre. Our chief scientist said he'd dreamed of a solution to Jamison's conjecture. That's some kind of mathematical problem I don't understand. We all had strange dreams on the stuff, and we kept increasing the dose. The chief warned us to keep it down, but we ignored him.

"Well, it wasn't long 'til the first death. One of the lab technicians tried a super dose, and it killed him. That sobered us up a bit, but then two more died. Soon, there were only enough of us left to get the ship back home. We decided to leave right away. The Commander ordered us to leave all the Xeno behind, but I managed to smuggle this box out. I knew I could sell the stuff back home if I could find somebody to help me get enough of it.

"On the way back, all of our scientific staff died, and the computers crashed losing all the data on the Q Tribe. We barely made it back on a skeleton crew. I was a cook, but I had to learn how to manage the life support system. The investigation was routine. Everybody lied about the Xeno. They said it was some kind of disease they had there we weren't immune to.

"Somebody told me about this guy named Regen being back from wherever you went, and I heard all the stories about you. So, here I am."

"That's quite a story," Padopolous says.

"Yeah, and I believe it," Regen says. "I only want t' do one thing before I make any decision."

"What's that?" Mallan asks.

"I wanna get the stuff analyzed by a doc I know first. I'll give you ₵1,000 for half o' that box."

Mallan agrees, and Regen heads back to the Velvet Saddle.

★ ★ ★ ★ ★

Herion sits up in bed and holds her arms out for Regen's embrace.

"I missed you," she says.

"How are you feelin'?" he asks.

She smiles weakly. "A little better. Doctor Morova is due in a few minutes to check up on me. I'm glad you're here to hear what he has to say. How did the test flight go?"

"Great. Padopolous knows what he's doin', that's for sure. No problems at all. I got somethin' t' show the Doc after he finishes with you." He holds up the vile of Xeno.

"What's that?"

"It's Xeno, and if it ain't an illegal drug, it may be our fortune."

Herion gives him a quizzical look. "What do you mean?"

"Well, you don't want me smugglin' dope, and this here stuff is better'n dope, but I don't think it breaks any laws on the books now. That's why I want Morova t' check it out."

"Where did you get it?"

"That's a long story. I met this guy…"

"Am I interrupting something?" Morova asks.

Herion smiles at him. "No, no, come on in."

Morova greets Regen and begins to examine Herion. He uses several instruments and draws some blood. He asks many questions but seems satisfied with her answers.

"What's the verdict, Doc?" Regen asks.

Morova addresses Herion. "You're recovering nicely. You should be up and about in a day or two. We have a new procedure ready if you're willing to try it."

Herion turns away and frowns. "I don't know. I'll have to think about it."

Regen produces the Xeno. "I got some stuff I need you to check out for me, Doc."

Morova takes the vial and looks at it for a second before opening it and sniffing the contents. "What is it?"

"It's a medicine o' sorts. I need to know if it's legal. Can you check it out for me?"

Morova hefts the vial. "Sure, but I don't need this much." He produces another vial from his case and transfers half of Regen's vial to his. "I'll let you know. I'll be back to check on Herion in a few days, and I'll have your answer by them."

"Sounds great, Doc."

Morova turns to Herion. "Maybe you'll have an answer for me by then too?"

"Sure, Doctor. See you then."

★ ★ ★ ★ ★

Two days later Morova is back. He hands Regen a chip saying, "There's nothing in that stuff that's on any controlled substance list, but that's the best I can say for it. It has some compounds we've never seen before, and some of them look like they could pose problems in large enough doses. We'd have to perform a whole battery of tests to be sure, and that would take months and cost a lot of money. Besides, we'd need a lot more of the stuff, and the chemists say they weren't able to synthesize those compounds."

Regen claps Morova on the shoulder and smiles broadly. "I was hopin' you'd say that. Did you try it?"

"Of course not. I don't take strange chemicals."

"You got any left over?"

"Only a small amount."

"When you get home, put just a pinch in a glass o' water and drink it down. Be sure you're on a couch or in bed first. You'll pass out, but I guarantee you'll have a great dream."

Both Morova and Herion eye Regen suspiciously, and Herion speaks first. "What are you getting the good doctor into?"

Regen raises his right hand and shakes his head. "It ain't gonna hurt him. I tried it, and I'm okay."

Morova snorts and turns to Herion. "Have you decided on another treatment?"

"What can you tell me about the side effects?" Herion asks.

"Each time we thought we'd minimized them, but you seemed to suffer anyway. We've done our best, but I can't guarantee anything. Without lab animals to test the cocktail on, we can't be sure of much. I won't give you false hope."

"I hear what you say. Give me another week to recover and

ask me again."

With that, Morova leaves, and Regen moves closer to Herion. ""I'm gonna tell this guy I'll take him to that planet where the Xeno is. I looked it up in the charts, and it's only two days away at Warp 300. We should be able to get there and get back in a week's time. Will you be okay?"

"I'll be fine. I'm glad what you're going to deal in isn't illegal."

"If this stuff works out like I think it will, we'll be in deep clover in six months."

Chapter 33

Regen stocks his ship with all the knives, pots, pans, colorful beads and cloth he can find. He refills his arsenal with laser pistols, rifles and various types of grenade also. By the end of the week, Regen Mallan and Hitler are on their way to KCC 1257. Once they are on trajectory, Regen begins pumping Mallan for information.

"Tell me more about these Q people," Regen asks.

"They're pretty primitive. When we got there, they were still using stone tools. We gave them knives and axes plus pot and pans. They weren't hostile to us at all. They worship a female sun god and sacrifice animals to her."

"Tell me about how they look."

"Their skin is a golden bronze color, and they have black eyes. The funny thing is their hair. It's blonde to silver color. They aren't bad looking, but they have heavier lips and wider noses than most races. Otherwise, they look about like us."

"What about the women? Did they offer any women to you?"

"That was strictly taboo according to our leader. We were told to stay away from the women and not take one even if offered. There was a strict no sex rule."

Regen cocks his head to one side before speaking. "You said your group tried the Xeno. Didn't that make some guys want to screw the women?"

"Nope, we knew it'd mean jail time back home if we were caught, and there wasn't much privacy in their caves."

"I'd think the women'd go crazy on the stuff."

"That's a funny thing. Only the men of the Q Tribe were allowed Xeno. The women were forbidden to try it. "

"Well, that doesn't matter. My main concern is how do we talk to these people?"

"That's easy. The Q Tribe language did get incorporated into the translator data base. I got us two translator modules for the language."

"They got any skeens on that planet?"

"No, Hitler will be the first, but you'd better keep him on the ship. They kill anything they don't like the look of, and Hitler sure fits that description."

★ ★ ★ ★ ★

Two days later, they land on KCC 1257 where Mallan indicates the Q Tribe villages are located. They don costumes made to Mallan's specifications, but Regen makes sure he has a laser pistol hidden inside his top and in easy reach.

"What now?" Regen asks.

"We need to pay a visit to Wotgar, the local chief. He'll need a bribe, so take a bolt of the good cloth and three on the bead necklaces. He's already got a knife, an axe and some pots."

Regen pulls the items from their stores and releases Hitler. Mallon is surprised by the skeen's presence.

"Are you going to bring him along?"

"He goes where I go. Besides, if they know he's my pet, they'll know not to kill him if they see him out hunting."

"Sounds like a plan to me. Let's get going."

The walk to the local chief's cave is not long. The tribe recognizes Mallan, and they flock to him expecting gifts. Several dogs looking more like wolves begin to bark loudly when they see Hitler and the women recoil in horror while the men reach for spears, but Regen assures them the creature is a pet and will not harm them. Mallan tells them gifts will come later, and we are here to see Wotgar.

Regen is immediately impressed with the women. They are rather tall with obsidian eyes and straight black hair that hangs down past their shoulders. Their skin is a soft golden brown, and their bare breasts are high and firm with dark brown nipple areas. The only nod to modesty is a skirt reaching to their ankles and fastened with a wide leather belt. Many of the skirts are made from what Regen guesses is cloth traded in Mallan's earlier venture, but some are well worked leather.

The chief soon appears and embraces Mallan before turning to Regen. He has a colorful feather headdress and sports a necklace of claws from some beast they probably hunt for food. Ivory earrings grace each ear. He's quite handsome on a par with the beauty of the women. He's bare chested and wears a leather skirt ending just above his knees. In contrast to the barefooted women, he has sturdy sandals strapped to his feet.

"Who is this with you?" Wotgar asks.

"This is Regen and his pet Hitler. Please instruct your men about Hitler so they will not kill him. We have gifts for you."

Wotgar points to Hitler. "That is a very odd-looking dog."

Regen suppresses a smile and says, "He ain't a dog, he's a skeen, but I guess you could think of him like a dog if you like."

Regen presents the cloth and the necklaces. The chief places one necklace around his neck and passes the rest to one of the women behind him.

"We welcome you back Mallan. My people are hungry for your trade goods."

"We have all you want, your excellency, and we will trade for

Xeno as before."

The chief's face takes on a troubled look. "It is not yet time for the otiza harvest, and we may not use our meager supply for trade until after the harvest."

Regen turns off his translator and moves closer to Mallan. "Ask him how long we have to wait. I got a sick lady back home."

Mallan responds with his translator off. "I'm getting to that. Keep your pants on."

"We understand, your excellency, but when will that be?"

The chief spreads his arms wide and almost chants his response. "When the first moon is full and the yellow moon has turned to black, the golden pods will be in sight."

Regen again turns off his translator. "How many moons has this rock got?"

Mallan replies in like manner. "Four. The first moon is the largest and rotates at a near synchronous orbit. Most of the time it's on the other side of the planet from here. It rises here only once a year and it's only visible for six of their months. The yellow moon is farther out and has a lot of sulphur on its surface. The third moon is all rock, and when it eclipses the yellow moon it looks to them like the moon's turned black. The fourth moon is out beyond the other three and very small. It's hard to see without a telescope."

"Well, when does all this happen?" Regen asks.

"That's what I'm going to ask him, be patient."

Mallan turns to Wotgar. "When will this be?"

"In three more sunrises this will happen. Then the women will pick the otiza pods, and our shamans will perform the Xeno ceremony."

Once more Regen turns off his translator. "Let's just trade for what they got on hand and get outta here."

"You heard him. They won't do that."

"Looks like we're stuck here then," Regen says.

Wotgar speaks again. "Will you trade for this until the Xeno is ready?" A nearby woman hands him a leather bag, and Wotgar shakes out a handful of stones that gleam brightly in the sunlight.

Regen takes one of them and inspects it closely before speaking to Mallan. "They look like diamonds, but they're rough. Rough diamonds don't shine like that."

"I didn't see those when we were here." He also takes a stone and scrutinizes it. "Where did you get these?" he asks Wotgar.

"They are found in some caves, but we could not get them lose until we had your tools. We wanted them for necklaces, but we cannot drill through them. Are they not beautiful?"

"They must be some kind of quartz," Regen says.

"Whatever they are, they may be worth something to the jewelers back home. I say we take them in trade," Mallan says.

"Okay, but only 'til we can get Xeno," Regen says.

★ ★ ★ ★ ★

The trading is going well, but Regen becomes enthralled by one of the Q Tribe women named Amarina. She seems to be amenable to him, and he consults Mallan.

"What do you know about makin' love to the women here?" he asks.

"Like I told you, we were strictly forbidden to fraternize, but they don't seem to have anything like marriage. From what we could tell, each man has three or four women who serve him, but it seems they trade them back and forth a lot."

"What do you think they'd do if I got cozy with Amarina?"

"Hard to say what they'd do, but what about Herion?"

"On Phoenicia the women didn't care what you did. She wouldn't mind."

"I think we'd better play it safe until we can talk it over with Wotgar."

"Okay, but she sure does light my fire."

★ ★ ★ ★ ★

The moons are finally in alignment, and Wotgar allows Regen and Mallan to watch the women harvest the otiza pods. All of the tribe's women and children pick up baskets at the crack of dawn and sing a cheerful song as they walk a few kilometers to a long valley. A forest of coniferous trees covers the valley floor, and dark green vines wind up the trunk of every tree. They seem to do no harm to the tree, but only search for sunlight filtering between the lime green needles. Yellow-brown pods covered in hairy fuzz hang in profusion on each vine, and the women and children gather them into their baskets.

Regen follows Amarina while Hitler forages in the brush for a snack. At one tree. Amarina reaches for a pod near the ground, and Regen notices a movement near her hand. Hitler notices the same thing and lunges for the spot, grasping the head of a green snake in his mouth and shaking it violently until it ceases writhing. Amarina recoils into Regen's arms, and he savors the touch of her golden skin.

When she recovers, she tells him, "That a virtana. It kill me if dog not kill first."

Regen smiles as he continues to hold her in his arms. Amarina does not seem to mind and doesn't resist. "Hitler's a skeen, and he's pretty good at killin' varmints," he says.

Her obsidian eyes seem to glow softly as she stares into his, and her lips part slightly as she says, "You save me. I belong you now."

Regen quickly smothers her mouth in a kiss, and Amarina pushes him away roughly.

"What you do?" she says, wiping her mouth with the back of her hand.

"Holy Astarte, I thought you wanted me to kiss you, that's all." Regen says.

By this time a circle of women and children have gathered attracted by the commotion and the sight of Hitler devouring his kill. Mallan joins the group.

"They don't kiss, Regen," Mallan says.

Regen turns to Amarina. "I'm sorry. In my country that is the way we comfort women."

The watching throng begins to giggle, and Amarina's frown turns into a smile. "I forgive," she says as she resumes her chore of picking the pods.

★ ★ ★ ★ ★

The harvest is gathered, and the procession back to the home cave is as jubilant as the march that morning. Regen carries Amarina's basket while she embraces his free arm. Several of the women giggle as they point out the sight to their friends.

Once back, the women and children crack open the pods and dump the pea-like seeds into clay pots which are then collected by the tribe's shamans and taken deep into the cave.

The shamans are a colorful lot. Their skin is daubed with red and white pigment in various designs. No two are alike. They wear a headdress of plaited vines and white blossoms like roses. Their noses are pierced through the septum with some kind of small bone, sharpened on both ends. A large stone resembling iron pyrites hangs from a leather thong around their necks. They chant a guttural dirge as they work. When Regen tries to follow the shamans, his path is quickly blocked by two brawny warriors wielding formidable clubs.

The sun is setting, and the tribe begins to light their cooking fires. Mallan turns to Regen, "I'm not too keen on their food. I recommend we go back to the ship now."

"I suppose that's best since they won't let me watch 'em make the stuff. Let's go before it gets dark."

They take their leave of Wotgar and start to walk back to the ship. Regen is surprised when Amarina rushes to his side.

"I go too," she says.

"No, honey, you stay here with your people," Regen says as he gently pushes her away.

"No, no, I belong you. You save me. I yours." She grasps his arm in an iron grip.

Regen turns to Mallan. "What do I do now?"

"I don't see that you have much choice. It must be a custom of the tribe."

"Okay, we'll see what she thinks of a spaceship." He turns to Amarina, "Come on, darlin'."

They reach the ship just as darkness envelopes the land. Regen leads an awed Amarina aboard and sits her down in the cargo bay on a bale of cloth bolts.

"You hungry?" he asks. Amarina only nods her head yes as her eyes wander about the interior of the ship.

"I no see cave like this before," she says.

"Ain't no cave, darlin'. It's a spaceship. I'll get you some food."

Regen leaves her while he joins Mallan at the food synthesizer. "What do these people eat?"

"Mostly the meat from the things they kill, but they also have some berries and green stuff they gather from the land around the caves. I tried some of it, and it's pretty gamey."

Regen searches the food selection for something appropriate. "I guess pot roast is as close as I can come."

He orders two meals and places the food on a tray before returning to Amarina. The woman stares at the food and then looks to Regen with questioning eyes.

Regen sits on the bale and places the tray between them. "It goes like this, darlin'." He takes a fork and knife, cuts off a chunk of the meat and offers it to her. Amarina sniffs the meat and smiles while grasping the meat with her fingers and plopping it into her mouth. She chews loudly and cocks her head to one side as she savors the morsel.

"That good," she says.

Regen takes a small piece of potato on the fork and offers it. "Try this too."

Amarina accepts the potatoes as well as the carrots but shuns the knife and fork. Regen feeds her until she signals she wants no more. Water from a glass is also a challenge, and the bale gets a bit wet until she learns.

After the meal, Amarina stretches and yawns. "Where you sleep?" she asks.

"Whoa, darlin'. My bunk ain't big enough for both of us."

Amarina looks at him with an air of curiosity. "What is bunk?"

"It's a bed, where I sleep."

"You show me?" she asks.

Regen leads her to the crew cabin where Mallan is preparing for bed. He points to the lower bunk. "That's where I sleep."

She shakes her head vigorously. "No good. No furs. I fix bed. You come."

She drags him back to the cargo compartment and tears apart a bale of furs they've taken in trade. Carefully arranging them on the deck she stands back admiring her work.

"See, good bed. We go now." She drops her skirt to the floor with one deft move and reaches for Regen's skirt. As she comes closer, Regen notices she has a heavy aroma.

"Whoa baby, we gotta do one thing before we can make love."

She looks at him with a blank stare, and he leads her back to the crew compartment. Mallan is in his bunk reading, but he reacts to the sight of a naked Amarina.

"Wow! She's worth taking home to mother if you can trust father."

"Yeah, but she's in need of a shower."

Regen takes her to the shower tube and shoves her inside before she can react. Once inside the transparent tube, she begins to pound on the enclosure and yell her distress. Regen turns on the shower cycle and warm water pours over her golden body. The water calms her down, and she revels in it until the soap cycle begins. She scoops some suds in one hand and raises it to her nose. This induces a sneeze which blows the suds away. She scoops another handful and tastes it, screwing up her face in a distorted mask and causing her to spit several times. The rinse cycle produces more enjoyment, then the drying phase elicits more screams as her long hair blows high over her head.

Regen opens the tube and helps Amarina out. Her scent is much more pleasant.

"How you make river run in small cave?" she asks, pointing to the shower tube.

"It's called a shower, and every spaceship has one."

"Sho-wah," she says as she stares at the device.

"Yeah, showah," Regen echoes. "Now we can go to bed."

He leads her back to the fur bed and they make love without kissing.

Chapter 34

They trade for crystals and furs for two more days before Wotgar announces the Xeno is ready. Under Mallan's guidance, they trade the rest of their items for Xeno. In the end, they manage to take aboard 200 kilograms of the drug besides another 200 kilograms of the crystals and several bales of furs.

"Looks like it's time to head home," Mallan says.

Regen points to Amarina who is busy feeding Hitler one of the rats from his store of cages. "What do I do with her?"

"We need to say goodbye to Wotgar. You can ask him about it."

That afternoon they walk to the cave and call for Wotgar. The chief embraces each of them.

"We are sorry to see you go, but I understand you have no more trade goods. Please come back soon."

Regen pulls Amarina up beside him. "I only got one problem, your excellency. I can't take her back with me. What should I do with her?"

Amarina kneels before her chief, and Wotgar lifts her to her feet.

"Amarina is a fine woman. I trust she served you well?"

"Damn well, I got no complaints, but she wouldn't understand my world at all."

"I see, but it is an easy matter. Amarina is a desirable woman. Many of my men would bid highly for her."

"You mean auction her off?" Regen asks.

"Exactly. Her previous man will certainly be the highest

bidder."

"Hey, I didn't buy her from him. He can have her back for nothin' if she wants him."

Wotgar laughs heartily. "You saved her life. That was the payment, and she has no say in the matter. It is our law."

"Who was her former master?" Regen asks.

"His name is Mandoro."

Regen turns to Amarina, "Would you like to go back to Mandoro, darlin'?"

Amarina thinks for a moment before answering. "He is good man, but his kazan no like yours."

This causes Wotgar to double over laughing.

"What's so funny?" Regen asks.

Wotgar recovers and points to Regen's crotch. "What do you call that thing?"

"It's a penis, why?"

"In our language it is a kazan. Yours must be quite different from ours."

Amarina nods agreement, "Yes, I show you." She holds up one hand curled into a fist then extends the middle finger bent toward her palm. "Our men go like this." She straightens her middle finger. "Same size only stiff, but your kazan go like this." She grasps her extended finger and grips it loosely, moving that hand away to twice the length of her finger.

By this time, she's drawn a crowd, and they begin to laugh as loudly as the chief. Wotgar recovers again, "You may have spoiled her for any of our men, Regen. but we will see. Come here Mandoro."

A well-built young warrior bows before his chief. "My chief," he says.

"Would you have Amarina back after hearing that?" Wotgar asks.

"I have mourned her loss these many days, my chief, and I will pay whatever the stranger asks to have her back."

Regen sees true sincerity in Mandoro and notices a sympathetic response in Amarina. These two obviously belong together. "Then you may have her as my gift," he says. "But if the next time I come, I hear you have mistreated her, I will let my dog devour your insides." He signals Hitler to take a menacing pose, and the tribe wails in response. He takes Amarina's hand and places it in Mandoro's.

Wotgar steps in, "I'm sure she will be treated well, Regen." He turns to the assembled tribesmen. "We must say goodbye to our friends and wish them good travels." He shouts something that does not translate, and the tribe echoes his words, then they begin to chant a song that does not translate.

Mallan speaks, "They sang that same song when we left. Kind of sad and happy at the same time isn't it?"

"I guess that's our cue to split," Regen says.

They return to the ship and rise into low orbit before launching for home.

★ ★ ★ ★ ★

Once back on Terma, Regen's first priority is checking on Herion. He's surprised to find her in bed.

"I thought you'd be up and about by now," he says as he kisses her gently on the forehead.

"I decided to let Morova try another treatment, but I'm beginning to regret the decision. The side effects are still pretty bad."

"A lot of nausea?" he asks.

"Not so much as last time, but I have a lot of cramping in my stomach area. It's painful sometimes." At that moment she doubles over and clutches at her abdomen. "There's one now."

"I'll call for the nurse," he says as he reaches for the buzzer.

Herion holds out a hand to stop him. "Don't bother. They don't have anything to give me for the cramps."

Herion winces with the pain, and Regen can almost feel it himself. "I got somethin'," he says as he reaches inside his tunic and produces a vial of Xeno. He drops a pinch of the powder into her water glass and fills it with water. The action of filling the glass dissolves the powder.

"Here, drink this."

Herion eyes the blue liquid with suspicion. "What is it?"

"It's Xeno. Morova says it ain't got nothin' dangerous in it, and it'll sure ease the pain."

Herion takes a tentative sip then downs the contents quickly. "Not a very pleasant taste."

Before she can say more, she collapses back on her pillows with her eyes wide open.

Regen rushes to her, remembering the Q Tribe did not allow Xeno to women. He checks for a pulse and is relieved to find a strong beat. He closes her eyes and waits. A seeming eternity passes before she awakens. She blinks her eyes several times and feels her stomach area.

"The pain and cramps are gone," she says before turning to Regen.

"Did you dream about anything?" Regen can't resist asking after his own encounter with Xeno.

"That was the best part. I dreamed I was back on Phoenicia resting on a beach and enjoying the sunset. I was all alone, but I was perfectly content."

"I'm glad it helped with the cramps. I don't know how long it will last," Regen says.

"We'll just have to wait and see," Herion says. "Tell me all about your trip."

Regen gave her all the details of his visit with the Q Tribe, including Amarina. Herion laughs heartily when told of the shower experience.

"We got a lot of these in trade." Regen showed her the crystals, and Herion takes one to inspect.

"I've never seen anything like this," she says. "Is it quartz?"

"Don't know. I'm taking these into Daq Vinas tomorrow to see if they have any value to jewelers. I know they're hard as diamonds. I checked that out on the trip back. They cut glass, and my best grinding wheels didn't phase 'em."

"Mariva should know who to contact about their gem value," Herion offers.

"I'll talk to her now that I know the Xeno helps you. I'll leave this here for when the stuff wears off. Least we can help with the side effects of Morova's potions. Remember, just put a pinch in a glass of water. I hope you're okay. The Q Tribe didn't let their women have it, and I don't know why."

"So far I feel fine, but stick around for a while longer in case."

Regen and Herion share lunch and the Xeno still manages her pain and cramps. Herion releases him to talk to Mariva.

He finds her in the casino part of the dude ranch.

"Well, Regen, I see you made it back okay," she says.

"Got somethin' to show you. Can we go to your office?"

"Sure, I just have to check the roulette tables first."

He follows her as she times the wheels and pronounces them

stable then follows her to her office.

"What have you got for me?" she asks.

Regen dumps a few of the crystals on her desk. Mariva picks one up and takes a loupe from her desk drawer. She inspects the item under a strong desk light.

"Looks like a diamond, but not the same refraction. Have these been polished or faceted in any way?"

"Nope that's how they are in nature on that planet. The Q Tribe find 'em in caves, but they couldn't get them out until they got steel tools from the first expedition."

"I can't tell you much more, but take them to a guy in Daq Vinas named Torom. He has a store on the main square. It's called Gem House. I trust him to give you a true evaluation." She hands the stone back to Regen.

"Thanks for the lead. I'll check him out tomorrow. I gotta get back to Herion now."

"How is she doing?" Mariva's voice has a sincere tone.

"She's started another of Moriva's routines, and was crampin' real bad. I gave her some Xeno, and that helped. I don't know how long it'll last, though."

"What is Xeno? Never heard of it," she says

"Sorry, that's a drug the Q tribe makes. I'll have to bring you some. It's pretty great stuff."

"I'm anxious to try it. Give Herion my love, and I'll look in on her tomorrow while you're gone."

"Thanks, darlin'. I'll keep you posted on the gems too."

Regen returns to find Herion mixing another glass of Xeno. "That wore off kinda quick," he says.

"The cramps are gone, but I've got a splitting headache now. I thought another dose of this might help." She holds up the glass which is slowly turning a light blue. "Do you think it's okay?"

"Dunno, I seen the Q Tribe men take it one after another, but they won't let the women have it for some reason. You're plowin' new ground, but give it a try."

Herion downs the mixture and once more lays back on her pillows. This time, she closes her eyes and falls asleep. Regen checks her for breathing and pulse and finds all normal. Still, he stays by her side. She's out much longer this time, and he begins to worry. He calls in the nurse.

"Will you check her over to see she's okay?" Regen asks.

The nurse checks pulse, heartbeat, blood pressure, temperature and blood oxygen level before assuring Regen she's just sleeping. Then she notices the vial of Xeno.

"What is that?" she asks.

Regen looks at the nurse sheepishly and stammers a response, "Th-th-that's a, a, a medicine I got from a shaman on another planet. He says it's good for cramps and headaches."

"Did you give her any of that?" The nurse places her hands on her hips and glares at Regen.

"Yeah, I did. It got rid of her cramps, but she got a headache and took some herself. I guess it made her sleep."

The nurse gives him the fisheye. "It looks like that's all it did, but don't let her have any more of that snake oil until Dr. Morova's had a chance to check it out. Okay?"

"I got ya," Regen agrees as the nurse leaves the room.

Two hours later, Herion is still out cold. Regen begins to worry a lot and calls the nurse back in.

"Say, darlin', do you think we ought to wake her up?"

The nurse consults her watch before answering. "It's almost time for dinner. It's probably time." She moves to the side of the bed just as Herion sits up violently and begins to scream.

"Help me," the nurse commands, and Regen helps restrain Herion. Her eyes are wide open and stare into some unknown space while she fights against her captors.

"Hold her while I get a sedative," the nurse again commands.

Regen uses all of his strength to keep Herion in bed while the nurse prepares an injection. She seems to be calming a bit but still utters a stream of Phoenician so rapidly Regen can barely understand it.

The nurse returns and administers the injection which calms Herion completely in a few moments. Regen lays her back on the bed carefully.

"What was she saying?" the nurse asks.

"Best I can make out she was really scared of somethin', but I don't know what ."

"She'll sleep for a couple of hours with that injection. Keep an eye on her and call me when she wakes up."

"I'll do that," Regen answers as he begins to wipe perspiration from Herion's forehead.

He keeps his vigil until well after sunset. Herion finally rouses and blinks nervously as she reaches for Regen's arm.

"Are they gone?" she asks in a voice shaking with fear.

"It's okay. Ain't nobody here but me," Regen soothes.

"They were horrible things. Did you kill them all?"

"Easy, it was just a bad dream. There weren't nobody else here. Must have been the Xeno. How do you feel?"

"Strangely enough, I feel good. Just a little tired."

"The nurse wants to look at you after you wake up. You ready for her?"

"Yes, call her in."

The nurse arrives and goes over Herion with a fine-toothed comb before pronouncing her back to normal. "You must have had one hellofa bad dream, lady," she says.

"It was horrible and so real, but I'm glad it was just a dream. What's for dinner?"

She and Regen order dinner, and they finish just as Dr. Morova arrives.

"The nurse tells me you had a shocking dream," he says.

Herion responds, "It was all that, but it was only a dream."

"She also says you had some sort of drug Regen gave you. She said you called it Xeno?" He directs the question more to Regen than Herion.

"It was, Doc. I thought it might help her cramps. It did that, but it also gave her a real nightmare."

"Obviously, it has some hallucinogenic effect. You say it helped your cramps?"

Herion responds, "It stopped them completely, and I don't feel any nausea either. Xeno does seem to have some therapeutic value."

"We'll just have to wait and see about that. Do you have any more of it, Regen?"

"I got 200 kilos back at my ship, but I plan to sell that to pay for the trip. I think I can get ₵2,000 a kilo for it once people try it."

"If you could spare me a kilo, I could do some research on it to see if it does have therapeutic value and maybe eliminate some of the hallucinogenic effects."

"It'll be a few days 'fore I can get you some, but I'll give you that much."

"Meantime, I don't recommend you give any more to Herion."

"I sure don't want to give her any more nightmares, Doc." Regen picks up the vial of Xeno and puts it back in his tunic.

Chapter 35

The next day, Regen rents a skimmer and drives to Daq Vinas. He finds the Gem House easily and asks for Torom.

A short, balding Andi emerges from the back of the store. Typical of his race, his ears are quite large, and his nose protrudes two centimeters out from his palid face. A fringe of gray hair surrounds his bald pate, and it is expertly curled. He wears an expensive suit in a fashionable stripe motif.

"How may I help you?" he asks.

"Are you Torom?"

"Yes, what can I do for you?"

"My name's Regen, and I got some gems here I want you to look at and tell me if they have any value." Regen dumps a small bag of the crystals on a black velvet tray. The Andie picks one up and studies it with a jeweler's loupe he extracts from a pocket in his coat.

"Hmmm, an unusual piece. Where did it come from?"

"Right now, that's my secret, but I'll tell you it ain't from anywhere on Terma."

"Hmmm, I'll need to do some analysis before I can be sure of their value."

"How much analysis?"

Torom places the loupe back in his pocket and picks up two more crystals. "If you can wait, I will have an answer in an hour or so."

Regen scoops up the other crystals and returns them to their bag. "I'll come back in an hour."

After slaking his thirst in a nearby bar, Regen returns to the Gem House. Torom is summoned by a clerk, and the Andie beckons for Regen to join him in his private office. Once inside the Andie asks, "Why did you bring these to me?" He hands two of the stones back to Regen.

"Mariva at the Velvet Saddle recommended you."

Torom nods his understanding. "Ah, Mariva. She has been my beneficiary more than once over the years."

Regen looks at the two crystals, "You took three. Where's the third?"

"Right here." The Andie reaches into a pocket and produces the most brilliant thing Regen has ever seen. It fills the room with a rainbow of color.

"Holy Astarte!" Regen exclaims. "How did you do that?"

"This crystal defied cutting or faceting with my normal machines and my best cutters. We had to use an experimental laser cutter. What you see is from only the few facets we were able to create in the time available. Can you imagine the brilliance of a fully faceted stone?"

"I never seen a diamond shine like that," Regen says.

"It is like a diamond. It is mainly silicon carbide, but there is another strange element involved, and it is much harder than the usual SiC substitutes. Does it have a name?"

"Nope, I guess you could call it a Q diamond."

"Q for queer?"

"No, Q for the Q Tribe who found it. The main question is what's it worth?"

Torom leans back in his chair and tents his fingers. "How many do you have?"

"I got 200 kilos of 'em."

The Andie's smile broadens. "Ahhhh, a nice number, and it makes them rare indeed. I will make you a business proposition, ah… What is your name again?"

"Regen."

"I've heard of you, and Mariva's endorsement is a plus in your favor Mr. Regen. What would you say to this? I will market these Q diamonds for you in consideration of 50% of sales. The other 50% is yours, of course."

Regen smiles. The deal is typical of an Andie, and he knows he can do better. "I had to go a long way to get these things. I gotta cover my expenses. Let's say 30% for you and 70% for me for this load. I'll go 40\60 after that."

Torom grunts in exasperation and rises from his chair. He begins pacing the floor.

"I too have expenses Mr. Regen. I must cut and polish the stones and set them in jewelry worthy of their brilliance. I must have at least 45% to break even."

Regen smiles at his consternation. "Once a gal sees a ring with one of these in it, she won't want no diamond anymore. They'll be breakin' down your door for Q diamonds and pay you whatever you ask. You ain't gonna be hurtin' at 40\60."

Torom frowns but offers a stubbly hand to Regen. "It's a deal. When can you get me the rest?"

"Start with these, and we'll see how it goes," he tosses the bag of gems to Torom. "Meanwhile, I'll wait while we have one of your people put this in writin'."

★ ★ ★ ★ ★

Regen's next stop is Jahallah's tent. Amalek, Padopolous and Mallan are waiting for him as he'd arranged. They welcome him, and Regen explains the deal with Torom.

"We need to set up how we're gonna operate with all the stuff we brought back from KCC 1257," he says. "The jewelry deal splits three ways between all of us except Amalek. We need to settle with you, Amalek, about the spaceship."

"No need. My father inspected your cargo. He will take all the furs and three kilos of Xeno for our payment," Amalek says.

"That's mighty generous of your father," Regen says. He turns to Mallan and Padopolous, "That okay with you two?"

"Don't worry about my share, Regen," Padopolous says. "I got a job in Daq Vinas working for Viron. They heard about our ship and called me in for an interview. They hired me on as chief engineer."

"That's great! They hired you even without a degree?" Regen says.

"Shhh, keep quiet. I told them I had a PhD from Phoenicia. They can't check it out, and as long as all of you keep calling me 'Doc', I'll have no problems."

"That calls for a drink," Amalek says as he claps for a servant.

The group enjoy some Gordian Bourbon while they laugh at Padopolous' subterfuge.

"Okay, the furs and the gems are taken care of. You still get a third of the gem business, Doc, whether you want it or not. I wouldn't feel right unless you got somethin'," Regen says.

"Whatever you say," Padopolous says.

"That leaves the Xeno. Mallan and I will split the take on that stuff. I don't know what it'll amount to, but I figure it'll be as good as Petro, and I was getting' ₵1,000 a Kilo for that. That means our load, minus Jahallah's take is ₵96,000 at least. Once the pushers see what this does and it's not illegal, I think they'll pay more than that. I just gotta get in contact with some of my old customers."

"Just remember, we need to keep where we got it a secret. The people on my expedition know about Xeno and where it comes from. Maybe we shouldn't call it Xeno?" Mallan says.

"Good idea. What do we call it?" Regen asks. The group goes into a pensive mood until Amalek speaks.

"What about Swena, that's Zunid for dream?"

"How about somni, Phoenician for dreams?" Padopolous offers.

His offer gets little response.

"In Brem, dreams would be snovan," Regen says. Again, his choice is met with little enthusiasm.

Mallan snaps his fingers. "I know, why don't we just call it Snow?"

"You got it," Amalek shouts. "It's easy to say and doesn't sound at all like Xeno."

"I like it," Padopolous says.

"But the stuff's brown, not white," Regen protests.

"Who cares?" Amalek shouts. "Petro doesn't look like oil."

"How about Dark Snow?" Regen asks.

Nods all around fix the new name for their drug.

★ ★ ★ ★ ★

Back at the Velvet Saddle, Regen finds Dr. Morova and his nurse checking over a peacefully sleeping Herion.

"How is she Doc?" Regen asks in a quiet voice.

Morova holds up one hand signaling Regen to wait. He studies a hand-held device for a moment before passing it to the nurse, then he signals for Regen to follow him into the hallway. Once there, he speaks, "Your Xeno is some kind of miracle drug. After she recovered from the initial shock, she's lost all side effects. My tests show she's recovered from the last treatment entirely and the protein has not mutated again. If I didn't know better, I'd say she was cured."

"Sounds to me that's just what you described," Regen says.

Morova shakes his head. "I can't be sure until I run a few more tests, but I sure want to do some research work on Xeno. What can you tell me about it?"

"First off, don't call it Xeno. Call it Dark Snow. Some other folks know what Xeno is, and if they think there's money to be made, they'll descend on that planet in force."

"Okay, but what planet is it from?"

"I'm gonna keep that secret too, but it's not that far away. The people of the Q tribe there make it from seed pods. It's a secret recipe only they know. They use it like we use Petro. I've tried it, and it gives you nice dreams."

"Did you see any adverse effects in the Q tribe?" Morova asks.

"They all seemed healthy, but they didn't let women have it. I worried about givin' it to Herion, but I figured it couldn't hurt her any worse than she already was. Looks like it did some good."

"Like I said, we'll wait and see. Meanwhile, can you give me a couple of kilograms of the stuff to analyze?"

"I 'magine so. I brought some in from the ship for you like you asked before."

Morova follows Regen to his rooms where the Bremen hands him a small bag of Dark Snow.

"Think that's enough?" Regen asked.

Morova hefts the bag in one hand before replying, "I think so. I'll let you know what I find out."

Regen bids the doctor goodbye and returns to Herion's

bedside. She's still sleeping soundly, but he notices her face is fixed in a broad smile. He busies himself with the latest news on the communication screen until she finally rouses.

"You're back," she says.

He turns off the screen and moves to her bedside. "Sure am, how are you feelin'?"

He bends over and kisses her gently on the forehead.

"Better than that." She grasps his neck and pulls him into a long kiss.

"You must be feelin' better," Regen says after breaking off the kiss.

"You won't believe the erotic dream I had. We've never done anything that great."

Regen laughs knowingly. "I guess that's why the Q tribe don't let women use it. The men could never live up to the dreams."

She smiles and takes his hand.

"I don't have that worry with you. I just hope the drug does the job. I think I want to get out of this bed."

Regen helps her up and watches as she gets dressed. He's amazed at the change and thanks the Q tribe for Xeno.

★ ★ ★ ★ ★

By evening, Herion is back in her bed, suffering the side-effects again. Morova is by her side along with Regen.

"Think we need another dose of Dark Snow, Doc?" Regen asks.

"I wouldn't advise it until I know more about the stuff. My lab's checking it out now, and I should know more by tomorrow. Meantime, I recommend continuing with the treatments we've been using."

"You're the doc."

Morova says his goodbye's and Regen stays by Herion's side when supper arrives.

Herion only takes a bit of broth, but she asks Regen, "How about some more of that Xeno stuff?"

Regen looks at her with a sympathetic smile. "Doc Morova said to wait 'til he knows more about it."

"To hell with him. All I know is it took away these pains and let me dream nice dreams. I'll risk it."

"Okay, I think it did you some good, so I don't see why not."

Regen mixes up another dose of Dark Snow, and Herion gulps it down. She falls back on her pillows with a smile.

"I can feel it working already. Kiss me goodnight."

Regen leans over and kisses her gently as her eyes close. Knowing she'll be out for the night he goes to their rooms for some sleep.

★ ★ ★ ★ ★

Regen's awakened the next morning by Dr. Morova.

"Get up, Regen. Herion's taken a turn for the worse."

"Is it bad, Doc?"

"Just get dressed quickly."

Regen complies and Morova leads him to Herion's bedside. She's delirious and thrashing about in the bed. All of the tubes and bandages are gone, and several blood stains mark her sheets. Two nurses are trying to hold her down with not much success. Regen rushes to her side.

"It's okay, darlin', I'm here," he soothes.

His words calm her down, and she grasps his hand in a death grip. She tries to speak, but no words come from her mouth, but he can see the anguish in her eyes. He leans over her and kisses her tenderly on her forehead.

"It's okay, it's okay," he murmurs. "I love you forever," he whispers.

A calmness comes over her, and her lips curl into a small smile. Her deep blue eyes soften as she manages a whisper. "I'm dying. Hold me."

Regen fights back tears as he takes her in his arms. "You aint dyin'. The Doc, here, won't let that happen."

Herion shakes her head and tears from in her sunken eyes.

Regen looks to Morova who only looks down at the floor.

"Aint that right, Doc?" Regen asks.

Morova leans close to Regen's ear and whispers, "Did you give her another dose of Dark Snow?"

"She begged me for it, and she was in a lot of pain. I thought it'd let her sleep."

"That's the problem. We found out why the Q Tribe doesn't give it to their women. It contains a secondary metabolite we haven't seen before, but it interacts with estrogen to produce a virulent toxin."

"Gimme that agin, Doc."

"Simply stated, it's poisonous to females."

"Why didn't the first dose do it?"

"I'm not sure. It must take some time to metabolize or it may require a larger dose. In any case, Herion is dying, and there's nothing I can do about it."

"Aint there no anti-toxin?"

"It'd take us longer to make it than Herion's got."

"Regen," Herion's voice is weak, and he moves back to her side.

"I'm here, darlin'."

"Hold me," she commands.

Regen takes her in his arms and begins to cry. "You're th' only thing in this universe I give a damn about 'sides Hitler, and I love you more'n Hitler. I always will, forever."

A smile lights her face as her eyes close, and she whispers, "It's nice to know I outrank Hitler. You gave up everything for me, and I love you for that. Your quest to save me was useless from the start, but you risked everything again to try. No woman could ask for more than I've had with you. Goodbye my darling."

He feels her grow limp in his arms. Morova moves closer and punches several buttons on the bedside unit, all to no avail.

"She's gone, Regen," Morova says.

The big Bremen continues to hold her close as he weeps unashamedly.

"She was a great lady, Doc," he says.

Morova places a hand on Regen's shoulder. "I know, and I know what she meant to you. Take some comfort in what she did for science. We learned a lot from her disease. Many of the medications we developed for her treatment have application in other cases. She will save many lives in the future."

Regen lays Herion down softly and folds her arms. "She'd like that, Doc. I hope that gives her some comfort wherever she's gone."

"What do you want to do with her?" Morova asks.

Regen thinks for a moment before answering. "I wanna cremate her so's I can have her with me all the time."

"I understand. I'll make the arrangements and let you know."

Chapter 36

Regen goes back to the apartment and releases Hitler from his cage before flopping into a chair with a bottle of Gordian Bourbon. The skeen seems to sense his melancholy. It moves to his feet and rests its chin on the big man's knee while cooing softly.

"She's gone fella. What're we gonna do now?" He strokes the leathery head of his pet tenderly.

They sit for a moment in silence before Mariva lets herself in.

"I heard about Herion. Want some company?"

"Sure, long as it's you."

She moves to him and places her arms around his shoulders. "I'm so sorry. I know how much you loved that woman."

"She was one of a kind. I never cared much 'bout what happened to any woman after I left 'em, but Herion stayed on my mind all the time. Now, I don't know how I'll ever get over her." Regen takes another long pull at his bourbon.

"You gotta go on. She'd want that."

"I know, I know." Another swig of bourbon, and he gently pats Mariva's arm.

"You been a good friend to both of us."

Mariva kisses him on the forehead and moves to another chair. "You thought about a memorial service?"

"Nope, but I guess I need to do somethin'. She'd want that."

"A Veminite bishop just checked in this morning. I imagine he'd do some kind of service for a reasonable price."

"Veminites aint so bad, even if most of 'em are gay."

"This guy asked about call girls first thing. I'll talk to him."

"Thanks."

"Are you going to bury her here or in space?"

"Neither one. I'm gonna cremate her so's I can keep her ashes close."

"Do Veminites cremate?"

"I don't know, but if they don't like it, we can find somebody else."

A knock on the door interrupts their discussion. Mariva opens the door to Padopolous.

He whispers to Mariva, "How's he doing?"

"He's pretty bad, but he'll make it. Come on in."

Padopolous walks to Regen's chair, and Regen rises to greet him, bourbon in hand.

The men embrace.

"I came as soon as I heard. I called Amalek and Jahallah, and they're trying to find Mallan. I'm so sorry."

"Thanks, Doc. Want some bourbon?"

"Yeah, pour me a shot or two, please.'

Regen finds a glass and some ice before pouring out three fingers of the bourbon. He knows Padopolous likes his bourbon on the rocks. He offers a glass to Mariva, but she declines.

"Too early for me," she says.

Padopolous says, "I don't suppose there are any priests of Astarte on this planet, but I could do the ceremony if you'd like. I had to learn it at Space Academy for burials in space."

Regen cocks his head to one side and his face brightens a bit. "You know, Doc, she was such a good woman the rest o' this galaxy could use some o' that goodness. I'm gonna have her cremated, an' I think I'd like ta spread her ashes in space. Is the ship space-worthy?"

"Sure, whenever you like. It wouldn't take many fuel rods for a burial ceremony, and I think there's enough aboard for that already."

"That sounds lovely," Mariva says. "There won't be that many people to attend. We could fit comfortably I guess."

"Plenty of room in the cargo hold, and the airlock's right there too," Padopolous says.

"I'll check everyone for a good date," Mariva says. "Who do you want there?"

Regen thinks for a moment before answering. "You, Doc, Jahallah, Amalek, Mallan, Morova and whoever else he can think of. Anybody else?"

Both Mariva and Padopolous shake their heads. "Can't think of anyone else," Mariva says.

"Thanks for settin' it all up Mariva. I think I'd like ta throw a party in her honor after the service. Nothin' too big, I can't afford a big party."

"Don't worry about that, Regen. The party's on the Velvet Saddle," Mariva says.

★ ★ ★ ★ ★

A few days later, Padopolous lands the ship just outside the Velvet Saddle. The funeral party is waiting consisting of Regen in a brand new suit, Mariva in plain black gown from the expensive shop in the hotel, Jahallah wears his most opulent robes and a jewel the size of an ostrich egg in his turban, Amalek is dressed in his finest silk outfit with a large gold chain across his shoulders, Mallan has opted for a dress suit in dark navy blue, Morova also wears a dress outfit in black and carries the urn with Herion's ashes, Two of the nurses who attended Herion also go along dressed in somber attire. Padopolous is the only surprise. He's managed to have a replica of his old Phoenician Space Force Admiral's uniform made for the occasion.

Padopolous pilots the ship to point in space free of Terman gravity and lets it coast while he moves to the cargo hold where the other passengers are seated on chairs temporarily fixed to the floor. The urn with Herion's ashes sits in the air lock with the lid removed. Padopolous moves to a podium and begins the ceremony.

"We are assembled here in the sight of Astarte to honor the Lady Herion, a past member of the Ruling Council of the planet Phoenicia and a widely recognized expert in animal science. She was a great lady as noted by the many awards she received during her lifetime, including the Astarte Prize for Science and the Minerva Award for Civic Achievement.

"We commit her ashes to the depths of space in sure and certain hope of uniting her soul with all those who have gone before to the fields of peace and plenty established by the holy hand of Astarte. May these mortal ashes spread throughout the galaxy so all they touch will know the peace and good wishes they bear. May we all be inspired by the life of the Lady Herion, and strive to emulate her in all we do. Rest in peace, good Lady."

Padopolous pushes a button on the podium, and the outer door of the air lock opens to space. Herion's ashes form a small cloud above the urn, and a soft wind blows them out into the blackness of space.

Regen cannot hold back his tears, and Mariva comforts him as Hitler rubs his legs and coos softly.

★ ★ ★ ★ ★

Back at the Velvet Saddle, the mood turns brighter after

everyone has a drink in their hand. The party takes their seats around a large table, and Jahallah rises to speak.

"Regen, you have helped to make me a very rich man, and your lady was one of the most talented and gracious women I've ever known. I have ordered a stella erected in the heart of the desert to honor you both. I give you this holograph of the stella to keep with you always."

He places a small disc on the floor and the holograph of a large stone stella arises from it. Portraits of both Regen and Herion are etched in the stone along with intricate Zunid designs and Zunid script.

"What's it say, Jahallah?" Regen asks.

"I'll read it. It says, 'Honoring the heroism of Regen of Brem and the majesty of his consort the Lady Herion. The kingdom of the Zunid has benefited greatly by their efforts on its behalf.'"

Regen stands and moves to embrace Jahallah. "That's mighty gracious of you, your majesty. I know she'd appreciate it."

Dr. Morova rises to speak. "Regen, I have obtained approval to rename our research laboratory the Lady Herion Laboratory. We will continue to research cures for the Cancers that evade our efforts."

Regen moves from Jahallah to Morova and takes Morova's offered hand. "Thanks, Doc, and thanks for all you did for her."

Regen turns to the rest of his guests at the table. "My special thanks to all of you for honoring Herion. She was a special lady. If she had died on Phoenicia, the funeral would have been attended by thousands, and a national holiday would have been declared, but this tribute is every bit as meaningful. Thank you."

Regen sits down and begins to weep unashamedly. Mariva rises and moves to embrace him. The other guests rise and file

262 M. L. Hollinger

past offering their condolences once more before taking their leave. Mariva stays with him.

"I don't want you to be alone tonight, Regen," she says.

He looks up at her with red, teary eyes. "I think I'd like that."

She leads him to her apartment and puts him to bed in her own huge bedstead then crawls in beside him. She folds him in her arms, and they soon fall asleep.

Chapter 37

The next morning, Regen awakens alone in the huge bed. He dresses in his formal clothes then goes to his own apartment to feed Hitler and change into something more comfortable. He releases Hitler to hunt in the wild countryside around the hotel before downing some Gordian Bourbon for breakfast. He finds Padopolous, Amalek and Mariva having breakfast in the hotel dining room and joins them.

"You sleep okay?" Amalek asks.

"Like a rock," Regen answers. "Where's everybody else?"

Padopolous answers, "Jahallah had urgent business back home, and Mallan was off to KCC 1257 for another load of gems. Morova and his nurses had to get back to the clinic. Mariva invited us to breakfast, and here we are."

"We were curious to find out what you planned to do now," Amalek says.

"I aint thought much about it, but now that you ask, I need to find out what those gems are worth first. I'll need some big credits for whatever I do."

"I'll buy your interest in those gems," Mariva says. "How much do you need?"

"I need to talk to Torom. I'll go to Daq Vinas today."

★ ★ ★ ★ ★

Regen enters the Gem House and is greeted by a joyous Torom.

"Ah, good to see you Regen. Come with me. You won't believe this."

He leads the Bremen to the back of his store and down to his shops. A smiling cutter comes at Torom's call carrying a small velvet-covered box.

"This is the ring I made with one of your stones," Torom says as he takes the box from his cutter. He opens the box, and Regen is almost overcome by the brilliance. He picks up the ring for closer inspection. He turns it over to view it from each angle.

"This stone's pretty small, but it still shines like anything five times bigger."

"Yes, I've shown it to some of my more affluent customers, and they've bid very highly for it. As you see, I can cut your stones several times and still have very desirable gems. The only problem is keeping them rare enough to maintain the price."

"That can be arranged. Mariva wants to buy my interest in the stones, and she'll keep 'em stashed away safe. You just tell me what they're worth."

The Andie rubs his chin a bit before answering. "My highest bid on this ring is ₵30,000. With our arrangement of 60/40, your share would be ₵18,000. This gem is one of five we cut from one stone. You gave me but three stones weighing a total of four grams, and I can easily produce 12 gems from that lot, making your share ₵216,000."

It's Regen's turn to think, "I got kilos o' those stones, and more to come. How many you think you could sell and still keep the price high?"

"I must hold my sales to two per month here in Ausland, but I will sell franchises to other jewelers on Terma who could be contracted to do the same. I think there are six or seven other cities with possible buyers."

"Okay, let Mariva know when you want more stones. What

would you say to a price of ₡25,000 a gram?"

The Andie produces a calculator and runs some numbers. "I will pay only ₡20,000."

Regen smiles, knowing his own mental calculations came to that answer, but also knowing the Andie would cut anything he offered by at least 20%. "Done," he says as he offers his hand to the jeweler.

Torom takes his hand and says, "Done."

★ ★ ★ ★ ★

Regen finds Mariva watching the craps tables. "Can we talk?" he asks.

"Sure, in my office," she replies, and they leave the gaming floor.

Once inside her office, Mariva asks, "What did Torom have to offer?"

"We came to a good agreement. He's gettin' plenty for the cut and polished stones, but he needs to keep the supply down. I reckon he'll only want to buy around 15 grams a month at ₡20,000 a gram. Padopolous and Mallan each get a third of that leaving you with ₡100,000 a month. Right now, you got 100 kilos, and that much is worth at least ₡600,000,000. Your share'd be ₡200,000,000 but over several years. If you want my share, I'd take ₡2,000,000 right now."

Mariva looks at him with a soft expression. "You realize you could stay here and have the whole thing and me too?"

"You're the best part o' that deal, darlin', but ₡2,000,000'll get me to Bardour and Orianne. I think she'll be glad to see me."

"Bardour isn't a welcoming planet. You sure they wouldn't just blow you into space dust?"

"I helped her get her throne. She'll take me in, I'm pretty sure."

"Why don't you check it out first? It'd only take a couple of weeks to get a message through to Bardour and find out."

"Okay, darlin', I'll do that, but my mind's made up for Orianne."

★ ★ ★ ★ ★

Regen's answer comes back in two weeks by priority express. His hand trembles a bit as he touches the keys on his communicator keyboard. The message scrolls down.

Regen, I thought you were dead.

It's good to know you are well, but sad to hear of Lady Herion's death.

Please accept my heart-felt condolences.

You are always welcome on Bardour, but I fear you want more than simple asylum.

I will always have a warm spot in my heart for you and Hitler, but things have changed since you were last here.

I have found a true love who cherishes me and is content with being my consort.

I feared you would not adapt well to that role.

We were married two years ago, and we now have a son to rule after I'm gone.

There will always be a place for you to lay your head on Bardour, but you would have to give up drug running. Under our laws, I could not allow that.

I wish you all the happiness you have made possible for me.

Fondly,

Orianne Regina, Queen of Bardour

Regen sits back in his chair and strokes Hitler's leathery skin.

"Well, fella, that's the nicest brush-off I ever got. Looks like me and Mariva are gonna be a thing for a while."

THE END

Title: *The Adventures of Regen the Bremen*
•: Author: M. L. Hollinger
•: Publisher: TotalRecall Publications, Inc.
•: Paper Back, ISBN: 978-1-59095-111-8
•: eBook, ISBN: 978-1-59095-112-5

Regen is a Bremen. By nature he loves only his pet skeen, sensual women, money, and adventure in that order.

Regen is an earthy, pragmatic, drug smuggler who cares little for anything but money, beautiful women, and his own highly unusual pet. The animal is a skeen, and they are usually shot on sight for the pests they are. Most people marvel that Regen managed to tame such a nasty creature. On top of everything else, he named the skeen HITLER after a 20th Century Earth dictator with a personality as evil as any skeen's. Regen is a Bremen. Bremen are known for their tough exterior, sexual prowess, and their tendency to leap before they look. I hope you enjoy following this arrogant, self-confident, egotistical and narcissistic bastard through a series of adventures in disparate sectors of the galaxy.

Young Adult and Adult
Recommended age 14 and above

Title: *Josh and the Cargan*
- Author: M. L. Hollinger
- Publisher: TotalRecall Publications, Inc.
- •: Paperback, ISBN: 978-1-59095-125-5
- •: eBook, ISBN: 978-1-59095-126-2

Science tells us the speed of light is absolute, but is it? If physical objects can't go faster than 186,000 miles per second, maybe something else can.

Josh Smith is your average teenage boy. His hormones are raging and he can't wait to have sex with a girl. He also wants to be a rock star, and has an amateur band of his own. One evening after band practice he learns his rich, eccentric great grandfather, Charles Evans Bastin, is dead.

When the will is read, Josh inherits one of Charley's ugly sculptures while his father inherits the rest of the fortune. Back home, Josh accidentally discovers his sculpture is a CARGAN, a device used for interplanetary travel as a ghostly presence called an ENTITY. He travels to the planet destination of his cargan and finds it's a very exotic place indeed.

Young Adult and Adult
Recommended age 17 and above

Title: *Mauhad*
• Author: M. L. Hollinger
• Publisher: TotalRecall Publications, Inc.
•: Paperback, ISBN: 978-1-59095-105-5
•: eBook, ISBN: 978-1-59095-106-

A boy struggles to pass Mauhad, the manhood test of his people, and falls in love in the process.

Javik lives in a country surrounded by mountains and covered in old growth forest. His ambition is to become a warrior like his father, Tolda, but he must pass Mauhad before he can realize that ambition. When is father is killed saving the others in his raiding party, Javik despairs of ever reaching that goal without his father's training. Goldar, who led the raid when Tolda was killed, convinces the King to allow Javik to train with Tao Shan, the finest mentor in the kingdom. Javik finds himself among the sons of the wealthy and must adjust to the situation quickly. While in training he encounters a girl in the forest. She is Allana an escaped slave, but Javik falls in love with her. He convinces her to come out of hiding, and she teaches the sling to Tao Shan's students.

The First book in the Javik series.

Young Adult and Adult
Recommended age 10 and above

Title: *Love and War*
- Author: M. L. Hollinger
- Publisher: TotalRecall Publications, Inc.
- : Paperback, ISBN: 978-1-59095-286-3
- : eBook, ISBN: 978-1-59095-287-0

Allana goes in pursuit of a crown, and Javik is trapped into an unwanted marriage before the fates conspire to free him from all obligations except finding the woman he loves.

Javik goes off the war. He gains glory and gold in the war but returns home to find Allana gone. He's dismayed when Dana tells him she doesn't want him to follow her. He's also promised Tao Shan another year of training. He begins the training, and Tao Shan gives him a bonus by letting him in on the secret of a magic powder (gunpowder) and the weapon called a hand cannon.

The second book in the Javik series.

Young Adult and Adult
Recommended age 10 and above

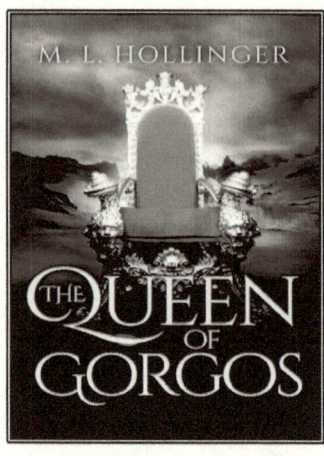

Title: *Queen of Gorgos*
•: Author: M. L. Hollinger
•: Publisher: TotalRecall Publications, Inc.
•: Paperback, ISBN: 978-1-59095-290-0
•: eBook, ISBN: 978-1-59095-291-7

Allana is held by the Turrek bandit King, Vargon.

Javik leaves to find her and learns of her predicament. With the help of her man Barinosh, Javik and his friends manage to free Allana and they set off to regain her throne. After many adventures Allana is crowned queen, marries Javik and they reign together.

Allana has begun her quest to regain the throne of Gorgos by establishing a high class brothel in another land with the help of a former madam who has been disfigured by a rejected lover. Allana gains a great deal of wealth and some allies, but she must cross the territory of a ferocious bandit king, Vargon, to reach Gorgos. She bribes Vargon with her body in order to secure his promise of safe passage, but he captures her in spite of his promise and forces her to marry him.

The third book in the Javik series.

Young Adult and Adult
Recommended age 10 and above

Title: *Josh Martin – Space Commander*
• Author: M. L. Hollinger
• Publisher: TotalRecall Publications, Inc.
•: Paperback, ISBN: 978-1-59095-282-5
•: eBook, ISBN: 978-1-59095-283-2

A bored teen-aged boy escorting his little brother at Disney World finds love and adventure on Space Mountain.

While waiting in line at Space Mountain, Buzz Lightyear presents Josh with a pin and suggests he'll enjoy the ride a lot more now. Josh and George board the sled, but Josh doesn't notice the cast member pushing a button on the sled. As they start the ride, Josh is suddenly propelled into another dimension where he's the Commander of a space ship. The ship is a battle cruiser, and receives an order to rescue a princess who has been kidnapped by pirates. With the help of the ships Executive officer and his staff Josh develop the perfect plan to accomplish the rescue. What could go wrong?